MURDER AT THE HOTEL

A gripping cozy crime mystery full of twists

JANE ADAMS

A Rina Martin Mystery Book 10

Joffe Books, London
www.joffebooks.com

First published in Great Britain in 2024

Cover art by Dee Dee Book Covers

ISBN: 978-1-83526-689-2

PROLOGUE

Derek had been gardening when the man arrived, working on the tall, raised beds beside the back door that he kept for seasonal bedding. He had been preparing the soil for the winter display. He worked patiently with trowel and a clawed, handheld cultivator that he found useful for teasing out the roots of spent nasturtiums and the last remnants of petunias and bidens, before mulching with fresh compost and using the same tool to work it in. This year, he was late with this particular task, but he had been ill during November and slow to recover. It was now mid-December and a trip to the garden centre had, he felt, set the world to rights. Once the beds were filled with primulas and winter pansies he would feel as though he'd properly caught up.

He was beginning to feel his age, especially on cold mornings when his body felt as stiff with frost as the icy garden. This was the cost of getting older, he supposed, though he was still fit and strong enough to chase around after his grandchildren and go walking with them along the beaches of the Jurassic coast, scrambling over the rocks in search of fossils. He was looking forward to Christmas Day, which he'd spend with his daughter's family, and Boxing Day, when they would come over to be with him.

1

Later today, he'd fetch the tree and decorations down from the attic, so he could send pictures to the kids for when they got home from school. They'd been on at him for days to get the tree put up, the same one their mum had when she'd been a kid. It was, like Derek, showing its age, but it looked bright and blousy enough when he got the tinsel on. It would do for another few years yet.

When the man arrived, Derek had done what he always did — taken him into the kitchen and made coffee. Derek disliked the thought of allowing him further into the house. Bad enough that he should occupy even this space in Derek's sanctuary. He had left the back door open, reluctant to offer even heat and comfort to this man. Derek had his thick fleece to keep him warm; it was his visitor's lookout if he'd got out of his car in just a shirt and lightweight jacket. They passed the time in desultory conversation, as though this one-time friend still felt the need to go through the motions.

"Have you seen—"

"No, I don't watch much television these days."

"Lousy weather. We'll have snow soon, they reckon."

And then, as he rose to leave not fifteen minutes after he had arrived, and stood expectantly beside the kitchen table, Derek had told him.

"I won't be paying any more money. I've given all I can. It's finished now."

And he had laughed, this man Derek had once reckoned as a friend. "Don't be so wet. You can't afford not to pay up. Because you know what'll happen. You've got a pretty daughter and she's got two lovely kids. I understand you're even fond of that husband of hers."

He leaned across the table, his face only inches from Derek's. "You remember what happened last time, don't you, Derek? It's others that will be made to pay, if you prove difficult."

He was so confident, so certain that Derek was too much of a worm ever to turn. But Derek had already made up his mind, had already played this out so many times in his imagination that now it came to it, it seemed almost as though he was watching a film of himself as he reached for the knife he had left on the kitchen counter and plunged it deep into the other man's chest.

He had not anticipated this exact play of events, his persecutor leaning forward across the table, so he was forced to thrust upward, but he seemed more observer than actor as he grabbed the shocked and now screaming man by the hair. Derek used the extra purchase this provided to pull him onto the knife.

The man jerked back, out of Derek's grasp, the knife still embedded in his chest. He was cursing and swearing and threatening Derek, his daughter, his family, but Derek barely heard him now. He reached for another of his kitchen knives, pulling it from the block and lunging forward, stabbing twice more as the man staggered backwards, falling out the half-open door and onto the slabbed patio, beside the raised beds. He fell hard, the sound of his body hitting the ground jerking Derek back to the reality of the moment.

The man lay still. But was he dead? Derek watched for signs of life, saw none, watched a little longer. Then — not because he felt uncertain but because the rage had descended once again, at the thought that this man had threatened to hurt his family — he grabbed the cultivator from where he had left it and raked it with all his strength across the body of his enemy.

Afterwards, rage spent and exhaustion taking over, he sat on the back doorstep and thought about what to do. When he had played this scene through in his fantasies, he'd never got further than the death of his persecutor, but he slowly came to realise that in getting rid of one problem, he had created yet another: what to do with the body.

In an old outhouse, which was now used for storing the lawn mower and his garden tools, was an ancient chest freezer. When his wife was alive, she had used it to freeze down the glut of vegetables and fruits they inevitably had, Derek having always been a keen gardener. It was a habit he had maintained in her memory, until his daughter had left home and it had seemed like too much trouble, just for one. The kitchen being too small to house it, the freezer had been kept in the outhouse. It was many years since it had last seen service, but when he plugged it in and switched it on, it bleeped once and buzzed back to life.

Derek opened the lid, wrinkling his nose at the mildew scent, though by the time he had returned with the body, the faint smell was dissipating and he could see the condensation beginning to form on the silvered sides of the box. He dropped the body in, arranging it for best fit, and then closed the lid. He couldn't leave it there for long; the risk of someone wandering into the outhouse and wondering why the old freezer was now on was too big a risk. But it would buy him some thinking time. It had been hard work, getting the knife out of the body. He figured it must have jammed in the rib cage, but he'd managed it eventually. Now, he ran hot water into the sink, added washing up liquid and a splash of bleach, and dropped both knives in. Filled a bucket with floor cleaner and yet more bleach and went outside to mop the patio. The act of cleaning, the routine task, calmed him until it once more felt as though he had simply acted in a role — one he had imagined and rehearsed and had now performed. Performed rather well, he thought.

He was surprised to find, as he scrubbed the knives and washed the coffee cups, that he felt absolutely no remorse. He had been pushed to this, had done it to protect his family. What was there to be sorry for?

CHAPTER 1

Rina Martin was not sure that she liked being confronted by a life-sized cardboard cut-out of herself, set close beside the overdressed Christmas tree, but she smiled benignly, took up her position beside her two-dimensional twin and posed for the photographs. If she was being totally honest, Rina could have done without this weekend. All she really wanted to do on this Friday evening was to go home to Peverill Lodge, put her feet up, drink tea, eat cake and watch some nonsense on the telly. But she had to admit that would have seemed somewhat ungrateful. Everyone had been so excited about the return of Lydia Marchant Investigates, and the release of the feature-length Christmas special cemented the success of the new series. The Palisades hotel, the lobby of which now housed said life-sized cardboard cut-out, had managed to procure the rights to a private screening to specially invited guests. Lord knows what they paid for the privilege, Rina thought. Privately she felt it was a nonsense, given everybody would be able to see it in a couple of weeks' time, but she kept her thoughts to herself. On top of that, the Palisades was running a murder mystery weekend, kicking off after breakfast on the Saturday morning, and Rina was an honoured guest.

The only compensation was that the Martin household, in its entirety, had also been invited to participate, and all had entered into the spirit of things with gusto. Looking across the lobby, she could see the Peters sisters, Bethany and Eliza, framed by the heavy swags of evergreen and red baubles that had been draped around the massive window, practically bouncing up and down with excitement. Their newly cut hair shone in the last rays of winter sun that streamed in through the curved glass. For the first time, they had embraced their grey, their young friend Joy telling them that the tone was very fashionable now. Rina had to admit the highlighted silver, cut in what she thought of as a modified bob, did look good on them.

Rina had been embracing her own grey for years.

Matthew Montmorency's steely mane had been tied back in a lush ponytail — another Joy influence. Joy had admired the effect at a late summer wedding, and Matthew had taken the praise on board. His ersatz twin, Steven, much smaller and plumper than his stage brother, seemed to have compensated for his lack of hair by donning a very snazzy waistcoat in scarlet silk and a smart grey blazer. He wore a spray of holly in his buttonhole.

"Look this way please, Miss Martin," one of the photographers requested. She bristled slightly at the *Miss*, but it was a common mistake, and the man was young and she was quite used to young people assuming that she had never been married, instead of simply long widowed. *Oh Fred,* she thought, *you would have loved this.* They had been wed for only five years when he had died, but he was still a presence in absolutely everything she did. She stroked her fingers affectionately across the face of the little watch that he had given her all those years ago, and which she now wore only on special occasions — or when she needed extra armour. It was her touchstone of those very happy times.

She posed for photographs and then for selfies, with guests and the cardboard Lydia, until the final rays of sun had faded, and the dusk had thickened into almost dark, smiling her best smile. She made certain to include her fellow actors from the television series: Jess Winteringham, who played her niece Adelaide, and Seth Collis, who played Otis Finch, Lydia Marchant's accident-prone sidekick.

Photo shoot over, Rina found she was being hailed by James Blake, who, together with his wife Lily, had bought and renovated the Palisades hotel. It was a beautiful Art Deco affair, created in 1932 on the site of an Edwardian manor and only enjoying a few years of heyday before the war began. After that soldiers, then refugees, then orphaned children, then medical patients had been billeted there. The poor building had never really recovered, Rina remembered, having known the then slightly shabby hotel for several years before James and his wife took over. From the 1950s it had been a hotel again, but had never quite reclaimed its glory, until now. The hotel — decked out for the Christmas season, swathes of evergreen and ribbon on the grand staircase and the twinkling stars of fairy lights anywhere Lily and James could manage to fix them — looked just a little smug at being so cherished — and maybe just a tad embarrassed by all the bling.

"The team have arrived," James told her. "They're really eager to meet you."

Rina assumed this particular team must be those who were organising the murder mystery weekend. There were several "teams" in the hotel this weekend. There would be the team of actors organising and performing in the murder mystery, then a small clutch of guests, who had booked to share the celebrations, and her own little team from Peverill Lodge. She glanced back across the lobby at her cardboard cut-out self. Lydia Marchant, smart, matter-of-fact, dependable with her fitted jackets, tweed skirts and big handbag. The writers of Lydia Marchant had deliberately channelled the supremacy of Miss Marple in her various incarnations — and in fact, Miss Marchant occupied the same approximate timeframe as many of the Marple television series: just post-war, a time of austerity, rationing, common sense and practicality, with a little glamour in the shape of the occasional femme fatale. It was somewhat ironic, given the location, that the *literary* Miss Marple, as opposed to the majority of the film and television versions, had been created for a short story in 1927, only a little before the Palisades had been built. In one sense, it was the Blakes who were getting things right.

Rina really liked her alter ego, and to be quite honest, she didn't feel she had to do that much acting. In recent years she had found herself channelling that other self in real life, when strange and often tragic events had turned up on her doorstep. Like Lydia Marchant, she'd had to roll up her sleeves and get on with dealing with them.

She followed James through a pair of impressive wooden doors — pale blond wood with a strongly figured grain, set with geometric finger plates — and into the smaller of the two dining rooms. This had been one of the last spaces to have been refurbished. They were planning to use this rather elegant, high-ceilinged room as the centre of operations, leaving the larger bar and restaurant, with its small stage at one end, available for evening entertainment. Unlike the larger dining room, that looked out over the driveway and circular lawn, this room had a wonderful view of the sea, afforded by a run of tall French doors that in summer stood open and allowed guests to spill out onto an elegant terrace. At this time of year, they were kept firmly closed; the wind blowing in off the sea was often strong and usually frigid and as she passed the windows, Rina could feel the chill seep through the panes. It was a shame, she thought, that there was no way to both keep the original, small-paned, metal-framed doors and install double glazing. She felt the urge to close the heavy, green velvet curtains. The last of the evening sun had faded rapidly and it was already getting dark, the sea invisible; Rina saw no reason for leaving the curtains open and letting the heat out. This room had so far escaped Lily's decorations, being, for the moment at least, closed off to the public. Rina had no doubt it would get the fairy light treatment the moment this was over.

In keeping with the setting, the murder mystery weekend was to have an interwar theme in terms of style and dress, and Rina was amused that they would be celebrating a post-war TV series with a distinctly pre-war weekend of entertainment. But then, the Palisades was now noted for its flapper-themed dances and events, so she supposed that was what was expected by the clientele.

Beside the door, as they came into the small dining room, a long table had been laid with hot water urns and the makings for tea and coffee and assorted herbal concoctions, together with biscuits and snacks. A group of half a dozen people were gathered around a table at the other end of the room, sorting through boxes and cases, while others came struggling in with further crates and trunks, one fully large enough to hide a body in, Rina thought. As she and James approached, two people broke away from the rest, advancing with broad smiles and outstretched hands. Rina shook hands and James made the introductions.

"Rina Martin, this is Fliss Cameron, who runs this little troupe of entertainers." Blake's smile was broad, but Rina knew him well enough to recognise a kind of reticence in the tone. He doesn't like this woman very much, Rina thought. She studied the tall blond with interest. Handsome, not soft enough to be pretty, and with steely grey eyes that assessed Rina just as assiduously as Rina was assessing their owner.

"And this is William Toons, who is going to be our victim this weekend." Blake's tone was warmer this time, and Rina smiled at the dark-haired man with the very dark eyes and the two days' worth of stubble. Was that for the role, Rina wondered, or was he under the mistaken apprehension that women liked that sort of thing. Rina had nothing against beards, only against men who didn't commit.

"So happy to meet you," William Toons said. "And in such a setting. Isn't this a marvellous place?"

He was practically dancing with puppy dog enthusiasm. He could have competed with the Peters sisters. Briefly, it made him look very young, almost childlike, though Rina guessed he must be in his mid-thirties. When Fliss Cameron spoke and took the attention away from him, Rina was conscious of the sudden emptiness in his expression as he stepped aside.

Interesting, Rina thought, and sad. Something had damaged this man, and the damage was permanent.

"I wonder if you'd like to see our playbook," Fliss Cameron was saying. "We have a number of storylines, and our company can switch between them at a moment's notice, depending on how the guests react to the scenes we give them. It's a bit of a balancing act, staying in control so nothing goes completely off-piste, but allowing for natural flow, so to speak."

Rina made a quick calculation. Did she really want to get involved? Reading through the 'playbook' sounded like that was what she was being invited to do. But would a refusal offend?

She smiled her sweetest smile. "It all sounds splendid," she said. She leaned in confidentially. "But if you don't mind, I'd love to just relax and join in the fun without knowing too much. It's not often an opportunity like this comes up."

She felt immediately sure that this had not satisfied Fliss Cameron, and she felt a pang of guilt that she had disappointed the woman — but not enough to change her mind.

Fliss Cameron nodded. "Of course. Splendid," she added, echoing Rina. "I hope you enjoy the weekend." Her attention was caught by two of the helpers still struggling with the trunk that Rina had spotted. "No, not there, Pete. That needs to go into the library."

"And where's that?" the man called Pete asked, and Rina noted the irritation in his tone. "I thought you wanted it in here."

"Shall we leave them to it?" Rina asked Blake.

He nodded. "Might be wise."

As they beat a retreat, Rina glanced back at the busy little scene, noting that William Toons was now occupying himself making tea and coffee for the assembled troops. He had a list and was working his way through it. "Nice to meet you," Rina said as they passed.

"Oh, and you too." The smile was back, and Rina got the impression that he meant what he said. "Just thought I'd make myself useful," he added, indicating the refreshment table.

And create a valid excuse for keeping out of the way, Rina suspected. It was a strategy she had often employed when committee meetings were getting a little tense — or when she was trying to avoid someone without making it look too obvious.

Interesting indeed, she thought. And then she wondered if being the victim in one of these weekend events classified you as a star in the drama, or as a bit player. Toons had been introduced to her as though his was an important role — and indeed, you couldn't have a murder mystery without a murder — so presumably he wasn't required to pop his clogs in the first act. She realised belatedly that she wasn't even sure how these things worked. Did the murder happen just once, and the investigation then take the whole weekend? Or would there be a chance to work through different scenarios in the playbook, as Fliss Cameron had called it? She almost wished now that she'd taken up the offer of an advance read.

Almost.

Returning to the foyer, she saw that her other guests had arrived. Tim and his fiancée, Joy, were chatting to the Montmorencys. Tim, a magician specialising in close-up magic and mentalism, performed several nights a week at the hotel, and she knew he was looking forward to just being a guest on this occasion.

Well, the gang's all here, or at least those able to make it. She wished Mac — Inspector McGregor, to give him his proper title, and his partner, Miriam Hastings, could have been there. They had been away all week on a rare holiday. Miriam's mother had been celebrating a 'significant' birthday and the family had been summoned, en masse, to help her enjoy it. They were due back tomorrow. Also absent for the moment were young George and Ursula. They were now eighteen, and Rina had known them since they were twelve, and counted herself fortunate that they still enjoyed her company as much as she enjoyed theirs. They should be along later, for the dinner and the screening, when Ursula had finished her shift. Both were juggling work and studies, and Rina sometimes wondered how they coped. They had opted out of the weekend, citing work and study commitments, but Rina also suspected they hadn't fancied the idea very much.

She thanked Blake and wandered over to see her friends. At least, if she got bored, she'd have some good company. Glancing at her watch, Rina noticed it was only just six. Another hour until dinner, then the screening at nine, and then dancing and a buffet from eleven until one. Rina felt weary just thinking about it. Everyone would be staying overnight, and then those lucky enough to be escaping the murder mystery would be checking out on the Saturday morning, leaving Rina and her friends, the actors and paying guests behind, plus the half dozen who had won the weekend as a raffle prize. Already Blake had told her how much this little group were looking forward to spending time with her; Rina quailed at the thought. She must have already met them when she posed for all those photographs, but she hadn't clocked which guests they were at that point.

"Rina my darling, how are you holding up?"

She turned and smiled as Jess Winteringham, held out her arms for a hug. In her early thirties, Jess played Adelaide Marchant, Lydia's niece. The role was her first big break. Rina could remember how nervous the young woman had been in those first days. They had become good friends since. Jess was tall and willowy with dark, curly hair and a warm smile.

She had Rina's co-star in tow. Seth Collis was a bear of a man in his mid-sixties. His character in the series, Otis Finch, was a man who would like to have been Lydia's love interest — Lydia was immune to his charms — and who helped her solve her mysteries. Or, more often, hindered, when he got the wrong end of the stick and alerted the criminal to Rina's suspicions.

"Rina, m'dear, you're looking rather lovely. I've just been talking to the mistress of ceremonies for the weekend."

"Fliss?" Rina guessed.

"Quite so." He leaned in, confidentially. "And I've got to say, I almost wish I was buggering off tomorrow morning."

Rina laughed.

"It will probably be fun," Jess said, but she sounded doubtful.

"There's still time to run away," Seth commented.

Jess grimaced. "I'm sure it will be fine. It'll make a change to watch someone else performing. I must say, though, I'm very surprised to see Will Toons here."

Will? Oh, William Toons. "Do you know him?"

"I worked with him once. Before the . . . you know, before the scandal." She lowered her voice and glanced around, as though worried someone might overhear.

"Scandal?" Rina asked.

"Oh, you must remember. About five years ago?"

So, after she'd retired. Or, as it turned out, after she'd *thought* she'd retired — the sudden return of Lydia Marchant being something of a serendipitous surprise.

"I didn't really keep up with things," she said, knowing that sounded rather lame. The truth was, she'd rather determinedly left that part of her life behind and taken on the role of Rina Martin, proprietress of Peverill Lodge Guest House. The fact that the guests were permanent residents, people Rina regarded as family and who were never likely to leave — Tim excepted — was beside the point. She had taken to the role so well she'd almost fooled herself into thinking she wanted nothing more.

Then Lydia Marchant had been revived, and she had admitted to herself that she had, in fact, sorely missed that part of her life. She dredged her memory for any reference she might have filed about William Toons. Came up with a blank, beyond recalling a not very successful sit-com about ten years before.

"Wasn't he in that Sleepy Lawns thing?" It had, if she remembered correctly, been set in a rather upmarket retirement home.

"He played the son of the owner," Seth reminded her. "The series didn't last, but it got him noticed. He did a

13

couple of films after that. A rom-com and something more action-y. I forget—"

"Midnight Deadline," Jess said. "Or was it Deadline, Midnight? Or am I getting it mixed up with some old black-and-white film?" She wrinkled her nose, thinking hard. Gave up. "Either way, it was pretty average, but he was doing OK. Then there was the scandal."

"You're going to have to remind me," Rina told her.

"Well, to be fair, he was exonerated," Seth said. "Not that it helped his career much. You know what they say about mud. It definitely sticks. He was accused of a sexual assault on an underage girl. By the time he managed to prove that he wasn't even in the country at the time, he'd been tried in the court of public opinion and his name was dirt. It didn't help that his then-girlfriend was much younger than he was. She was a model or something, and the girl who made the accusation was a younger sister."

"The girlfriend believed her," Jess added. "Until someone actually took the time to check where he was when all this was supposed to have gone on. If I remember right, he was on a flight, mid-Atlantic, didn't get back into the UK until several hours later." She shrugged. "Something like that, anyway."

"Do you know why the girl made the accusation?" Rina asked.

"Well, to be fair," Jess said, "someone definitely attacked her. And it happened in Will Toons's house. She was staying over with the girlfriend. She seems to have assumed he got back and came to her room." She shrugged. "It was enough to kill his career for a while, but I'd no idea he'd been reduced to doing murder mystery weekends." She must have seen Rina's faint disapproval at her tone, because she added, "Believe me, I know what I'm talking about. I did a fair few events like this when I was starting out. In the end I preferred bar work."

"We've all done jobs we'd rather forget," Seth agreed. "But I did a stint on a costume drama with Will, and frankly, I'd be shocked if anyone that worked with him believed the gossip. He simply wasn't the type to do something like that."

Rina saw the flash of annoyance that crossed Jess's face. "I suppose he was exonerated," she said. "It must have been a very difficult time for everyone involved."

"Well, quite," Seth said.

"Of course it must," Jess agreed.

Rina sighed inwardly. The fact was these two actually liked one another a lot, but at times they competed for attention like teenage siblings, usually for Rina's attention. She could cope with them both on set, had a genuine affection for the pair, but sometimes . . .

Tim was heading in Rina's direction, and she excused herself gratefully and went over to meet him halfway. The gossip had added to her sense that she really didn't want to be here. That she wanted to don her Rina Martin of Peverill Lodge persona and relax for a while in the company of real and cherished friends, not just professional ones.

"You looked like you needed rescuing," Tim said.

"I was heading that way," she admitted. "I've got to admit, I'm not looking forward to any of this."

"Well, to cheer you up a bit, George just texted, and he and Ursula are only a few minutes away. So apart from Mac and Miriam, just about everyone that matters will be here to help you celebrate." He reached out and gently touched the watch on Rina's wrist. She smiled.

Fred was there in spirit, Rina thought, and he would have been so proud. The thought brightened her mood. Had Fred been here, he would have enjoyed every minute of the weekend, because Fred had possessed a talent for that. For wringing every ounce of joy out of just about any situation. Rina made up her mind that she should be doing the same. Fred had loved Christmas, even though, as performers, it was often their busiest time of the year. He had relished the preparations and the food and even the tackiest of decorations. One year he had come home, triumphantly carrying a tiny silver tree which he'd set down on the windowsill with the jubilant air of a magician producing an extra-large rabbit from his top hat.

"I was passing the Queen's Head," he'd told her. "The landlady had thrown it out. It was standing on the pavement, waiting for the dustcart."

"So you rescued it?"

"Well, I couldn't let the poor thing get wet. It had started to rain."

Rina found herself smiling at the memory. and she reminded herself, as Fred would have done, that this weekend would not be happening had it not been for her success as Lydia Marchant, and a good many other people had also benefitted. Surely that was something to celebrate.

* * *

Rina was relieved that Blake and Lily had put her on a table with her friends, instead of insisting they have a top table for honoured guests. Seth and Jess had been seated with members of the Fliss Cameron Theatre Company; others of that group had been placed with the half dozen Rina assumed were the raffle prize winners. She could hear Seth holding court even across the room noisy with voices and laughter and the chink of cutlery and china, and the soft but relentlessly upbeat seasonal music. Seth's pronouncements mostly seemed to be along the lines of "I remember an episode of Lydia Marchant, when we—"

Fliss Cameron looked bored and tired, but the rest of the company seemed happy to be entertained. William Toons didn't seem to be saying much. He chatted amiably enough to the guests on either side of him and watched Seth's performance with a look of mild amusement on his face, but Rina could tell that his attention was wandering, and she could not help but wonder where to.

Every now and again one or other of the guests would look her way, catch her eye and raise a glass or beam a smile. She did her best to be dutifully happy.

George was sitting next to her, wolfing down bread rolls. Rina, familiar with George's food requirements, had held onto the bread basket after the first course was cleared, together with a dish of butter. As a child, George had often gone hungry, and had never quite lost the habit of loading up on calories when he could. How he had remained as skinny as he had was beyond Rina. Now, as a young adult, he had a very physical job as an apprentice boat builder in a yard near Lyme Regis, working three days a week and attending college on the other two. He was thriving, and Rina found it hard to reconcile how much he had changed in the past few months. He had grown and filled out. His hands were calloused and capable, and there was a confidence to him that made her feel very proud.

Across the table, Ursula and Joy were chatting happily. "How's she doing?" Rina asked.

Back in early summer, they had almost lost Ursula when a very troubled woman had tried to kill her.

"She's doing OK," George said. "She still gets the occasional nightmare, but it's not nearly as bad, and since we moved into the flat, she's been a lot happier."

Ursula and George had grown up in care. On leaving, they had been housed in tiny studio apartments for a time, but two months previously, they had finally managed to find a place together. The bedsit was tiny. Bijou, if you were being kind; cramped, if you were being honest. Too small and inconvenient to be a decent holiday let, Rina supposed, but within cycling distance of George's work and Ursula could drive to uni. It was right at the top of a tall and narrow Victorian town house, on the third floor and with a private entrance via an external metal fire escape, the landing of which was now decorated with pots of winter pansies, courtesy of Rina. The door leading back into the house could be bolted from the inside, and Ursula had hung a very heavy chenille curtain she'd found at a charity shop, so she could pretty much forget the door was even there.

"It's like an eyrie," she had told Rina. "It feels like it would be difficult to invade."

"Anyone that tried would be out of breath by the time they ran up the stairs," Rina agreed. Fortunately, George had been on hand to carry the compost and pots up to the top landing; Rina had only had to carry the plants.

"Her course is going well. I think she's even enjoying it. And she's made some friends. I've even met two of them, so she must think they're OK."

"And you?"

"Couldn't be happier. I mean, really. College is different from school, and everything I'm learning has a practical application. We're doing all right, I think."

"I think you are." The next course arrived, and George abandoned the rolls and set about the fish.

They were so different, Rina thought, glancing across at Ursula, who was slicing her own fish with delicate precision. They had been friends and allies, though, since meeting at Hill House when they had both been just children, and an item very soon after that. Rina, knowing what they had both been through, fervently wished them both all the happiness in the world.

She picked up her own knife and fork. The salmon looked nice, but she wasn't really hungry. The soup and roll had been all she'd really wanted, and there were still two courses to come, plus the threatened buffet later on. Lily and Blake had really gone to town on the catering. She wondered absently what a weekend like this would usually cost, especially as everyone was encouraged to dress up.

Ursula was wearing the beautiful flapper-style dress she had been gifted after she had been a bridesmaid in the late summer, when Joy's mother, Bridie, had remarried. Joy, who had been maid of honour, was wearing hers, too. She suspected Bridie Duggan might also have helped out when they had rented the flat. Something Joy had said made Rina suspect that she had paid the deposit and maybe stood guarantor. Rina would gladly have done the same, but she had been away, recording the new series, when the two had found the flat. Bridie and her new husband, Fitch, were good people.

She poked unenthusiastically at her salmon. Perhaps she could quietly slide her own portion onto George's plate.

Rina could not quite explain the knot in her stomach, that nervous, sick feeling she used to get before an audition, and which occasionally made an appearance before filming more complex scenes. But what on earth was there to be nervous about now? The screening would be straightforward, and the rest of the evening should be relaxing enough, if she let it be. She could just sit on the sidelines and gossip with her friends and watch everyone having a good time.

No, she thought, it was almost certainly something about the weekend; the thought of having to spend the next two days on her best behaviour when all she really wanted to do was rest and relax.

"Do you want my salmon?" she asked George, who had now demolished his own and was looking to threaten the bread rolls again.

"If you don't." He whisked it onto his plate. "Those two really don't like one another, do they?" he commented, as he sliced the fish and doused it in hollandaise.

"Who?"

"That woman over there and William Toons. Is he in this thing this weekend?"

"The murder mystery, yes. I'm surprised you recognised him. I don't think he's been in anything for a while."

"He made two classic horror films, back before he was famous. Supporting actor on Night of the Vampire — that was a remake of a 1960s film; we saw them both on the same night. Then he was the lead in a low-budget thing called Passing Evil. We went to see them when they were on at the local art house last Halloween. They did a marathon run of forgotten films. The second one was based on an M.R James story, the one about passing the runes? Ursula recognised the story, and then we looked it up."

He paused to deal with the salmon. Ursula would have recognised it, Rina thought. From the sound of it, she'd have taken exception to the term 'classic,' but she should have guessed that George would have recognised William Toons. George loved his films.

She glanced over at the table where the actor sat, opposite Fliss Cameron. Both were speaking to their neighbours, turned slightly away from one another. She wondered what George had observed to give him the impression that they did not get on. George, having grown up watchful and wary, waiting for the next explosion of violence, was good at reading people.

Her thoughts were interrupted by the waiting staff, removing the fish course and bringing in the next. "What did you mean when you said they don't like one another?" Rina asked, when the servers had left. "The woman is Fliss Cameron, by the way. She runs the Cameron Theatre Company and the Cameron Players. They'll be doing the . . . whatever it is they do this weekend."

George paused in the act of applying gravy to his turkey — a nod to impending Christmas, Rina assumed, as it was only ten days distant. "It was when they were coming in. Ursula and I were looking for our seats and we checked out that table over there first. This Fliss Cameron and William Toons, they came in behind us, and she was having a right go at him, telling him he was lucky anyone would employ him after what happened. And he was saying that what happened was in the past and he didn't need her to find work for him, that he was doing fine now. But it wasn't what they were saying so much as how they said it, you know? All gritted teeth and false smiles." He grinned at Rina. "I hope the acting's better than that over the weekend or you'll be tearing your hair out."

So did she, Rina thought. Frankly, she couldn't wait till it was all over.

* * *

As the long case clock in the lobby struck midnight, the chimes loud enough to be heard in the large dining room next door, Rina had to admit that the evening was going better than expected. The screening had been a success, and the live sextet were very good and had encouraged people onto the dance floor, including Rina herself. The band was playing mostly 1920s jazz and swing, with some arrangements of more modern tunes that Rina recognised from the radio. Some dancers were strictly ballroom, she noted; some were making it up as they went along, but no one seemed fussed either way, and the atmosphere was pleasant. Rina began to relax a little.

She had danced with Tim and with her on-screen sidekick Seth, and was now feeling in a much better mood. She had been additionally cheered by a message from Miriam and Mac, wishing her well and congratulating her on this most recent success — and telling her they were looking forward to being back home. A week of unadulterated family celebrations, Rina gathered, though lovely, was also proving a tad exhausting.

Now, just past midnight, Rina was content to watch others having a good time.

The large tables they had used for dining had been broken down into their component parts, long napery removed and swiftly arranged at the periphery of the room. Rina was now seated at one of the small tables, Tim on one side of her and Seth on the other. The raffle prize winners had approached at various points in the evening, still a little too overawed to do more than say how happy they were to meet her — and Seth and Jess, of course. Or, rather, Otis and Adelaide. She felt a little sorry for her earlier sourness; they had obviously all made an effort for the occasion, the women in vintage style gowns and the men in smart lounge suits, and a few in period evening wear. All were obviously excited at spending the weekend in such esteemed company.

Now, looking around the room, Rina saw that most people really had taken time, and probably expense, to dress up. Most of the women had made at least a nod to the 1920s, and the men looked smart and elegant, even though the choice of costume was more conventionally modern. Joy and Ursula both looked spectacular in their bridesmaid dresses; genuine black beaded silk from the interwar era that Joy's mother, Bridie, had found and had expertly refitted for them.

"They've got some stamina," Seth commented, following her gaze. "I don't think I ever had that much, even at their age."

Rina nodded. Both girls loved to dance. If Miriam had been there, she'd have joined them. Their male partners were less enthusiastic, but the girls did quite well without their input anyway, sometimes partnering one another as they attempted to emulate their ballrooming elders, and other times just free-styling it. They looked, Rina thought, quite beautiful.

Across the room, the Peters sisters were chatting to two women Rina did not know, but assumed were either guests or part of the theatrical company. Matthew Montmorency had found himself a partner. A woman in a very blue dress, matching shoes and a matching blue rinse, who could foxtrot as well as Matthew. Steven sat with his pocket chess set, glancing at his 'twin' from time to time and, Rina knew from experience, quite content to be just absorbing the atmosphere. Time was, Steven would have liked to participate, but his knees were now too painful. Their original act, she recalled, had been a song-and-dance routine, with a lot of comedy and pratfalls. Like Rina they had started out in end-of-the-pier shows, albeit a good few years before. Later on Rina had joined a repertory company. She had fond memories of travelling the country, trying to remember which role she was playing that week. It had often been hard, but she'd not have traded any of it. Apart from losing Fred, of course. After his death, it was only her friends who had kept her going.

"Penny for them," Seth said.

"I was thinking just how long we've been around and how much has changed," she said.

He lifted his glass — the most recent of many that evening — and toasted her. "Profound thoughts for this time of the evening," he said. He turned to Tim. "Rina tells me you're a bit of a performer yourself?"

A bit of a performer, Rina thought, as she excused herself and made for the lady's room. Tim's magic act was amazing, and the only pity was he wouldn't get to demonstrate that this weekend.

Fliss Cameron was out in the reception area when Rina arrived there. She was speaking on her mobile and had the other hand over her ear to block out the noise from the main room.

Rina moved swiftly on. Coming back out of the ladies, she was surprised to see Fliss still in the lobby. She had finished her call and seemed to be gathering herself before she went back to join the festivities. She looked weary and distracted, not quite the capable woman in charge that Rina had encountered earlier. Rina pretended not to see her and spent a moment searching for something in her bag, giving the other woman time to set her smile in place before acknowledging Rina and asking if she was enjoying herself.

"I am, rather," Rina told her. "More than I thought I would, but I've got to admit I'm ready for a breather. Everyone seems to have a lot more energy than I do."

Fliss smiled, and it was nice to see a genuine smile on the young woman's face. "I don't believe that for a moment," Fliss said. "Lily describes you as indefatigable."

"Well, I certainly feel fatigable at the moment," said Rina. "And you? Are you having a good time? I imagine it's quite a responsibility organising something like this."

"It's . . . demanding," Fliss agreed. "Though I really enjoy these events once they're underway, and I see everyone getting involved and trying to work things out. That makes it all worth it. The night before, though, that's always a trial. I find myself going over and over everything, worrying that something's been forgotten."

"It's all going to be wonderful," Rina reassured her. "And I've got to admit, I'm really looking forward to not knowing what's going to happen. It's going to be such a refreshing change."

Fliss smiled at her again, and Rina got the impression that she was genuinely pleased at Rina's words — and that she'd finally been forgiven for not wanting to read the playbook in advance.

CHAPTER 2

Rina was up bright and early on the Saturday morning; she and Matthew Montmorency had been out for a bracing walk on the cliff path before breakfast. Rina had become much more of a morning person since her retirement, and even though that phase of her life seemed to be on hold, she still maintained the habit of starting the day at the crack of dawn. The rest of the Peverill Lodge household was less keen, but Matthew enjoyed his walks and going out for a good yomp first thing in the morning had become something of a recent habit.

"Steven looked a little uncomfortable last night," Rina commented, as they returned to the hotel. The sun had been shining when they set out, but grey clouds were now gathering and threatening rain.

"His legs were painful, but he had a hot bath and used the liniment the doctor gave him. In the end, he slept well enough."

"That's good. I must admit, I'm George-style hungry this morning."

"Not surprising, considering you fed most of your dinner to him last night. I can't imagine where he puts it all. There's not a spare ounce on him."

"Well, he can get seconds at the buffet this morning. I'm going to eat all of mine. Matthew, do you know anything about Fliss Cameron?"

"Only what Blake and Lily have told me. She's their regular for events like this one. Though I understand this is the first time they've tried to extend the action over an entire weekend. Trick to do, I'd have thought. Why? Is that nose of yours twitching?"

"Not especially. George noticed that she and William Toons seemed at odds over something."

Rina recounted what she had overheard, and Matthew nodded sagely. "Lovers tiff, perhaps . . . though your instincts are that it was more serious? Rina, you've just come back from filming the next series. You're exhausted and your brain is still in Lydia Marchant mode. Don't you think you may be looking for trouble where none exists? Mostly," he added, "because you really don't want to be here."

She looked sharply at her old friend. "It's not that obvious, is it? Lord knows I'd not want to upset Lily or James. They've put a lot into this weekend."

"And will profit nicely from it. Especially as Lydia Marchant herself is present. But no, you're behaving perfectly. Only those of us who know you well will notice anything amiss. Now, I'll go and get Steven to stir his sticks and I'll see you at breakfast. And remember, we're here to have a good time, so put a brave face on it. Get that smile unpacked, as Milly used to say."

Milly Wright. Lord, Rina remembered her so well. Milly had run a troupe of dancers, exercising and drilling them with the method of a drill sergeant and the passion of a racehorse trainer. What was it about this weekend that was calling to mind all of these old memories? At this rate, she'd be wallowing neck deep in nostalgia before the weekend was through.

* * *

25

Breakfast over, Rina waved George and Ursula off and took a moment to assess herself in the lobby mirror before making for the small dining room, where they had been instructed to assemble. She had, she realised, channelled a little of Lydia Marchant's look, though her heathery tweed skirt was less tailored than Lydia would wear and her sweater softer. For her role as Lydia Marchant, Rina's slightly wavy hair was straightened and set in a more mannish style than she wore it today. *Mannish*, now there was a lovely old-fashioned word. Lydia's makeup was sparse and au naturel, though she did like a touch of lipstick when she was preparing for battle. As did Rina, she thought, amused, as she dug in her bag to find her own, refreshing it with the help of her compact mirror. The compact was another old friend gifted to her by Fred. Thus armoured, she straightened her spine, squared her shoulders and sailed off to join the party.

* * *

"We really should get moving," Joy said.

Tim threw a smile at his fiancée and continued with his poking. "I'll only be a minute," he told her. "I didn't get a proper look at this room when Lily and Blake were doing the renovations and the murder mystery people are bound to want to be using it this weekend, so I may not get another chance."

"And they can't start without us, so you've got—" he saw her glance at her watch — "three minutes. No more."

They were in the newly restored library, a beautiful, high-ceilinged, almost square room with tall windows that looked out over the sea. The other walls were lined with books and ancient library steps, with locking wheels and a small, railed platform at the top, allowed access to the higher shelves. One corner was currently occupied by a large wicker basket that he guessed belonged to the theatrical company. He'd had a poke inside, but it contained only costumes and props. The library was, Tim thought, emphatically not art deco, one of the four rooms in the Palisades that had been retained from the building that had stood on the same spot before the hotel.

Tim had known there had been a big house up here on the cliffs but had assumed that it had all been demolished to make way for the hotel. He had been surprised and delighted when Lily and the architect in charge of the restoration had shown him the plans; the newer structure of the hotel had been grafted onto sections of the existing building and a new facade and wing added, which was now the main body of the hotel. But the library had remained intact, as had what was now the small dining room next door and the master bedroom above the library. The small dining room had originally been two rooms: a study belonging to the owner and a second office, originally used by the estate manager. These two rooms had been knocked into one at some point during the war — or so the architect thought, when the hotel had briefly become a hospital for injured officers. During the hotel build, it had been given the art deco treatment, and now it was hard to visualise it ever being anything else.

The master bedroom above the library had originally also had a dressing room and an en-suite bathroom. Blake and Lily had reconfigured the space so that the large dressing room was now their bedroom and the old bedroom now a private sitting room. They had kept the bathroom — and the oversized bath — but improved the plumbing. Tim had been up there a few times and knew that the art deco influence stopped at the sitting room door. After that, it was like stepping back in time, through a heavy wooden portal and into an era of Edwardian affluence and style.

He rather liked it, though he found it ironic that most guests at the Palisades came for the authentic 1930s experience, albeit with more modern plumbing. They might have been taken aback by the styling and decoration of the Blakes' private quarters. He wondered if they'd have also been surprised to find a state-of-the-art kitchen, all stainless steel and white tiles, or if they secretly expected to find an interwar kitchen, complete with lead blacked range and irascible cook.

"Time's up," Joy said. "Tim, we can't keep people waiting. If you're hoping to find a secret passage, you'll have to come back later."

He shook his head. "I don't think there'd be room, not between this and the small dining room. The wall between is thick, but there's not enough space for — oh." He saw her grin and realised she was teasing him.

"No," Joy agreed. "I saw you measuring it earlier; there isn't the space. If there was a secret door, it would have to lead downward, into the cellars." She must have seen the change in his expression as he realised she was correct, because she grabbed his hand and pulled him towards the door.

"Later, Marvello," she told him, invoking the stage name he had used back in the days when he had still been clowning at children's parties and picking up cabaret work as and when he could. He had alternated between Marvello and the Great Stupendo, depending on his audience. Now he used his own name. Tim Brandon, Illusionist, and no longer hid behind an orange wig and clown makeup or an attempt to conjure a connection to an earlier golden age of stage magicians. Tim had, largely thanks to the influence of Rina and Joy and the regular employment of Lily and James Blake, stepped out from those particular shadows and allowed himself to stand in the spotlight. He was supremely grateful for the opportunity.

He allowed himself to be dragged out of the library and into the small dining room next door. He and Joy arrived at the same time as Rina.

"George and Ursula get off OK?"

"Ursula has work this afternoon; I think they want to get some shopping done first. George didn't look too impressed at the idea."

They fell silent as someone at the front of the room rang a little bell. Tim looked towards the sound; Fliss Cameron, in a very smart, green, 1930s suit, stood by the window, her smile a bow of deep red lipstick.

"Welcome," she said. "In a few minutes we will begin our weekend of murder and mayhem and mystery. I've just got a few bits of housekeeping to attend to, and then we'll all adjourn to the library, where the first act of our little performance will take place. You'll then break up into groups to discuss what you've seen and, we hope, speculate as to what comes next."

The red smile widened as though in anticipation.

She looks a little self-satisfied, Tim thought. Though, despite himself, he was intrigued. He'd been involved in enough real-life mysteries that he'd expected to feel slightly jaded when it came to someone making this up. Surprisingly, though, he realised he was quite looking forward to solving a murder when there was no real body involved.

He glanced around the room. Rina was standing near to the door as though ready to make a break for it. She was, he felt, far less thrilled. The Montmorencys and the Peters sisters had gathered in a corner. Matthew looked serious and attentive, while Steven had found a comfortable chair, and Tim guessed he'd be disinclined to move from it until absolutely necessary. Bethany and Eliza were practically hopping with excitement. Tim smiled fondly; the sisters approached everything in life with that same level of enthusiasm and he loved them for it. He was surprised to find Seth Collins and Jess Winteringham, standing alongside the six people Rina had told him had won her in the raffle. Actually, she'd told him they'd won the weekend, but Tim was under no illusions; it was Rina they had come to meet; the rest was just pleasant window dressing.

There were others in the room: guests he had not seen the previous evening — the dinner and screening had been invitation-only, but a couple of whom he recognised from previous murder mystery weekends, when he'd done an evening set, and others who were regulars at the cabaret evenings and special events at which he performed. It felt very strange to be a guest this time instead of, essentially, staff.

He realised he had missed most of what Fliss was saying as the group began to move towards the door.

"What are we doing?" he asked Joy.

29

"Off to the library," she said. "To witness act one. Then we get to talk about it."

She didn't exactly sound thrilled, Tim thought. Then looked at her more closely. "Are you OK?"

Joy shrugged. "I thought I was," she said. "But it feels like I've had too much murder and mayhem in my life for real. It feels kind of crass, all of a sudden, to be making entertainment out of that. Maybe I should have gone with George and Ursula."

Tim blinked. He'd thought it odd that Ursula hadn't even tried to trade shifts so she could be part of the weekend, or that she had not encouraged George to come along anyway. "Oh, God, I've been rather dim again, haven't I?"

"Have you?"

Tim pulled Joy aside, allowing the crowd to pass them by. "If you want to leave, we can. Joy, I never even thought."

"I know."

To his relief, she didn't sound pissed off with him, just a tad resigned — which was almost worse. Ursula had almost been killed for real that June. They had all gone to a wedding in August that had also ended in violence. Joy had come into his life as a result of a murder and a kidnapping. Of course this weekend felt awkward and painful. The Lydia Marchant screening was different; crime on TV she could cope with, even enjoy, because it was quite literally going on behind a screen, and she had the option to switch off or go and make a cup of tea should things get too intense. This was a different kind of experience, one in which they had to participate, the actions of which they would have to analyse. It wasn't in any way real, of course, but he could imagine it would touch a nerve.

Did the Montmorencys and Rina feel the same? The Peters sisters? Was there something wrong with him, that he'd not even thought it might be difficult. That he felt nothing, when his friends and his beloved Joy felt such unease?

"I'm sorry." He clasped her hand. "Sometimes I'm a complete dunce."

She pulled his head down and kissed him, and for a moment he buried his face in the scented, strawberry-blond hair. "You are," she said. "But I love you anyway, and Rina needs us to be here. She's no more comfortable with this than I am. Come on, let's go and solve a murder, then we can go home and next week you can take me Christmas shopping as a penance."

Tim shuddered inwardly, but nodded. He figured that was the least he could do.

CHAPTER 3

A proportion of the guests had dressed up and were almost indistinguishable from the costumed actors. Rina half expected someone to step out from the audience and join the cast. Others, like Joy, were comfortable in jeans and a jumper or the equivalent.

Rina allowed her face to settle into an interested half smile, something she had become expert in over the years. She had been caught out on a couple of occasion by press photographers and had developed the interested-half-smiling resting face as a defence. It certainly came in handy now.

As the guests crowded in, the three actors had taken their positions for the first scene, holding them until Fliss signalled that everyone was present and then the action began.

Glancing at the program and list of dramatis personae — the 'witnesses,' as Fliss had called them — Rina guessed that the older lady in the black dress and pearls was probably Lady Beers and the younger couple her son Gregory and his sister, Daisy.

She was quite impressed that they plunged straight into the action, picking up in the middle of a bad-tempered discussion.

"He can't be allowed to get away with it," Lady Beers declared.

Daisy shook her head. "The consequences are too ghastly to contemplate. He has to be stopped."

"But how?" This was Gregory. "The blasted man has evidence. And he's not afraid to make use of it."

"This is your fault, Gregory. If you'd listened to me, none of this would have happened."

"And I suppose you never even flirted with the devil. Damn it, Daisy, if it hadn't been for you, I'd never have got mixed up in his circle to begin with."

"You should both have had more sense," their mother told them tartly. "I'm glad your father isn't here to see this. He'd have died of shame."

"I doubt it, Mother." Daisy's voice was sharp. "He'd have had to crawl out of the bottle for long enough to notice, and when was the last time that happened?"

"Daisy! Don't you dare speak of your father like that."

Daisy shrugged. "If you must know, I was flattered when Lord Thursby took notice of me. He was far more sophisticated and entertaining than those boys you introduce me to."

"Young men who might have offered you marriage, Daisy. Before you imperilled your reputation by getting mixed up with him. Now they just think you're fast!"

Rina tuned out a little. She could guess where this was going. It would only be a matter of time before this Lord Thursby was found dead, and the suspects — Daisy, Lady Beer, Gregory and probably a few others — were lined up for scrutiny. It would probably turn out that, in true Agatha Christie style, they all did it. She would have been quite happy with that.

She realised with a start that the scene was over, and Fliss was approaching her audience with a large cloth bag in her hand.

"Take a ball from the bag," she instructed, "and that will tell you what group you'll be in. Then you can go off with your group and discuss what might be happening and what might happen next. There are clipboards and pens on the side table in reception, so you can make your notes."

Rina's heart sank. She'd been hoping that the Peverill Lodge cohort could go off into a huddle and at least she wouldn't have to remain on her best behaviour. It seemed even that relief was to be denied. Glancing over at Tim and Joy, she could see the same dismay on Joy's face.

All right, she thought, *let's do this and do it right.* Professional smile in place, she dipped her hand into the bag and came out with a blue ball, held it up. "I'm blue," she said brightly. "Who's with me?"

CHAPTER 4

Lunch finally arrived, and Rina was able to rejoin her friends. The same loop of carols and Christmas music that had played the night before sounded softly in the dining room. That could get annoying before the weekend was through, Rina thought. The morning had not gone too badly. Her first group of five had included Joy and three of the raffle winners, and it soon became obvious that they were out to impress this doyenne of crime fiction. She was, Rina realised, far more Lydia Marchant to them than she was Rina Martin.

"I've not participated in one of these events before," Rina had told them. "But it seems to me that in the next act we'll get to meet Lord Thursby himself and see just how vile he is, and then, later this afternoon, we'll find he's been murdered."

"We've already got three suspects," Joy added. "Rina, do you think there'll be more?"

"I expect so," she said. "The writers will want to throw in a few red herrings, and the three possible suspects we've got so far are all a bit obvious."

There had followed what turned out to be a lively discussion regarding what this Lord Thursby might have done. "I'll bet it's blackmail, Genevieve," one of the lottery winners had said, and Rina had been happy to concur. Genevieve, a middle-aged woman with very dark cropped hair and very bright pink lipstick, had been ecstatic.

They had noted their theories down on the forms attached to the clipboards. The pages had been divided into columns, headed 'Suspect', and 'Motive', with a third column so they could record any other thoughts. Rina wondered how similar the ideas generated in her group would be to those in another. Perhaps this constant division and reorganisation of the guests was a good idea after all. It might stop people getting into a rut.

Though she would still rather have been with her own people.

A second scene had followed and then a second discussion. Lord Thursby, played by William Toons made his entrance, his manner sinister and threatening. Rina got the impression he was actually enjoying himself, and, though he didn't actually twirl his impressive moustache, he would have liked to. He made barbed comments about reputation to Lady Beers and suggested she look at her husband's accounts. She might find that her husband also owed him a great deal of money, and — casting a lascivious glance at Daisy Beer — that there was only one way out of their dilemma.

"Marriage!"

Daisy promptly swooned, and Lord Thursby did, in fact, give in to impulse, long fingers twisting the point of his expansive facial hair.

"Well, that was so much fun," Bethany announced, as she brought her buffet lunch over to the table. "Rina, why have we never done anything like this before?"

"Perhaps because we've been too busy solving real crimes," Eliza said.

"Oh." Bethany nodded wisely. "I suppose that's true."

"Richard and Mavis hope they get into your group this afternoon," Steven told Rina. "They're nice people, and very eager to meet the real Miss Marchant."

Rina smiled at him. "Well, if they don't manage to draw the same colour, I'll be sure to have a chat with them later."

Steven nodded. "For my money, it will be the daughter who did it. The man is a cad. Probably seduced her and now he's threatening marriage."

Eliza giggled. "Does anyone use the word 'cad' anymore? I think we should revive it; it's such a pleasantly explosive word."

"Indeed it is," Matthew agreed. "Tim, Joy, how did the morning go for you?"

"Well, apart from being in separate groups both times, I suppose it was all right," Tim said. "Though we need a couple more suspects, at least, if this performance is to last the weekend. Keeping it in the family is all very well, but it makes for a bit of a tight plot."

Rina glanced at Joy. "And how are you?" she asked, as the rest of the group continued with their chat about plotting and suspects and the groups they had been in.

"I'm OK, thank you. I think Ursula was right not to come. It would have been triggering for her. The people are nice, and it's all been fun, but I keep remembering that Ursula was nearly murdered, and then, at Mum's wedding, all hell broke loose. It makes me feel . . . vulnerable, if that makes sense. Like my skin is too thin."

"If you need to leave—" Rina began.

Joy shook her head. "I'll be fine. It's interesting though, isn't it, how differently everyone reacts. I think for some people this is almost cathartic."

Rina nodded. She smiled over at Eliza and Bethany. For the sisters, that certainly seemed to be true. Matthew reached over and grasped Joy's hand and Rina realised that he had overheard. "We're all performers, my dear. We're used to separating reality from the parts we play, and this is all about playing a part. Tim as well," he added. "Mind you, I think he'd be happier if he had a wand and a pack of cards."

Joy laughed. Tim, hearing his name, looked up. "Sorry," he said. "Did you ask me something?"

Rina shook her head fondly and turned her attention back to her lunch. The players were eating in the small dining room and not mixing with the guests, in order, so Lily had confided, to keep the illusion going. Her mind turned back to William Toons and her sense that the man was, in fact, enjoying his performance. He had seemed a little out of sorts when she had first met him, intent on making refreshments for the rest and keeping out of Fliss's way — or that had been her impression — but he seemed at ease now.

Curious, Rina took out her phone and searched for William Toons. She had expected the first search results to be about the scandal of the false accusation and his attempted recovery from that. But, although this story was certainly there, it did not top the list. Instead, she was surprised to find that he had been working in America until very recently, playing supporting roles in a string of quite successful films. Not blockbusters, perhaps, but a mix of arthouse and full cinema releases. None of the big action films George so enjoyed, so maybe he'd not been aware of Toons's rehabilitation, but it was clear that he was not performing in a hotel whodunnit because his career was in crisis.

So, she wondered, why was he here? She would have to make a point of asking him. She had found no reference to anyone being arrested for the assault on the young woman. One article referred to there having been a house party, organised by the girlfriend. Several carried statements made by Toons' legal team, making it plain that their client had been totally exonerated. There was even a statement by the girlfriend and her sister, apologising for an accusation made 'in good faith' and for the unintended consequences of that.

There was something about this that Rina found both distasteful and disturbing. Yes, it was absolutely right that a man wrongly accused should be publicly absolved, but she had spotted nothing to suggest that the young girl who had been the victim of the assault had received any kind of justice. Perhaps that wasn't considered as newsworthy.

Fliss appeared in the doorway and rang her little bell, and smiled her bright red smile. "Five minutes, everyone.

We'll assemble in the hotel reception. Thank you!" Then she was gone.

Rina fetched herself another glass of wine. Five minutes, she decided, was just long enough to finish it before returning to the fray.

* * *

Scene three took place in the reception area. A young woman in a maid's outfit of black dress, white apron and frilly headpiece hurried across the area. She was intercepted by William Toons, in his role as Lord Thursby.

"Well, girl, did you get it?"

"No sir, I've not had a chance."

"You know what happens to people who let me down." He leaned menacingly over the girl, who cowered and whimpered an apology.

He really does want to twirl that moustache again, Rina thought, *like the villains in all those old silent films.*

The door from the small dining room opened and a tall man in a butler's uniform marched out.

"Is something the matter, sir?" he asked. "Run along now, Dorcas. If his Lordship needs anything else, I'll take care of it."

Dorcas, the maid, scampered off.

"May I be of service, your Lordship?" The butler's tone was cold and Thursby's attitude also shifted. He took a step back, lost the bluster.

"So, what's the butler got on his Lordship?" Matthew, standing at Rina's side, muttered.

What indeed? Well, that was at least an interesting twist.

Thursby slunk away, and a moment later Lady Beer sailed into the hall. "Is something wrong, Denbeigh?" she asked, looking after the retreating Lord Thursby with a frown.

The butler turned to her. "Nothing I can't deal with, your Ladyship. Lord Thursby seemed to think young Dorcas had something he wanted, but the girl put him right and I sent her on her way. I believe he is leaving us this afternoon?"

"Yes, thank goodness. But he'll be back, I've no doubt about that."

"Then we will deal with him, your Ladyship," Denbeigh said coolly. "May I suggest you have a quiet word with young Dorcas in the meantime?"

"Of course, Denbeigh. I'll speak to her later this afternoon."

Butler and mistress parted then, and the scene ended. Interesting, Rina thought, almost despite herself. Two more suspects and an old family retainer who could be counted upon to act on the family's behalf. So, was the murder going to happen in the next scene? She guessed probably so. Fliss would not want to hold out until the following day, not if she wanted time for an investigation to happen.

Fliss appeared with her bag full of coloured balls. Rina drew a red this time. She held it up so her new group could gather around her, and they withdrew to a corner of the main dining room. Matthew joined her, and Genevieve, along with the two delighted winners Steven had mentioned, Richard and Mavis.

"So," Rina said. "We now have two more suspects. I'll bet that butler has previous experience in fixing things for the family."

"What if it turns out the butler did it?" Mavis laughed. "That would be precious."

What indeed, Rina thought, reflecting that sometimes the old jokes were the best and the oldest clichés the most fun.

CHAPTER 5

The last breakout session had passed quickly, coffee drunk and mince pies devoured. Richard and Mavis had proved to be good company, though Rina suspected that, had the session continued for too long, the element of competition between those two and Genevieve for her undivided attention might have become a little wearing. She could hear the chat from the other group, set up in the opposite corner of the large dining room and was pleased to see that Joy seemed to be relaxing at last and having a pleasant time. Tim was in the third group, along with both Peters sisters and a couple of paying guests. The third group had possession of a tiny office and the fourth, with Steven, had disappeared into the small dining room just off the lobby.

When Fliss appeared ringing her bell, she'd already collected these two groups and they clustered in the doorway behind her, still chattering. As Rina reached the door, she could hear that some were still speculating about the direction the plot might take; others had shifted into more personal and random conversation. Fliss shooed them out of the doorway, so that the final two groups could exit. Rina caught fragments of conversation about someone's divorce and the birth of a new grandchild. She caught Seth pontificating "this reminds me of when we had the Lydia Marchant episode that started with the lost dog . . ." and overheard speculation between one older couple, about the supermarket still being open when they drove back home the following day. If a twenty-four-hour supermarket actually stayed open for twenty-four hours on a Sunday.

In Rina's experience, the answer was a definite no. Were they bored, she wondered? Or just saving their ideas about the drama for a more appropriate moment?

The reception area was crowded, with everyone milling about like children on a school trip. She felt a sudden anxiety for the safety of the overlarge Christmas tree and the consequent urge to get them to form an orderly crocodile. Rina had moved away from the main jam, and so when Fliss ordered them all "to the library," she was among the first to get to the door.

"Wait for me." Fliss's voice was imperious.

"So, this is to be the body scene, I'll bet." Genevieve sounded excited. "She's not made us wait before."

She was probably right, Rina thought, and that would fit, planning wise, allowing for discussion to take place over the high tea they had been promised for half past four, and the investigators arriving for the final session of the day, just before dinner. Then the investigation could happen on the Sunday, before guests departed the following evening, after yet another high tea.

Fliss swung open the door. She stopped, gasped, the colour drained from her face. Rina was briefly reminded of a clown: red lips, totally white skin. Sure that the woman was about to faint, she drew Fliss aside, handing her over to Genevieve, and then peered in through the door.

"I didn't do it. I found him like this." William Toons, dressed as wicked Lord Thursby, knelt beside the body of a man Rina did not recognise. His hands were covered in the dead man's blood.

CHAPTER 6

Rina turned in the doorway to face the other guests, half closing the door to block their view. Almost everyone, she realised, had assumed this was just a very dramatic part of the action and were craning their necks to see into the room.

"Everyone back to the main dining room," Rina ordered. "Tim, call the police. Joy, see if Mac's back in town. Genevieve, get Fliss sat down and then get Lily. She's a trained first aider. Fliss is in shock. Best call an ambulance, too." Though it was too late for the man in the room.

There were protests. Some guests were still assuming this was part of the act and the ripple of laughter at Rina's performance, the suggestion that Lydia Marchant was taking charge, trailed off into nervous giggles and then silence as Tim, speaking into his mobile phone, began to shepherd everyone away. Others were cross at Rina's high-handedness, at being told what to do. Fliss was moaning softly, and Rina looked impatiently at Genevieve. Mavis came to the rescue, taking the shaking woman by the shoulders and steering her towards the small dining room. The rest of the acting company were emerging, drawn by the unexpected sounds.

"What's going on?" the actress playing Lady Beer demanded.

At that, Fliss began to wail. "He's dead. There's blood. Someone killed him."

"Now, now, enough of that." Steven had taken one of Fliss's arms and he and Mavis led the distraught woman into the room. Rina could hear the wails continuing as they closed the doors.

Confident that her Peverill Lodge family could deal with the situation, Rina ducked back into the library. William Toons had moved away from the body. He was standing beside the window, backed up to the props box Tim had examined that morning, staring at his hands.

The blood, Rina noted almost absently, was not fresh. Not yet dry — as evidenced by the reddish brown on Toons's hands and cuffs, but not fresh either. She could see extensive wounds to the chest and lower abdomen, and noted that whatever had been used to inflict these wounds had torn and dragged raggedly through the fabric of his clothes, but there was almost no trace of blood on the carpeted floor. The shirt was soaked red and the green jacket the man wore stained brown, but Rina would bet her house that he'd not been killed here, and he'd not been killed within the last hour or so.

"Let's get you out of here," she said to Toons. "Walk around the side of the room; that's it. I'm not coming in any further. We've already contaminated the crime scene enough."

"I didn't do it. I just found him like that," Toons was distraught.

"And I believe you," Rina told him sharply. She wasn't entirely certain that was true. He could have killed this man earlier and dumped the body here, then "found" it when he came to get ready for his own death scene. But that would be for someone else to determine. For now, she just wanted to get him out of the room.

"You believe me?" He sounded shocked, almost affronted, then relieved when he said, "You *do* believe me."

"Let's just get you out of here," Rina told him again. "Come along and don't touch anything."

He did as he was told, taking a path close to the wall, but with his hands tucked almost comically across his chest.

"That's the way."

Rina nudged the door back open and released William Toons into the hall. Tim and Joy were standing at the foot of the stairs. Lily and Blake were with them.

"Rina, what's going on?" Lily demanded, her face pale and a look of shock on her face as she noted the blood on William Toons's hands.

"Lily, can I put William in your office?" Rina asked. "I think he needs to be somewhere quiet. Can you make sure no one goes into the library until the police arrive?"

Lily looked as though she wanted to argue, to tell Rina that there couldn't possibly be a body in the library; that things like that just didn't happen at the Palisades. But she nodded and stood aside.

"Mac's coming over." Tim said. "Joy managed to get hold of him. He and Miriam had only been back an hour. Sergeant Baker and Andy Nevins are on their way, too, and an ambulance. I thought the local police would be quicker than getting someone here from Bridport or Exeter."

"Good thinking. Lily, I know you've done first aid training. Could you take a look at Fliss? I think she's had a big shock. They've got her in the small dining room. And I think maybe we could all do with tea and coffee. Everyone's going to be upset."

"I'll take care of that," James told her. He looked shaken but seemed relieved to have something to do. "Is there really someone dead in there?"

Rina nodded. "Not anyone I recognise. Not anyone staying here, I don't think, and I know all the staff, at least by sight, so I'm pretty sure it's not one of them—"

"Well, I suppose that's something," James said, and strode off to deal with refreshments.

Rina escorted William Toons to the office. He'd said nothing since they had left the library. He was shaking and kept staring at his hands as though not quite believing what he saw. Rina settled him close to the radiator and he pressed his back to it as though suddenly frozen. Rina was relieved when, a moment or so later, Joy knocked at the door. She was carrying a blanket, which Rina wrapped around Toons.

"I knew he'd be cold," Joy said. She had, Rina knew, had her own experience of shock following violent acts.

A car pulled up outside the hotel and two familiar figures got out, both dressed for the weekend rather than in their usual uniforms. DC Andy Nevins, with his red hair and freckles and gangly frame, saw Rina and waved as though this was a social call. Sergeant Frank Baker shut his door and nodded at her. Behind them, an ambulance appeared.

"Mac called to say he was only minutes away," Joy said. "Miriam's coming with him. She wants to make sure the scene is secured before the CSI arrive. It's weekend; it may take a while for a team to get here." Miriam, DI MacGregor's partner, was a senior CSI.

Rina nodded; that was all good. "You sit tight," she told Toons, who had clutched the banket around himself, his bloodied hands now out of sight. She followed Joy out into the lobby.

They could hear raised voices coming from the large dining room as Frank Baker and Andy came into the lobby. Frank glanced over at the source of the noise.

"I take it you've got the guests corralled in there?"

Rina nodded.

"Well, I'll go and settle them down," Frank said. "Andy, take a look and see what we're dealing with. For the purposes of the investigation, you'll be FOA."

Andy nodded. As first officer attending, he'd be responsible for assessing and protecting the scene and gathering initial information. "Did you find the body, Mrs Martin?"

"No, the person who first saw the body was William Toons. He's an actor on this murder mystery weekend. He'd gone into the library to get ready for his scene and he found and touched the body. He's in Lily's office. The next person was Fliss Cameron, who runs the acting troupe. She's in the

46

small dining room." Rina pointed at the door. "I was next. I went just inside the doorway and coaxed Mr Toons out. He was very distressed, as was Fliss."

Andy nodded. "Right, let's take a look and then speak to witnesses. That'll be you as well, Mrs Martin."

Rina nodded. She'd known young Andy since his probationer year in the police, so just over five years, yet despite that, she could never get him to call her anything but Mrs Martin. He could never quite manage "Rina".

Sergeant Baker opened the dining room door. Tim and Joy exchanged a glance and then followed him, wanting, Rina guessed, to be with the rest of the family. The sounds of raised voices and irritation grew louder and then subsided as the door closed. Frank Baker's own voice rose above the hubbub. He managed, Rina noted, to sound both cheerful and commanding, which was a good trick in anyone's book. Andy Nevins opened the library door and looked inside, then stood in the doorway taking notes. There was, Rina thought, no need for him to go in and check that life was extinct. The extent of the wounds and the stillness of the body told him that.

So why, Rina wondered, had William Toons been drawn to do so? Why had he not just seen the dead man and backed out? Probably with some appropriate screaming or yelling to accompany the action. To have crossed the room, knelt by the body, touched the blood . . . that spoke of a more personal connection. The need to touch, to check that a life was ended, even when that was self-evident. And to have closed the library door before doing so — that was a complex set of actions.

Another car drew up outside and Rina could see Mac and Miriam inside. She waited for them beside the large glass doors.

"Are you all right?" Miriam asked, giving her a hug.

Mac bent and kissed her on the cheek. "Can't leave you for five minutes, can I?"

CHAPTER 7

Rina knew that soon enough the Palisades would be the location of a full-scale murder investigation. That Mac would call on reinforcements and quite possibly someone else would take over, as the Frantham contingent of law enforcement numbered exactly three officers, and they were all currently present. Mac, however, and his colleagues, had between them an unenviable amount of experience in the investigation of violent crime, so it was possible that he would remain as senior investigating officer. She paused to wonder if he really wanted to be SIO, heading up a major investigation, so soon after he'd come back from what was probably a rather trying family holiday.

She stood in the office doorway as Andy Nevins took a preliminary statement from William Toons. She had intended to leave, but Toons had become panicky at the idea, so she stood now, half present and half not, listening as Andy asked the shocked man what had happened, the other part of her attention drawn to the activity across the reception area.

Miriam always had basic kit in her car, ready for those occasions when she was called out from home and first to arrive. Rina watched as, outside the library door, she stripped the plastic from a fresh coverall and donned that and a mask

48

before entering the room. Behind Rina, William Toons recounted how he had gone into the library to prepare for his scene. The idea was that he would be found dead on the library floor, fake blood on his chest, clutching a knife. He touched his pocket. "I've still got the fake blood and the knife in my pocket. It's just a stage prop."

"Leave it there for now," Andy told him.

The police would want to examine it anyway, Rina thought.

William Toons explained that he had opened the door and seen the man already lying there and, he said, he had frozen.

"I had this stupid thought," Toons said, "That there'd been some kind of mix-up. That maybe I was in the wrong room, but I couldn't remember Fliss ever saying anything about two bodies. I wondered if she'd written an extra scene and not told me. Then I thought, oh, she's replaced me and no one bothered to let me know. And then I realised, this wasn't acting, this wasn't someone pretending to be dead. This was someone who was really dead."

From the corner of her eye, Rina saw Andy nod encouragingly. "So, once you'd realised that, why didn't you go and get help? Call the police. Or at least warn the guests not to go to the library?"

"I . . . I don't know. I think I wanted to see if he really was dead. I think I didn't quite believe it."

Rina glanced at William Toons. *Yes, you really* did *want to see if he was dead, didn't you? I think you hoped it was the truth.*

She sensed that Andy had picked up on this too, because his next question was asked with careful emphasis. "And you say you have no idea who this man might be? You don't recognise him? You've not seen him before?"

"I . . . no. I don't know who he is. I've not seen him before. At least, I don't think I have."

He's covering himself, Rina thought. He can say later that he might have seen this man. That he might have spotted him hanging around the hotel. But why?

Again, Andy seemed to be following the same train of thought.

"A hotel like this is a busy place," Andy said. "You didn't spot him among the guests at any time? Or outside in the grounds? A couple of public footpaths come through here, from the cliff path and another through the woods at the back, so—"

Toons frowned and shrugged. "It's possible," he said. "I just don't remember if I did."

Andy nodded again. "Why did you touch him, Mr Toons? Forgive me for saying so, but that's an unusual thing to do." He, softened his tone, managed an almost conspiratorial half-laugh. "You know, most people find a dead body and run screaming."

William Toons smiled. A brief and fleeting smile, but one, Rina thought, that spoke of relief at this sympathetic young officer. This probably not very experienced young man. Rina almost smiled, too — at the misconception.

"I suppose I wanted to make sure he was dead. I suppose it was in my mind that he might not be and that I should call an ambulance for him. I really don't know what I thought."

Andy nodded again and, even though he was recording the conversation — with Toons's agreement — jotted something down in his notebook. "And you'd closed the door when you went into the room?"

Toons shrugged. "I don't remember doing that. I suppose I must have done."

"All right, so what happened then?"

"Then I heard noises outside, and I realised that the guests would be coming in for the next scene. And then the door opened and Fliss saw . . . saw me and the dead man, and I realised I'd touched the body and I had blood on my hands. Well, you've seen I had blood on my hands. I'd really like to wash them, if I could."

Andy nodded again. "I'll get that organised in just a minute." He had taken photographs of the bloody palms and then produced some wet wipes and allowed Toons to wipe the blood away. The wet wipes had then been bagged, Andy doing this in a most casual manner and with an encouraging smile. Procedure, he had said, and William Toons had nodded absently, as though that word made everything all right. Andy had labelled the bag while Rina handed William a cup of tea. She'd been slightly surprised that Andy hadn't asked Toons to allow Miriam to take scrapings from his nails, again just as procedure. Rina had observed that the word acted as an open sesame for many people who had found themselves caught up in unexpected violence. Perhaps, she mused, it was because it was used to effect on so many television programmes that it had become almost a soothing expectation that procedures would be carried out.

So she had wondered about the nails. But when she had handed Toons the mug, she had seen what Andy must have noted. That the nails were bitten short, almost to the quick. There was nothing much to scrape.

"I'm going to have to ask you for your clothes and shoes," Andy said gently. "It's possible you picked up some evidence of the killer when you were in there, especially as you got so close to the body. Will that be all right?" He had already obtained foot covers from Miriam and placed them on Toons's feet.

William Toons nodded weakly. "I'll need something to put on. There are clothes in my room. I can go up."

"Don't worry, sir, we'll find you something," Andy said. "So, tell me what happened next," he added, distracting Toons from the idea of stripping off and not being able to get his own clothes to change into. Rina knew they'd have to check Toons's room and all his belongings first. It was totally possible that he was just an unfortunate witness, but the possibility had to be considered that he was in some way involved. Due diligence would have to be observed.

She noticed that Miriam had come out of the library and deposited her camera back in its case. The sound of other vehicles pulling up on the gravel drive attracted Rina's attention. Mac went to the door to greet the new arrivals.

A CSI team exited from a van and two familiar figures got out of the car, DI Dave Kendall and DC Yolanda Connors. Andy, his attention totally focussed on William Toons, did not look out of the window or acknowledge his girlfriend. He and Yolanda, who worked with Inspector Kendall, had been seeing one another since late spring; they were talking of getting a place together. She assumed Mac must have called DI Kendall, and that other officers would soon be arriving.

William Toons had half turned at the sound of the cars, but Andy gently pulled his attention back. "And what happened then?"

"Then Mrs Martin — Rina — came into the doorway, and she pulled the door half closed and I told her I just found him like that and I hadn't done anything." The panic and fear were back in his voice. "She told me to come out of the room, to keep by the wall and not touch anything, and then she brought me in here."

"Thank you, Mr Toons," Andy said, as a patrol car pulled up in the drive and two officers emerged.

"Now, Mr Toons, you've been really helpful. You see that car that's just arrived? Well, if you can go with the two officers, they'll be taking you to Bridport and someone will probably ask you all the questions I've just asked, again. I know it's tiresome, but that's the way these things work, I'm afraid."

"But I just found him! You can't think—"

"Mr Toons, no one is suggesting anything. It's all just procedure. It's like a checklist and if we don't all go through the checklist, then we can have trouble later on, if some little thing we didn't double-check proves to be important. You see?"

Andy's voice was soothing, admirably calm, and that calm transmitted itself to Toons, who assented reluctantly, making no further protest. But then, she thought, Andy'd had good teachers: Mac, Sergeant Baker and, she liked to think, a little input from herself.

Miriam came over with a white coverall, still in its plastic wrapper. Rina hoped it was, larger than the one Miriam was wearing. Andy pointed towards her.

"This is Miss Hastings," he said. "She's got a coverall for you to put on, over your clothes, before you get into the police car. You remember what I said to you about maybe picking up evidence when you knelt down and touched the body? Well, this will help preserve that evidence. Then when you get to the police station someone, another CSI like Miss Hastings, will need to take your clothes. Don't worry, we'll find you something to wear," he smiled reassuringly. "You all right with all this, Mr Toons?"

Rina wondered absently what would happen if he said no, but William Toons just seemed resigned.

"Can Rina come with me?"

What was she, Rina wondered, suddenly a good luck talisman?

"I'm sorry, no. We need to ask Mrs Martin some questions, too. You'll see her when the officers bring you back."

A few minutes later, Rina watched as William Toons was helped into the police car. He looked very ill at ease, but then so did most people forced to pull a too-small bunny suit over their clothes and sit in the back of a patrol car. He'd hung onto the blanket, she noted.

"I think he knew the victim," Rina said to Andy. "Or at least knows who he is."

"I don't doubt it," Andy said. "But did he kill him?"

Rina did not have the answer to that one.

CHAPTER 8

Rina caused something of a stir when she re-entered the large dining room to join the rest of the guests, with all eyes turning in her direction. The players had now joined them, along with Fliss who looked pale but composed and was sipping what looked like a large brandy. Rina wondered how many had preceded it.

Her family was seated at a table by the window. They waved and smiled as though Rina was a late but welcome guest at a party, earning looks of disapprobation from the rest of the room. Rina smiled back and then seated herself in the space Matthew had been saving for her.

"I'll get you some tea," Bethany said. "Or would you like something stronger?"

I could do with a double whisky. Light on the ginger. But she shook her head. "Tea would be lovely."

"So, what's happening?" Eliza leaned over and whispered conspiratorially. "We saw them take poor Mr Toons away. Is he a suspect?"

Bethany returned with the tea and set it down by Rina's hand. The sisters now regarded her with equal intensity, heads tilted slightly to one side. They had, she thought, been a double act for so long that even now, long into retirement, their actions automatically mirrored one another.

"Truthfully, I don't know. He is, at the least, a material witness. Andy talked to him, just so he could get the facts down, but he's been taken to the police station for a proper interview, and he's got to hand over his clothes. That's why he was wearing the overalls. It's possible he picked up some evidence at the crime scene, so they'll need to examine him and what he was wearing."

"We saw Mac and Miriam arriving," Matthew said. "Have you had a chance to speak to him?"

"Only to say hello, really. He looked tired. I think the family gathering must have been lively."

"Miriam's family do like their parties," Steven said, "and Mac isn't exactly an extrovert, is he?"

No, he wasn't, but then, neither was Miriam. Her sister always said she must be a changeling; even as a child she'd been resistant to the family exuberance, often creeping off upstairs to read her book once she'd done her social duties. After a while, they seemed to have just accepted that was just the way she was. Rina had met Miriam's parents and sister; she'd liked them a lot, especially the sister, but imagined a full week of them might be hard work.

"Mac will be through later, to tell everyone what's happening. I imagine there'll be some kind of preliminary interviews, but I doubt they'll keep people here for longer than necessary."

"Well, most people will have alibis for almost all of today," Bethany said. "Or at least those who made it down to breakfast. After that, we were all watching the play and in our groups. And I think everyone was present at lunch. Of course, we didn't get high tea." She looked quite disappointed about that.

"Though it depends when the poor man was killed, of course."

"Do you have any sense of that?" Tim asked.

"Not really. Though the blood on William Toons's hands wasn't fresh. Not fully dried, obviously, but not, I'd have said, from fresh wounds."

"Oh, Rina, it's just horrible."

Rina turned to look at Joy. The young woman looked sick and distressed. She reached across the table and took her hand. "Yes," she said, "it is. Whoever he was."

She became painfully aware that their table was the centre of attention. They had kept their voices down, but those sitting closest were straining to hear and making no secret of it. Rina spotted Frank Baker heading in their direction, a smile on his face — but Rina, knowing him well, suspected they were about to get a gentle telling off.

"I know, Sergeant Baker," she said, as he arrived. "No more speculating."

"If you wouldn't mind, Mrs Martin," he agreed. "We don't want people talking about it too much. You know how ideas and memories can then get muddled."

Rina nodded. She could almost feel the collective sigh of disappointment from the rest of the room. They had been hoping for a break in the monotony of waiting. For the chance of overhearing some juicy bit of gossip.

The room was, in fact, almost uncannily quiet. Eager to speak with her friends, Rina had not noticed that at first, but as Frank Baker went off to chat to another group and Yolanda escorted two of the female guests to the toilet, she was suddenly struck by the level of discomfort. By the realisation that no one was to be left alone to gossip or allowed to leave unattended. That Sergeant Baker's gentle platitudes and Yolanda's cheerfulness were masking their careful management of these witnesses who might just as easily be suspects. Until they could be questioned, and their whereabouts ascertained for the time the man had probably been killed, they had to be warehoused, conversations controlled, calm maintained.

She really did now wish she'd asked for the whisky in place of the tea.

Mac had told her that they intended to make use of the small dining room as their incident room. Lily and James Blake had loaned the police a part of their refurbished stable block for a previous investigation, but Rina guessed this incursion was definitely not as welcome, especially as the hotel was now likely to be closed for several days while the investigation was in its initial phase. She felt for the Blakes. They'd worked so hard to get this place up and running and into profit; Rina fervently hoped that there would be no long-term impact on the business.

Lily and James were now busying themselves ensuring their guests had refreshments. This effort was already flagging; after all, there was only so much tea or coffee or alcohol even a large group could drink, especially in such a tense atmosphere. Glancing at her watch, Rina noted that it was almost dinner time, and the growling of her stomach reminded her that the promised high tea had not occurred, the discovery of the wrong body having interrupted proceedings. As the kitchens were in a separate wing, she guessed that preparation had been allowed to continue, as the scent of food had been wafting along the corridor. She anticipated a wave of reluctance, as everyone assured one another they couldn't eat a thing, before they realised just how ravenous they all were. She made a mental note to be up first with her tray. It was her experience that the adrenaline rush that was an inevitable adjunct to incidents like this made people unexpectedly hungry.

She wondered what Mac and Miriam and Dave Kendall were doing and wished fervently, as she accepted another cup of tea from Lily, that she could be a fly on their particular wall.

* * *

At that point, Mac and DI Kendall were assessing what they currently knew, which wasn't a whole lot. There had been no identification on the body. Miriam, though reluctant to commit, had suggested the man had been dead for perhaps two or three hours and definitely killed elsewhere. She was troubled, though; the body temperature was lower than she expected it to be, given the still-wet nature of the blood. On that single basis, she would have estimated death to have taken place two or three hours before. There was no sign of rigor, but the body temp had dropped to a level she'd have expected at a much later point, and for a body lying in a much colder environment. It didn't add up. She hoped a more thorough examination by the newly arrived team and then the post-mortem would help to make sense of this anomaly.

One thing she was pretty certain of, the man had not been killed where he was found.

"There would have been a lot more blood, had he been killed in the library," Kendall agreed. "The blood isn't fully dried, so we have to assume whoever carried him into the library would have been contaminated by it. They must have had somewhere to dispose of the stained clothing, in which case, we might strike lucky and find it in the house."

Mac laughed. "That would be considerate of the killer."

"Or they left quickly, before anyone saw them, blood-stained clothing and all."

"Which would not have been difficult," Mac said. "There are several exits from the hotel, and most of the guests would have been involved in this murder mystery thing and out of the way. Staff will have been about their regular duties, so anyone who knew the layout and the usual routine could have avoided notice quite easily. Once out of the house, they could have gone through the woods at the back and, if they'd left their car parked on the lane, could have been well away within, what, ten minutes."

"You're making the assumption they were familiar with the place."

Mac saw Kendall considering this. Finally, Kendall said, "Most likely you're right. The Palisades isn't positioned to attract passing trade. You have to know it's here. But that knowledge is going to be shared by anyone who ever stayed here, or anyone who ever worked here, and that's a sizeable list."

"True," Mac agreed.

Kendall shrugged. "OK, so we assume a familiarity with the building and its exits, and that they left through the woodland, where there's better cover. The cliff path is too open; there's too much risk of someone spotting them. The road from the Palisades down to Frantham, likewise. Anyone walking up the drive, in bloodied clothes, would run the risk of being spotted from the house. So, the likelihood is they left by the woods and the back road. We might get lucky and have someone notice a parked car. Isn't there a layby?"

Mac nodded. "So hikers can access the public footpath. Cutting through the hotel grounds is a quick way onto the cliff path. It's busy in the summer, and the hotel bar is open throughout the day. They serve sandwiches and the like in the bar during the summer months, when they do get passing trade, from walkers and hikers and families. At this time of year, though—"

Kendall nodded. "And our dead man is definitely not one of the guests?"

"I've shown his picture to the owners, and the staff. No one recognises him as a guest."

"You think they recognise him as something else?"

"I got the impression that Lily half recognised him, or at least thought she did, but she wouldn't commit. I'll have another talk with her later."

"So, next step is to figure out where everyone was immediately before the body was found, and for, say, three to four hours before. If we need to extend the timeline later, we can, but it depends what the post-mortem tells us."

"Whoever killed him wanted to be sure," Mac observed. He picked up the tablet and regarded the images Miriam had taken of the body, enlarging so that he and Kendall could examine the injuries. It was not an edifying experience. The dead man had been stabbed at least three or four times in the chest, and the wounds to the abdomen had ripped and torn as much as they had stabbed, exposing muscle and intestine.

"Whoever carried him in here was strong," Mac said. "He's no lightweight and he'd have been a literal dead weight. Whoever it was would also have been a right mess by the time they finished. You think it might be worth getting a cadaver dog out in the woods?"

"You hoping for another body?" Kendall asked.

"I'm wondering if there might be a blood trail," Mac said. "The killer can't have avoided brushing up against the undergrowth, even if they risked taking the path. It gets pretty narrow in places. As I don't know of any bloodhound packs around here, I wondered about a cadaver dog."

Kendall, he noted, still looked slightly sceptical, but he nodded. "I'll have a word with the dog handlers, see what they think, but it might be worthwhile." He glanced out of the window. Mac, too, noted the leaden sky and heavy clouds. "Though it looks like we're in for some snow. That could make it difficult."

"If we can establish a route the killer took, through the woods or across the adjacent fields, we'd have a better chance of identifying any vehicle they might have used to make their escape." And, Mac thought, they must have used a vehicle to get themselves away. There were no houses within easy walking distance of the hotel and no remote outbuildings that he could think of, where someone might have changed their clothes.

There were stables and ancillary buildings attached to the hotel, of course, but these had all been converted into additional accommodation in the past couple of years. One stable block had become self-catering accommodation, and the old coach house was now converted into the very modern kitchens, and had been joined to the house by a short passageway.

Backup had now arrived, the sound of tyres on gravel announcing the arrival of two more cars and six officers being dropped off.

"Right, we get everyone in for preliminary interviews. Establish whereabouts for the day, get their rooms examined and get rid of everyone that can be got rid of, as soon as possible," Kendall said. "I'll inform the troops that you're the SIO and you can brief me this evening. Meantime, I'll get us some space back in Bridport."

Mac nodded. "It's interesting, isn't it, that the next scene in this little drama was to be the finding of a body in the library?"

Kendall laughed. "Someone has a twisted sense of humour."

"Probably, but it does make me wonder, why bother? If you want to dispose of a body, there's a nice selection of cliffs around here, and several places where parking is available close to the cliff path. This time of year, you could chuck someone in and be pretty sure not only of not being seen, but that they'd be taken out to sea and likely never found. Or, if they were, it would be after a good battering by the tide and cliffs. Unless the dead man was actually killed on the premises, then the killer brought them from the road, which is a good ten minutes away, even if you're not conveying a body. It seems unnecessarily complicated."

"So, you think someone is making a statement. Maybe trying to cause specific problems for the Blakes?"

"Maybe. Maybe even for William Toons. Maybe they knew he'd be the one to find the body."

"For that, they'd have to know the schedule for the weekend."

"True," Mac agreed, "and maybe I'm being fanciful, but—"

"But maybe you're not."

The newly arrived officers were filing in, and Kendall turned to greet them and to introduce them to Mac. He recognised a few familiar faces and prepared to brief them before Kendall departed. He was tired, from the busy week, from the drive home, from the prospect of the rest of Saturday and all of Sunday spent in lazing and relaxing with his favourite human being suddenly snatched away from him.

As though on cue, Miriam appeared in the doorway and then made her way over to him.

"I've handed off to Barry," she said. "I'm not due into work until Tuesday and they'd have to pay me overtime, so—"

"So you're off home."

"I'll come and get you when you're done here. We can pick up a takeaway and maybe watch a film?"

"That would be good, but I don't know how long I'm going to be."

"So Dave's landed you in it," she said. "Meanwhile he gets the rest of his weekend."

Dave Kendall, standing next to Mac, grinned at her. "I'm providing resources." He gestured in an exaggerated manner at the new troops.

Mac bent to kiss her. "I'll be home as soon as I can. I'll catch a lift with someone," he promised, grateful — not for the first time — that she understood how these things went. Sometimes it was Miriam who got called out unexpectedly; sometimes it was him. On odd occasions, it could be both.

He watched her walk back across the room, knowing that he wasn't the only one. Miriam with her long dark hair and blue eyes was beautiful. She was also clever and funny and kind and kept him vaguely sane.

He turned his attention back to Kendall and stepped forward to brief those newly arrived. Andy had joined them, while Sergeant Baker and Yolanda were still holding the fort in the dining room, and, Mac knew, keeping a lid on the speculation while also paying attention to the gossip. People trusted Frank and instinctively wanted to confide in him, and Yolanda was learning fast. She had a knack of listening to people as though genuinely interested in them. No, he thought, she *was* genuinely interested in them and that was a useful skill. She'd come a long way from the young woman he had first met a few years before, experiencing the countryside for the first time and disgusted at the thought she might need wellies.

"DC Nevins was first officer attending," he said, beckoning Andy forward. "He's spoken to the witness, William Toons, who found the body. Mr Toons has been taken to Bridport to make a statement — as a witness, for the time being, not as a suspect. Andy?"

Mac stepped back, giving Andy the floor. Listened as attentively as the rest of the room as Andy described his conversation with William Toons and fielded questions from the floor with the efficiency of an officer twice his years, Mac thought.

Then they prepared for the long haul of room searches and interviews to begin.

* * *

Rina looked up as Mac came into the large dining room to let the guests know what was going on. They had all been aware of the comings and goings, and Sergeant Baker and Yolanda had done a lot of the groundwork for him. They had spoken to the guests and suggested that the police might want to take a quick look at their rooms.

"There's a possibility," Sergeant Baker had told them gravely, "that the killer might have needed to get rid of evidence very quickly. I know all your rooms would have been locked, but it's just possible our man gained entry."

Frank Baker had also acquired a stack of printer paper and assorted pencils and pens, and encouraged everyone to write down their timelines for the day. Most people had set to the task with a modicum of enthusiasm; at least it gave them something to do.

"Everyone's been very cooperative," Rina heard Yolanda tell him, as she handed over a tray laid out with room keys to Mac. "I told everyone it would be a very quick inspection; they won't even know anyone was there."

"I'll pass the message on," Mac said dryly. He sent a quick smile in Rina's direction and then took up position at the end of the room, where he thanked everyone for their help, commiserated on the distress caused and assured the guests that they'd be on their way as soon as possible.

"I've got a number of officers waiting to take your statements," he said. "We need to know where everyone was this morning. I understand from Sergeant Baker that you've already started on this, so thank you all very much. If you could think about what you were doing and where you were from about six a.m., that would be a real help. And, of course, if you saw anyone acting suspiciously, either last night or today, then if you could report that as well."

The rattle of trolleys in the hallway told Rina that food was arriving. That would improve morale, she thought.

Mac assured everyone they'd have time to eat before the interviews began and responded to a handful of questions, while food was set out on the buffet tables at the end of the room. He assured everyone once again that they'd get the formalities over with as soon as possible, and then went on his way.

"I don't think he's got a clue what's going on," Bethany said sadly.

"No, but he'll sort it all out in the end," Eliza told her. "Mac's good at putting things right. Just like Rina."

CHAPTER 9

Mac went with Andy to examine William Toons's room. He wanted to get a feel for the man, though he had no real expectation of finding anything significant. The photographer had just finished when they arrived, and a gloved and suited CSI had finished examining the belongings. They had nothing of interest to report.

"Suitcase is empty, clothes are in the wardrobe and two drawers, but there's nothing you wouldn't expect to find for a man staying over the weekend in a hotel. Nothing beneath the mattress, or in the mattress, nothing concealed in the headboard, not unless he could insert it without doing any damage. There's a diary on the bedside table and a paperback book he seems to have scribbled some notes on, but that's it."

Mac thanked him, and he and Andy donned gloves.

Once the CSI had gone, Andy repeated the search, giving a running commentary to his boss. It was not because of any doubt about the work of the investigator, but just that Andy knew by now that having an inventory helped them both to get a better idea of what they were dealing with.

"Winter coat, quilted, undamaged lining." He patted it down, satisfying himself that nothing had been concealed. The contents of the pockets had been bagged: a used tissue, a bottle

65

of hand gel, some loose change and a pinecone. Mac, who was still in the habit of picking up acorns and conkers and beach pebbles, felt a momentary tug of fellowship with Toons.

"Three shirts, two jumpers," he reported, and then the usual underwear and socks in the drawers. Mac didn't bother asking Andy to lift the mattress again. The CSI would have made a thorough examination of that.

The bathroom proved no more interesting. Toiletries, toothbrush, an unused pack of supermarket own brand pain-killers and a packet of antihistamines.

Andy noted these. "It's not exactly hay-fever season, is it."

"No, but Miriam takes them when her dust allergy flares up. They're not just for hay fever."

Andy nodded. "Anything in the diary?"

"It's just a pocket diary. There's appointments and the odd phone number. This weekend is listed as *Fliss's thing*, and there's the post code of the hotel, so presumably for his satnav."

The book mentioned by the CSI turned out to be a political thriller Mac had heard of — the cover told him it was about to become a major Hollywood film. Was William Toons going to be in it? He had evidently started reading it; a bookmark stuck out about a quarter of the way in, which proved to be a supermarket till receipt that listed ibuprofen, the book and a sandwich deal. They had been bought on the previous Thursday, so just prior to Toons' arrival at the Palisades.

He flicked through, looking at Toons's notes. He'd underlined several sentences — using the pen on the bed-side table, presumably. Beside one underline he had written '*motivation?*' A little further down, '*would Maddison suspect yet that Paul was playing away?*' A quick flick through the pages revealed that both Maddison and Paul were characters in the novel. Perhaps Toons was simply preparing for a role. Mac would have to ask him.

He set the book aside, bagged the diary and told Andy he thought they had seen all there was to see. But then, because he was used to being thorough, Mac bagged the book as well, sealing it in an evidence bag, and then taking it and the diary and the contents of Toons's coat pockets away with him.

* * *

"Mind if we join you? I'm bored to tears. The sergeant says it's all right."

Seth Collis, Rina's co-star and her on-screen niece, Jess Witherington, looked hopefully at her.

"Of course not," Rina said, and everyone shuffled up, Tim finding extra chairs for the newcomers. It made the space around the table a little crowded, but a bit of rearranging and the disposal of trays soon sorted that. Rina poured wine.

"How are you both holding up?" she asked.

"Well, to start with it was just like hanging around between scenes," Jess said. "Then it all started to get really boring. I mean, what can you talk about if you can't talk about the murder?"

Rina smiled at her. "At least we've had lots of practice in hanging around," she said. "I think it's been harder for everyone else."

"But I've usually got a book to read or some knitting," Jess said, "and Seth has his crosswords and his boxed sets."

That was true, Rina thought. Seth kept a tablet with him and was usually deep into some crime drama or historical series, cut off from the rest of the world by his rather expensive headset.

"How much longer do you think they'll keep us?" Seth asked.

"Well, it's after seven now. I can't see the interviews being done much before midnight."

"So, we'll be here overnight," Seth said glumly. "You think we'll be allowed to go to our rooms?"

"So long as they don't expand the crime scene. If the only areas of interest are the library and the adjacent areas, I don't imagine it will be a problem. Though I expect they'll want everyone to use the back stairs."

"I don't know what any of us can tell them. We were all together for most of the day. It's not like any of us had time to kill anyone."

Rina wondered if she should remind Seth that they were not supposed to be discussing the murder. It also occurred to her that it didn't really take long to kill someone. Though, she frowned, in this case, whoever had placed the body in the library would still have had to clean themselves up and then get back to whatever they were doing. That would be the thing to take the time. Unless they'd done the deed very early that morning, of course. But there was still the issue of getting the body to the library. Had the body been positioned early in the day, they'd run the risk of it being discovered before William Toons went to take up his position.

"Penny for them," Tim said.

"Oh, I was just wondering how likely it was that anyone wandered into the library before the body scene was due to happen," she said. "So I suppose I was wondering how long the body had actually been there."

She sipped her wine and thought about it. Silence reigned for a moment or two, and then Eliza asked Seth about series three of Lydia Marchant, due to begin filming in the spring. Rina listened with half an ear as the conversation turned to their various careers and away from the events of the day.

No, she thought, on balance, it was unlikely anyone involved in the murder mystery weekend had killed the man in the library, but the thought that both William Toons and Fliss Cameron knew a great deal more about him that they were letting on refused to go away.

"Do you think they suspect Will?" Jess asked, in almost a whisper. "They took him away."

"He found the body," Rina told her. "So they need to get a formal statement and to examine his clothes, just in case he picked anything up at the crime scene."

"You mean like fibres or something?"

Rina nodded. "I expect he'll be back soon. The poor man was very shaken up."

"I don't suppose he's comfortable dealing with the police. I mean after the last time."

"I don't think many people are comfortable with being interviewed," Rina said. "I think most of us feel guilty, even when we're not. It's like driving when a police car's following, even if you know you're not doing anything wrong, you still drive with one eye on the speedometer."

Jess laughed. "I suppose so."

Rina studied the younger woman. She did indeed look anxious. Was she really just nervous about making a statement, and quite naturally upset by this turn of events, or was there something more?

"You said you worked with Will Toons?"

Jess nodded. From the slight change in her expression, Rina guessed that he was the chief subject of her anxiety.

"And what was that like? What were you both in?"

"Oh, I learnt a lot. It was a summer, Shakespeare-in-the-park kind of thing, except it wasn't Shakespeare. It was Chekov, and we were in the gardens of this big stately home up in Yorkshire. We did the rehearsals in one of the tithe barns and then open-air performances, until it rained so hard for two days you couldn't see your hand in front of your face. Then we had to move back into the barn for the performances.

"People still came, though. It really was in the middle of nowhere and the roads were like rivers, but we got a full house, even on those nights."

Rina smiled at the sudden enthusiasm in the young woman's voice. She was about to ask what role Jess had played, but her expression changed, and Rina could see the anxiety return. "What was Will Toons like to work with?" she asked instead.

"Oh, to work with, he was fantastic. Kind and encouraging and really supportive. We were an inexperienced cast, most of us straight out of drama school or, like me, in the second year. This was like paid work experience."

"At least it was paid."

Jess nodded fervent agreement.

"And when you weren't working?"

Jess's expression twisted into one of distaste and, Rina thought, remembered distress.

"Well, it wasn't like he pressured anyone, but we were all young and I think flattered by the attention. A couple of the girls, well, you know."

Rina nodded. "And you?"

Jess shrugged. "Rina, you know what it's like sometimes when you go along with something just because you can't think of a way of getting out of it?"

"Did he threaten you?"

"No, not like that. It was just . . . look, I was nineteen and not very experienced and a bit overwhelmed and I'd had too much to drink and I wasn't very good at saying no back then. I suppose a bit of me also wanted to think this was special. That he'd singled me out, even though I knew he hadn't. He was good looking and successful and, well . . ." She looked anxiously at Rina, clearly uncomfortable talking about this episode.

Rina nodded. "I think we've all been in situations we regret. And when the other person involved is in a more powerful position, it can be very difficult."

"Can't it just! Well, the following day, it was like he hardly knew me. I felt humiliated, I suppose, and angry. I wondered how often he'd done exactly the same thing. I mean, he'd not forced me to do anything, but I still felt like I'd just been used. I was young, I'd had too much to drink, I was really out of my depth."

"So, when you heard the allegations about the sexual assault, you found it easy to believe," Rina said.

Jess looked uncomfortable, but nodded. When Seth and Jess had joined the group, and the extra chairs accommodated around the table, Rina and Jess had found their seats pushed back a little and the slight separation had, Rina thought, been enough for Jess to feel she could confide, albeit in a voice not much louder than a whisper.

"Did you expect him to remember you, when you saw him this weekend?" she asked curiously.

Jess frowned, and for a moment Rina thought she was offended by the question, then she nodded, sheepishly. "I guess a small part of me did," she confessed. "He really upset nineteen-year-old me. Oh, I suppose I wanted some kind of apology or at least some sense that he wasn't still as careless of people's feelings as he was back then. I suppose I wanted to feel that he'd learnt lessons. That he'd changed."

"I can understand that. And do you think he's changed?"

Jess nodded. "I think he's unhappy."

And for a moment Rina felt she'd glimpsed that younger version of Jess, the girl who'd fancied the older, more successful actor and allowed herself to believe — or been encouraged to believe — that he could really care about someone like her. She'd seen the same power play so often and the same outcome and had met enough women who'd got into relationships, convinced that they could change their particular . . . cad. Yes, the Peters sisters were right, *cad* was a lovely, explosive word, even if she did think a much stronger one, with a few added expletives, might be more appropriate for the likes of the younger William Toons. However, to be fair, people did change, did mature, and the impression she had of Will Toons was a man who had learned some hard lessons, and grown older and wiser as a result. She hoped she was correct. Mentally, she compared Toons to the many men and women she had known who went through their entire lives seeing others as just commodities to be used and thrown away, who never changed or gained insight or empathy, and found that she didn't believe Will Toons to be one of them.

"You do know—"

"That he's not worth my time, or even worth time spent thinking about it? Yes, I know. I'm not nineteen any more, and it takes a lot more than a few acting credits to impress me."

That hadn't been quite what Rina had intended to say, but she nodded. It would do if it made Jess feel better. None of this made William Toons a murderer, though. But she recalled the look on his face when he told Andy that he just wanted to be certain the man was dead. In that wish, she was certain, he had been utterly sincere, and he had also been utterly relieved.

CHAPTER 10

The CSI had completed their examination of the library and Mac took Andy with him to view the crime scene. There was little to see. The body was still in situ, but the mortuary ambulance waited outside, and Mac had no wish to delay the removal longer than was necessary. He had studied the crime scene photographs in depth, but seeing the body brought home the brutality of the attack.

"There seem to be several stab wounds to the chest," Andy said. "The bloodstains on the shirt make it hard to see, but there are three or four tears in the fabric, where the blade penetrated. But the wounds to the abdomen look different, don't they?"

Mac nodded. There was nothing neat or clean about those wounds. It looked, fanciful though the idea was, as though a giant claw had dragged across the man's belly, clawing through skin and muscle and intestine. The smell was powerful, disgusting. It made Mac wonder again about why Wiliam Toons had approached the body, laid hands on it. It wouldn't have taken a genius to realise that this man was well and truly beyond help.

"You'd be able to smell the corpse as soon as you opened the door." Andy seemed to pick up on his thoughts. "Whoever attacked him wanted to be sure he was dead, didn't they?"

Mac nodded. He stood and told the constable hovering in the doorway to inform the undertaker that the body could be taken away. He turned his attention to the rest of the room.

"Nothing looks to have been disturbed," he said. "There's very little blood on the carpet, nothing anywhere else." He pointed to the large trunk which now stood open in the corner. "The CSI found nothing in there, either. No blood, no weapon, no bloody clothing. In fact, no sign anyone's touched it since the actress playing Daisy Beer, Connie Bligh, took her costume out of it this morning."

"So, our dead man wasn't brought in by the company. Or, at least, not in the chest."

"It seems unlikely." Mac turned to watch as the body was collected. Carefully laid in a white sheet and then in the mortuary bag, which was placed on a gurney. He had been a large man, he thought. Tall and well built, not the sort to be taken down by just anyone. It would have taken strength and probably an element of surprise.

"It will make our lives simpler if his fingerprints are on record," Andy said, as the gurney was pulled away.

Mac agreed. It would at least give them a place to start.

CHAPTER 11

Rina glanced at her watch. It was almost eleven and she was still sitting in a corner of the large dining room waiting to go home. As one of the principal witnesses, she'd been an early interviewee, had given her statement, answered questions, had her fingerprints scanned for elimination purposes and then returned to the dining room. Once there, she'd been told to sit at a table on the opposite side of the room to those still awaiting their call.

Sergeant Baker had gone off to assist his boss, but Yolanda remained, cheerfully telling everyone that they'd not be kept much longer, chatting to guests about their families and admiring pictures of dogs and babies. She was, Rina thought, a little body of brightness moving through the gloom. DI Kendall should be proud of her — Rina would be certain to tell him so.

Rina could have left; the police were done with her, but the thought of returning to Peverill Lodge without the others left her cold. People came and went, most just went to make their statement, then returned to the dining room only briefly, drifting through self-consciously as they headed for the back stairs and their rooms. Some came back down again with packed cases, and Rina glimpsed them through the glass panels on the end doors, as they headed out of the side door near the kitchens. She then heard cars leaving as the guests fled. This was not a weekend they'd forget in a hurry. Others, those who had made a little free with James and Lily's hospitality, and who would have been neither safe nor legal to drive, went to their rooms and stayed there. Breakfast was likely to be a sombre and hungover affair, Rina thought.

Lily brought her more tea. James had been among the latest batch taken through to the small dining room, and Lily had already made her statement. Rina felt that if she drank any more tea she'd be drowning from the inside, but she accepted it with good grace, knowing that Lily was just trying to distract herself.

"I don't know what this is going to do to us," Lily fretted, her voice low and shaky.

"You'll be surprised," Rina told her. "A little notoriety, even of a terrible sort, always draws a certain crowd."

"Yes, but what kind of crowd?"

Rina had no answer to that one.

Eliza and Bethany returned and came to sit beside her. "Well, I'm glad that's over," Bethany said. "That young officer seemed terribly confused. He kept asking me to repeat myself."

"The one that talked to me kept telling me to slow down," Eliza complained. "I asked him why they don't teach shorthand anymore. He didn't seem to know what I was talking about."

Rina hid her smile. "Matthew and Steven have just gone through," she said. "Along with Tim and Joy, we should be able to leave when they get back."

"Well, I'm going to get myself a drink," Eliza announced. "Would either of you like anything?"

Bethany and Rina declined. They watched as Eliza marched over to the end of the room and, in the absence of anyone to do it for her, helped herself to a large gin and tonic.

"Did someone upset her?" Rina asked. She had noted the bright pink blotches on Eliza's cheeks and the general air of agitation.

"She got a bit flustered," Bethany said. "When she gets tired, she can't always get her thoughts in order; you know that."

Rina nodded, but made no comment. There had been a few times recently when Eliza had seemed a bit confused, or it had taken her a moment to grasp what she was being told. It worried Rina a little, and she knew it concerned Bethany a great deal, but they would cope. It wasn't as if anyone at Peverill House was going to go through anything alone.

Tyres on the gravel caused everyone to look towards the double glass doors that gave a view onto the hall. Two officers came in, with William Toons.

"It must be snowing," Eliza observed, as she returned to their table. She gestured with her glass towards the three men.

"Must be," Rina agreed. Across the room, the dining room curtains had been drawn against the night, and she had lost track of both the darkness and the weather. Toons and the two officers brushed small, polystyrene-like flakes from their shoulders and hair.

William Toons was let through into the dining room and Yolanda took charge of him. After a quick conversation, he was brought over to where Rina and the Peters sisters sat.

"I'll get him a drink," Bethany said. "He looks frozen through."

William Toons did indeed look cold. He was dressed in a washed-out grey tracksuit and had a different blanket wrapped around his shoulders, the hotel one presumably being kept in case it had picked up anything from his clothes, Rina assumed.

"You look to have had a bad time," Eliza said. "Did they grill you like they do in the movies?"

She meant American movies, Rina thought absently. Eliza always made the distinction; films from elsewhere were simply "films," American films were always "movies," categorised quite differently in Eliza's head and fulfilling a quite different set of expectations. She had a fondness for film noir.

William Toons laughed, though it sounded strained. He gratefully accepted the double whisky Bethany poured him. They had certainly all been drinking the profits tonight, Rina thought.

"Thank you, but they were very polite, very British, I suppose. They wanted to know everything I'd done since six o clock this morning."

"Oh, us too. I mean, who can remember every detail? I had to go back and forth so many times, just to be sure I had it right," Eliza told him. "I'm Eliza, by the way, and this is my sister, Bethany. Rina you already know, don't you?"

Toons shook their hands. He was visibly relaxing now. The Peters sisters could have that effect on people; there was something slightly fey but also charming about them that either put others at their ease or had them running for the hills. Rina had, for a long time, used these alternate reactions as a basic assessment of worth when meeting new people. Her opinion of Will Toons rose slightly.

She watched as he picked up the whisky glass and cradled it between his hands. Bethany had not asked what he wanted to drink, just assessed this as a whisky moment. She seemed to have got it right.

Toons sipped his drink.

"So, you can leave now?" Rina asked.

"I can, but I'm too bushed to drive tonight. Apparently, it's OK for me to go to my room, so that's what I plan to do. Try and get some sleep and then leave in the morning. Do you have far to go?"

"No, we're just in Frantham. We're just waiting for our friends."

"That's the small town down the hill? I saw signs for it when I was driving over." He frowned suddenly "The police are hanging on to my diary and a paperback book I was reading. Why would they do that? I've done nothing wrong."

"I imagine they're just trying to build up some background," Rina said. "Will not having the diary be a problem?"

"Not really. I've got everything important on a calendar on the fridge. I just copy things into the diary so I can keep it with me. I'm not very good with electronic calendars and such. If I can't see it, it ceases to exist."

He laughed, sounding slightly embarrassed at that admission. Rina, who also had a calendar on the fridge and another in the hall, told him she thought it was a sensible idea. She didn't tell him that she also had an electronic calendar on her phone, integrated with her emails and notes, shopping lists and everything else she needed at her fingertips.

"It must have been a terrible shock, finding a body like that," Eliza said. "Rina found a body in the summer. We were all at a wedding. It did rather spoil the atmosphere."

Toons looked a little bewildered by this; Rina didn't blame him. She said, "You didn't recognise him from anywhere. I mean, now you've got over that initial shock, you can't recall seeing him?"

He shook his head. He looked suddenly uncomfortable again. "The police kept asking me that. They seemed bothered by the idea that I'd touched the body. That I'd closed the door. But, I mean, people do strange things when they're shocked, don't they?"

"They do," Rina agreed but there was a shift in tone and a discomforted look in Toons's eyes that caused her to wonder.

Tim appeared in the doorway, Joy and the Montmorencys behind him. It was time to collect their things and leave. On impulse, Rina searched her bag for her notebook. She wrote the address and phone number for Peverill Lodge on a page, tore it out and gave it to Toons.

"I'm sorry your performance was cut so short," she said. "If you find yourself in Frantham, feel free to come and look us up."

He looked surprised. "Thank you."

"I was intrigued to find you taking part in something like this," Rina said. "You seem to have been the toast of Hollywood, these past few years."

He laughed at that. "Slight exaggeration. But I've been doing all right out there. No, but Fliss and I go back a long way. She set this thing up with a group of aspiring actors, to earn us all a bit of cash when we were starting out. The company is all different now, of course, but I do the odd thing when I'm back in the country. It's usually fun."

Rina would have liked to have asked him more. Who else had been part of the original company? Had Fliss not made it to the big time, as Toons had done? Did that bother her? Had the rest moved onward and upward? But her family was waiting to leave, and taxis had been called for. She had been eager for the off, but now she felt a tad reluctant as she went to her room to collect her bag and coat. She would have to Google the question, she thought. There was bound to be something, somewhere, about the early days of the Cameron Players.

CHAPTER 12

It was one in the morning by the time Rina and her cohort got home to Peverill Lodge. Tim and Joy had joined them in the taxis, neither feeling up to navigating the narrow winding roads back to their little cottage and, she sensed, just wanting to be with family. Tim could go up and collect their car the following morning. He would want to check in with James and Lily anyway.

Rina made hot chocolate for everyone and they gathered around the dining room table, relieved to be home, sobered by the idea that they'd had another brush with murder.

"What did the police ask you?" Tim asked, Rina being the only one to have actually seen the body.

"What happened. So I told them. I was standing behind Fliss when I saw her go pale and start to scream. I thought she was going to faint, so I pulled her out of the doorway and when I looked in, I saw a very obviously dead man on the floor and an equally obviously distressed William Toons crouched beside him. He just looked at me and said he hadn't done anything, that he'd found the man like that."

She shrugged. "I still can't fully understand why he didn't just back out of the room and get help. It wouldn't take a genius to see that the man had to be dead, so why go further?"

"Unless you're right and he knew him."

"Even then. The man was evidently dead and equally evidently, it wasn't natural causes." She drained her mug. "I'm off to bed. Thankfully, we don't have to solve this one, and Mac is in charge so we know it will be done well. No doubt we'll all know more in a few days."

But she was already suspecting that wasn't going to be the case.

* * *

Mac had arrived home about an hour after Rina and her friends. Miriam was in bed, watching an old film on her laptop.

"There's Chinese takeaway in the fridge, just needs heating up," she told him.

"I don't think I could face it. Lily kept us all fed, so I've had sandwiches and too much coffee."

He sat down beside her on the bed, knowing he'd have to summon the energy for a shower, but wondering where he was going to get it from.

"Anything?" Miriam asked.

Mac shook his head. "Almost everyone staying at the hotel was involved in this murder mystery weekend and there was barely five minutes together that they couldn't account for. The handful of other guests were certainly in the dining room at breakfast. Three of them went walking first thing, and met and chatted to other hikers on the cliff path, so if we have to prove an alibi, there are potential witnesses. The final two are on honeymoon. They stopped at the Palisades overnight on their way to Cornwall. Didn't get in until 10 p.m. Friday and ordered room service at nine this morning. They then checked out at eleven but stayed on for lunch and left around two. Lily has their home address and mobile, and we spoke to them on the phone, but it's stretching it to suppose they stopped off in order to commit murder and then stayed for lunch."

"Any closer to TOD?"

"No, Barry agreed with your findings. The body temp definitely seems off and so we're keeping a broad estimate on time of death. We're timelining from 6 a.m. on Saturday morning, just to err on the side of caution. Even taking account of body temp, the fact that the blood was still congealing and not fully dried, suggest it's unlikely he was dead before that, but until the post-mortem, that's all we've got to go on."

"Staff? But no, I can't believe that. We know the people who work there."

"And someone could say that about every murderer there's ever been. What a nice, quiet man he was, or how she never had a bad word to say about anyone. But I know what you mean. Anyway, like the guests, they've all found it easy to account for their time. No, he was killed somewhere away from the hotel and then brought there. The big question is, why? The other big question is when. Though we think we've narrowed that down slightly."

"Oh?"

"It can't have been before nine in the morning. Lily and Fliss went in to do final check and one of the actors came in to collect part of her costume from the big box, and there was definitely no body. There's someone in reception all the time between seven and eleven, in case anyone needs assistance checking out. It's usually Lily; she uses the time to catch up on paperwork. They get some people checking out before then, but they usually just drop their room key into the box on the counter. It's like an old-fashioned letter box."

"I know the one."

"Most have breakfast and then go. Lily likes to make sure they've had a good stay and so on. Usual checkout is by ten, but some guests ask for an 11 a.m. departure, like our honeymooners. Lily saw them load their car and then they sat in the bar and had coffee and then stayed for lunch. The only time the reception area is almost guaranteed to be empty, or at least not consistently manned, is between twelve and two thirty. Anyone needing assistance between those times can just ring the bell, and as you know, the office is just off the lobby. Lunch was a buffet, and at twelve sharp yesterday, everyone participating in the murder mystery weekend trooped into the large dining room. All other guests had left.

"Check in time is three," Mac said. "Lily usually makes sure there's someone available for the odd person who arrives early, so from two thirty on, but this weekend no one was booked to arrive on the Saturday afternoon. Between twelve and just after two, which was when the third scene of the mystery was played out, actually in the reception area, that space would be empty. It would have been possible for someone to come in through the old delivery entrance and get to the library without being seen. That door is rarely locked, except at night, because it's handy for the staff to use as a shortcut to the self-catering units in the old stables, or the kitchen delivery area."

"And if you're right, and our killer brought the body through the woods, then he'd be able to see if there was anyone in that courtyard area. If it was clear, he could nip in through the back door," Miriam said, though Mac could see she was frowning. "It's a hell of a risk, though. It would only take someone to glance out of the window at the wrong moment, or cross the yard, or come out into the reception."

"Which deepens the mystery of 'why bother? It feels personal, deliberate. So, who did they have a grudge against?"

"Apart from our dead man."

"Apart from him. Are they trying to ruin the Blake's reputation? Or were Fliss Cameron and her players in their sights? Or William Toons?"

"What's happening with him?"

"He's back at the hotel and free to leave tomorrow, with all the rest who've chosen to stay overnight. Some couldn't wait to get going, but there were more than a few who'd made too much of Blake and Lily's booze to be able to drive. We've no obvious reason to hold any of them, Toons included. And until we get an ID on our body, no alternative leads either."

"Something will break," Miriam said. "Something always does."

Mac got up, stretched, headed for the shower. "I certainly hope so."

* * *

William Toons had gone to his room, but he had not stayed there. He had taken the time to shower and change out of the grey tracksuit the police had lent him. He wasn't sure what to do with it. Should he drop it off at the police station?

Leaving it where it lay on the bathroom floor, he pulled on some of his own clothes and then padded along the corridor to Fliss's room, guessing she'd not be asleep, despite the lateness of the hour.

She'd been drinking heavily, he realised when she opened the door. In fact, she still was. Her eyes were red, and her cheeks flushed. She looked both exhausted and too hyped up to even think of sleep.

He eyed the glass in her hand. "Haven't you had enough?"

"No such thing as enough. Not tonight. I'm celebrating."

"Why didn't you tell the police you knew him?"

"Why didn't you?"

It was a fair point, he thought. Despite the amount he guessed she'd had to drink, her voice wasn't slurred and her gaze seemed remarkably clear and direct. True, she was flushed and a little unsteady on her feet, but he got the impression that, despite her insistence that she really was celebrating, or at least she was trying very hard to get drunk enough to pass out, it wasn't working. A couple of times in his own life he'd reached that point, when it seemed that some weird reaction had refused to allow his brain to accept just how absolutely pissed he was, when his body knew perfectly well. Both times had been when he'd been pumped full of adrenaline and utterly overwhelmed by shock.

The second had been the night Terri had accused him of assaulting her. The first . . . well, that was long before.

"Who do you think killed him?" he asked. He watched her carefully as she took another sip of her drink. A sip, he noted, as though now she had suddenly grown cautious. Cautious of him? Or of the question?

"Whoever it was, I want to shake his hand. It's a pity neither of us had the guts."

"Do you think . . . do you think Derek could have?"

"Derek?" She laughed. "Derek wouldn't be capable. Derek just takes it; he doesn't put out."

The expression sounded crude. William Toons frowned. She was probably right about Derek not being capable of actual murder. Of other things, yes, but this?

"Ok, then who?" he asked, though anything was possible. True, it would have been out of character, but Derek had been pushed about as far as he could go. He was broke. William should know; he'd subbed him often enough in the past couple of years. Not that he'd ever expected to get any of it back. He'd long since written the money off as a gift. After all, they were all in the same boat, it just so happened that Toons had more to give — and boy, had he had to give. He didn't even want to do the sums.

Fliss seemed to have been considering his question. "If it wasn't Derek, then it must have been someone else that bastard was blackmailing. Though how the hell he found out about me in the first place, that I've never understood."

"And I've told you over and over again, it wasn't me."

"Then it's got to have been Derek. Give that man a bottle and he'd run his mouth about anything."

"You know that's not true." Will's protest sounded hollow even to him.

"I don't know anything of the sort."

William Toons sighed. "We should have told them. They'll find out sooner or later who he is, and sooner or later they'll find out we knew him."

"*Knew* him," she said, "when we were all kids. Not a surprise we didn't recognise him after all these years."

He could hear it in her voice that the alcohol was finally getting to her. She slumped down on the bed and lay back. He rescued the glass before it hit the floor.

He sat down beside her on the bed and watched her sleep, wondering if he could drink himself into oblivion as well. He ought to be feeling better about all this. He ought to be dancing with joy that, after all this time, the man who had tapped him for thousands of pounds was now out of his life. But somehow, he couldn't quite believe it.

More than that, he had lied to the police about recognising him and he was beginning to realise that they suspected that. So who *had* killed this man who had persecuted him and Fliss for all these years? Will, Fliss, Derek and who could guess how many others? And why had they brought the body to the Palisades and dumped it there? Despite the blood he had got on his hands and clothes, Will had watched enough true crime on the telly to know there hadn't been enough blood in the library for it to have been the scene of the murder. There'd have been blood on the carpet, wouldn't there? Splatter on the walls and ceiling. No, this man had been killed somewhere else and then brought to the hotel, when it was known Will and Fliss would both be there. But why? To make what point?

He wanted to call Derek, to see if he had any ideas and maybe just give him a heads up about the murder, but what if the police were keeping tabs on his calls? He could tell them, quite legitimately, that Derek was an old friend, that they'd known one another for years, and that was true. The fact that he'd only communicated with Derek a handful of times in the past decade, and that had only been when Derek had needed money, though . . . how would that look?

No, best not to call. Best to give it a few days for things to calm down and then go over there.

Toons pulled the duvet across Fliss's unconscious form, then returned to his room, hoping to sleep.

* * *

On Sunday morning, Mac returned to the hotel just as breakfast was finishing and asked to see Fliss Cameron. She'd not come down to breakfast, Lily told him, but she'd not checked out either, so was probably still in her room.

"Almost certainly nursing a hangover," James added. "She wasn't half putting it away last night."

Lily went up to roust Fliss and Mac settled in a comfortable chair in the lobby, beside the large window that looked out onto the in-out drive.

The day was bright but very cold and more snow was expected later. In the hotel reception, the Christmas tree dominated, fairy lights switched on even thought it was morning, their twinkling light catching the silver stars and red baubles. At home, they tended to switch the lights on only in the evening. It seemed a waste to have them on in daytime — though to be fair, neither he nor Miriam would have been home to see them anyway, whereas here, presumably the guests expected such excesses.

He glanced up as conversation drifted down the stairs and Fliss and Lily came slowly into view.

Mac stood, "Miss Cameron. How are you feeling this morning?"

"I'll bring you both some coffee. You can use my office," Lily said, clearly not wanting even familiar police officers hanging around in her lobby, where her guests might see them. He wondered if he should remind her that Yolanda and the rest of the team would be arriving shortly to take up residence once more in the small dining room.

Not, he decided, if that would jeopardise the arrival of coffee.

He led Fliss into the little office and sat her down, facing the desk. Mac took Lily's seat behind.

"Now," he said, "obviously this isn't a formal interview, and I know you made a statement last night, but I just wanted a chat this morning, see if you'd got over some of the shock and ask if you might have remembered anything else?"

She shook her head. "I told the officer everything last night. I don't know any more than what I said then."

"You were upset," Mac said gently. "Sometimes when the shock recedes, we realise that we've taken in more than we thought. Miss Cameron, are you certain you've never seen the dead man before? Just in passing, perhaps?"

She looked at him, a momentary confusion on her face as though she was torn between different responses, but then Lily arrived with the coffee, and she shook her head. "I never saw him before," Fliss Cameron insisted. "I'd have remembered, I'm sure."

Mac glanced up at Lily as she set the coffee on the desk, and for a second, he was certain that she was about to say something. "And what about you, Lily? Does he ring any bells?"

Did she exchange a swift look with Fliss Cameron? Mac thought so, but could not be sure. Lily shook her head emphatically. "I don't know who he is," she said. "I'll leave you to it."

Don't know who he is, Mac mused. *That's not the same as never having seen him.*

A few minutes later, he had given up on Fliss. She was insistent that she did not know the dead man and had no idea why someone might want to leave his body at the hotel. "How can it have anything to do with me?" she asked, though Mac had not implied that it had. It was a response he found interesting. "I just run murder mystery weekends. It's just a game, a fun event. It's not like real murder."

No, he thought, *it isn't.* Though the sense of the body being staged, presented, almost as part of a performance, was not lost on him.

He let her go. Cars drew up in front of the hotel. Yolanda and two other officers got out of one. A man he did not know emerged from the other.

Mac watched as Yolanda approached the man and, presumably, asked what he wanted. It was too early for guests to be arriving, and Lily hadn't mentioned anyone having an early check-in. A moment later, the man was on his way, parking up outside of the entrance to the driveway, one of the officers following him and standing, sentry-like, eying the intruder.

Mac went to reception to meet her. "Press?" he asked.

Yolanda nodded. "It's only surprising we didn't get them arriving last night."

"I left a patrol car on point," Mac said. "I let them go when I got here. They were well into overtime."

She nodded. "I'll arrange for a proper cordon," she said. "Now one reporter's arrived, the rest will soon follow."

Mac nodded and let her go. He should probably have kept the patrol car in situ until the team had arrived, but he knew how hard it was, sitting hour after hour, waiting for nothing to happen. He knew the other officers were due at any time. Going through to the small dining room, he noted that Lily had replenished supplies of tea and coffee. He must try and get her reimbursed for that. She had followed him in.

"If anyone wants breakfast, there's plenty left over on the buffet," Lily told him. "Most of the guests that didn't leave last night went off really early, and the ones left don't seem interested in eating. It would be a shame to see good food go to waste."

He thanked her. He had no doubt that her offer would be taken up.

She looked tired and old this morning, Mac thought, not like the usual lively, energetic Lily. But then, having a body dumped in your library was apt to dampen spirits.

Gently, Mac patted her on the arm. "We'll be out of your hair as soon as we can," he promised.

CHAPTER 13

On the Tuesday morning after the disastrous murder mystery weekend. Rina was walking along the promenade on her way to do some shopping. The snow flurries that had begun on the Saturday night, and lasted through to the Sunday morning, had melted into slush and she was glad of her boots. When she had first moved to Frantham, Rina felt she had let her standards slip a little. She'd taken to wearing soft, slouch hats and even softer slouchy boots, even got herself a little basket on wheels to carry her shopping. Rina Martin had officially Retired, with a capital R.

Last winter, however, she had bought herself a rather smart pair of oiled leather knee-length boots, with a cosy lining, and dug out her warm blue coat with its military styling. For that Christmas, too, Ursula and George had brough her a rather gorgeous Fedora, with a little feather fan attached to the band. It might be old-fashioned, but it was very her. Catching sight of herself in a shop window, she felt she was now seeing a new and improved Rina, one that had regained her confidence and sense of self.

She turned at the sound of her name being called. James Blake was standing outside of the coffee shop. She went over to him.

"Rina, how are you? The police have finally gone and we're getting ready to reopen on Thursday. Lily is rehanging all the decorations and adding even more to that damned tree and now says she wants to give everything a deep clean. I've come out of the way; she's got every member of staff wielding industrial steamers and vacuum cleaners. I swear we're never going to get rid of the smell of bleach."

"Have the police let you clean up the library?" Rina asked. She put a hand to her head as the Fedora threatened to lift in the stiff breeze.

"Thankfully, yes. They gave us the number for a professional cleaning crew, and they've arrived to take care of that particular problem. I think Lily's relieved about that. Come and have a coffee," James added. "It's blowing a gale, and from the look of that sky, I'll bet we have more snow before the day is out."

She followed him over to the little Italian coffee shop that had been a feature of the promenade for three generations, and decided that she would also have cake. There was something decadent about eating cake mid-morning.

James ushered her to a table and went to get their order. He seemed relieved, she thought, which was not surprising. He seemed also a little overexcited, like a child who'd eaten too much sugar.

"It must be a major relief to get rid of the police," she said, as he set the tray down on the table. The scent of gingerbread and spice rose from both cake and coffee. Rina inhaled happily. "When did they go?"

"The last of them on Monday morning. Mac did his best to keep the disruption down, and that young woman, Yolanda, if she ever gets sick of being a copper and wants a job, she's got one. She kept all the guests happy and calm after Frank Baker left. Someone had to hold the fort here in Frantham, and I think Frank's been on his own this week. Young Andy's been up at the hotel. Just as well it's the off season. Anyway, most of them cleared out on Sunday afternoon, and the last of them, including Mac and Yolanda, went last night. They left a patrol car to deal with press, but I expect they'll be gone too as well. The staff have all be practising their 'No comments,' but most of the reporters seem to have drifted off as well. There's no shelter up on that back road, and it's bloody cold to be standing around or even sitting in your car."

"Do they know who the man was yet?"

She had spoken briefly to Mac on the Sunday, but he'd had little to tell her. Or that he could tell her.

"No. Still no clue. But they're pretty certain the killer came through the woods and dumped the body in the library. They reckon it must have been around lunchtime when everyone was in the dining room and there was no one on reception. They must have come in through the back door. Mac suspects that means they knew the layout of the hotel, which is an uncomfortable thought. We're getting a keypad put on that back door. That way, the staff can come and go, but we don't have to leave it unlocked."

It was a good idea, Rina told him. "Did all the guests get off all right?"

"Gone by Sunday lunchtime. Thankfully. I've not added up the bar bill yet. But everyone was surprisingly good about it all, and several left really nice messages in the visitor's book. There have even been a few complimentary reviews online, which helps enormously, as you can imagine. Of course, it's all over the news, and we've been fending off reporters. Yolanda was brilliant with that. A few turned up on the doorstep, but Mac saw to it they were sent away." He paused to draw breath and then said, "Rina, I've a horrible feeling that for some of the guests, it was the most exciting thing that ever happened to some of them."

"I expect they almost feel it was part of the mystery weekend," Rina said. "It might take them a while to process, I suppose, but at least no one saw the body. They won't have to live with that."

He looked suddenly serious. "Apart from you and Fliss and poor Will Toons."

"How was Fliss? She looked ill; I thought she was going to collapse."

"She calmed down. Lily did a good job looking after her. I think Fliss spent the rest of Saturday and into Sunday semi-sozzled, which is probably not the best thing for shock, but," he shrugged, "she's a grown woman, so what can you do?"

"So long as the police got some sense out of her."

James looked slightly embarrassed. "I think Fliss is quite good at maintaining when she's tipsy," he said. "She knows how to put it away, that's for certain."

Interesting, Rina thought. "William told me he and Fliss go back a long way. That he was part of the Cameron Players when she first started them."

"Oh, he was, yes. So were Milly Latimer and Greta Ericson and a few others that went on to bigger and better things."

"But not Fliss? She stayed where she was."

"Um, no, not Fliss. She did get the breaks, but didn't seem able to capitalise on them. I mean, she makes a decent living with the Players and her other enterprises. She runs a costume hire business. We use that for all our events, and she has a few other irons in the fire. Will has turned up at a couple of our previous weekends. He's a nice chap, never wants any fuss making. Just mucks in as part of the team."

"That's nice," Rina said neutrally. "He seemed to have survived that little hiccough in his career well enough."

"Oh . . . that. Well, yes. It was proven that he didn't do anything. I don't think he's got involved with anyone since, though. I suppose the girlfriend thinking he might be guilty soured the idea of relationships somewhat."

"And they never found out who attacked the sister?"

James shrugged. "Sorry, Rina. I couldn't tell you. I didn't really follow the case. I only met Will once the thing was all over. I'd not have had him in the hotel if he hadn't been exonerated, you know."

"No, of course not."

"From what I understand, there was a party at the house, people coming and going all the time, so I suppose it could have been anyone," he added.

"Hard on the girl, though, if no one was punished for what they did to her."

"No, no, of course. Tragic." He glanced at his watch. "I must push off," he said. "Got some things to pick up for Lily. Lovely to see you and I'm so glad you're not too upset by what happened."

He left and Rina finished her cake, ordered a second coffee and then ate Blake's, too. He'd not even touched it, and to let good ginger cake go to waste would have been criminal.

When they had left the Palisades, in the early hours of the Sunday morning, Rina had intended to take a look at William Toons's association with Fliss Cameron, but the intention had fallen by the wayside as they spent Sunday recovering and Monday getting back to normal. She made up her mind she would take up the challenge when she returned home.

James Blake's attitude also bothered her. She didn't really know him that well; Lily participated in local events more regularly than her husband, and Rina had come to like her very much. She wasn't really surprised that Blake had been more concerned about William Toon's reputation being restored — and hence him being a suitable visitor to the hotel — than he was about anyone being arrested for the sexual assault on a young girl. She guessed he'd have been appalled if she'd confronted him with the disparity in attitude. But she had been disappointed. He had definitely sunk a little in her estimation.

CHAPTER 14

Mac was glad to be back in his own little office but also irritated by the lack of any solid process made over the weekend. That morning, he had attended the post-mortem and for the first time got a proper look at the wounds that had killed the still-unidentified man. His fingerprints had been taken, but there was still no match. The best hope now was that public appeals for missing persons and a carefully composed image of the dead man, created by a police artist using photographs of the body, might elicit a response.

There had been discussion about releasing a photograph, but it had been decided this was not the best idea. The man had died in pain, and the agony and shock were described in his features. To confront any family or friends he might have had with such a discomforting image, or even to display it to the general public, was deemed inappropriate — much to Mac's relief.

The image they would be releasing was a great likeness; it was just a little less shocking. Though it occurred to Mac, looking at the picture, that he'd not been the sort of man you'd catch helping old ladies across the road. There was a hardness to the expression that he felt had nothing to do with inaccuracy or bias on the part of the artist. Rather, it seemed as though she was picking up something that Mac had sensed even behind that contorted grimace — that this was not a man to be crossed.

"What weapon would have been used? Or weapons," Mac had asked. The stab wounds to the chest were recognisably knife wounds, but those on the abdomen, now he could see them properly, looked even more as though they'd been inflicted by a giant claw.

"Well, the chest wounds, probably by a common kitchen knife, or similar. Single edge, maybe an inch wide. The wounds themselves look bigger, but I suspect that's because of the angle of both insertion and withdrawal. It's not straight in and out. More as though the victim was moving, and the killer had to pull the knife out as he fell. At least on what I'm speculating were the first three wounds. However, I'm pretty certain they were not inflicted with the same knife."

He had pointed to the stab wounds highest up in the chest. "We'll know for certain in a few minutes, when I open up the chest cavity, but that one there, highest in the chest, looks different. Chances are the knife got stuck in the ribs and the killer had to wrestle with it to get it out, hence the rather ambiguous size and shape of the wounds. The other two are more straightforward and almost certainly inflicted when the man was down on the floor. As you can see, the profile is narrower; the knife strikes pretty much straight in and out. Gruesome as it sounds, I'm led to think the killer had to use a different knife for those two, probably because he couldn't withdraw the first until the man was down."

Mac grimaced. "Both ordinary kitchen knives, you think?"

"Or similar. As you and I both know, around a third of murders every year take place in a domestic setting. It's likely this one did."

And as many other involved a knife taken from home, Mac thought. "And the wounds to the abdomen?" Mac shaped his hand into a claw, tried to visualise the weapon.

"You'd need a much longer middle finger." The pathologist pointed to the way the wounds were spread across the body. "And steel nails," he added. "Do you garden, Mac?"

"Miriam has house plants. Does that count?"

"So, you've never used a cultivator, one with three or five claws that break up the soil?"

Mac shook his head. But he knew a woman who would have done. He could ask Rina about such things.

"Apart from the tips of the claws, which can be quite pointed, they aren't usually sharpened, which would fit with the way this weapon seems to have been dragged through the body. Anyway, something of that basic shape certainly comes to mind."

As Mac reviewed the images now, he had to agree.

The post-mortem had continued, the marks on the rib bones supporting the pathologist's hypothesis of the knife becoming stuck before being withdrawn. Whoever did this was strong. Strong or in a fury, or both. Mac had known of even very averagely built people being capable of tremendous feats of strength or aggression when pushed far enough to explode.

Andy appeared in his office doorway and broke through his reverie, reminding him that it was after one. Time to go, to meet with Dave Kendall, perform at the press conference, present the image of the dead man to the world and then wait for the calls to come in.

The press conference had been timed for three: plenty of time for both local and national media to show it on the evening news and for the image to be widely circulated, along with the crime stoppers number. By six thirty, Mac estimated, the control room set up for the expected calls would be buzzing. Mostly with useless information.

He thought again about William Toons, who had found the dead man and behaved, in Mac's view, so oddly. Could Mac see him as a killer? Or as one of the killers? He was coming to the conclusion that there had to have been two people involved. The choice of weapons, the difference in strikes. How likely was it that someone would attack first with one weapon, and then drop that in favour of another?

"It's odd that there were no defensive wounds," Andy commented as they went out to the car. "Someone clearly took him by surprise."

"Or he considered them no threat, and allowed them to get up close. Andy, are garden cultivators sharp? The ones that look like a claw?"

Andy looked blank. "I'm not that keen on gardening," he admitted. "And Mum's never really trusted me with garden tools, not since I hoed an entire row of broad beans down by mistake. But she'd probably be able to tell you. Or Mrs Martin. Or Miriam; she knows a lot about gardening."

"I suppose it would have a long handle attached," he said. "So it would have to be swung."

"I don't know," Andy said. "You can get short ones. About the length of a trowel. Mum uses something like that for attacking weeds."

Mac put the question aside. It occurred to him — and the thought briefly amused him in a macabre way — that everyone he and Andy knew that might have experience wielding a three-clawed cultivator was female. Though, on a more sobering note, having watched Rina garden, he could well imagine how lethal a weapon it could be in her hands should she ever have need.

Rina wasn't the killer, but should he broaden out his ideas as to who might be? He was guilty of making the assumption that the assailant was male and strong. But if there were two of them, if the man was taken by surprise by individuals he saw as no threat, that changed the shape of events.

"There's another thing," he said. "Which throws our time of death into question. There were freezer burns on the hands and the back of the neck, places where the body had been exposed and in direct contact with ice."

"Freezer burns! Someone killed him and dumped him in the freezer?"

"A domestic chest freezer is the best guess. There were fragments of breadcrumbs, the sort you find on commercially made fish cakes, and fragments of a frozen pea under his collar. Whoever killed him dumped him in a freezer and then, sometime later, took him out and dumped him in the library at the Palisades. The internal organs were still not fully thawed, hence the anomalous body temperature. But the blood on the surface of the body had unfrozen, hence the semi-liquid state. Basically, we can't even guess when he was killed, now."

"That's a setback," Andy agreed.

"First thing we need to do is find out who our victim was, and when he was last seen," Mac said. "Then find out who hated him enough to want him dead."

Tonight should help, he told himself. In amongst the inevitable noise of false reports, mistaken identities and people who told themselves they were being helpful by reporting their neighbours as potential killers, there would be some concrete facts. Something, as Miriam had predicted, would break. Then they could move forward with an investigation that had stalled even before it had properly begun.

* * *

Returning home, Rina called the Palisades and spoke to Lily. "I've just run into James," she said. "He told me you'd finally got the hotel back to normal."

"Getting there," Lily agreed. She sounded harassed, Rina thought. "I've got to say, it's good to get cleaned up. Makes the place feel like ours again."

Rina made sympathetic noises, but it was clear that Lily was now intent on putting everything firmly behind her and not really in the mood to talk about death and bodies in libraries.

"Rina, I'm sorry, but I've—"

"Got to get on," Rina finished for her. "Of course you have, my dear. I'll not keep you. I just wanted to see how things were going and thank you again for what should have been a lovely weekend."

"Thank you, Rina," Lily sounded both gratified and regretful. "It should have been, shouldn't it?"

They said their goodbyes and Rina hung up. Something else was bothering Lily, she thought, but now was not the time to push. Lily would dig her heels in, insist that everything was fine and that she knew nothing more, and that would be that. No, best to wait.

So, what could she be doing in the meantime?

Rina recalled the mention of Fliss owning a costume hire business. It just so happened that Rina had an event coming up in the spring that required fancy dress.

Well, she didn't actually have one yet, but she'd suggest the idea as a fundraiser, to one of the many local community committees she seemed to have found herself on. A quick online search and she had the address. She was relieved to find that Cameron Costumiers was an actual shop and not just an online enterprise. Would Fliss be there today?

Rina glanced at her watch. It was just after two, so plenty of time before the shop closed at four. It was worth taking a chance.

Rina phoned for a taxi and was soon on her way to Bridport. If she was careful with her timings, she could get the bus back to Frantham at four thirty. Plenty of time to interrogate Fliss, do some browsing in the shop and have coffee and cake before returning home. Coffee and cake twice in one day, not to mention a spot of sleuthing? That felt like the type of guilty pleasure she could get used to.

* * *

Derek set his mobile down on the table and stared at it for a moment. He had been surprised to get a call from Will, even more surprised by the content of the younger man's call.

"I borrowed a friend's phone," he said. "I was worried, in case the police wanted to see mine and might ask who you were. I know I could tell them you're an old friend but . . ."

He had broken off, and Derek suspected he was well and truly regretting his impulse. "Are you all right?" Derek asked. "You sound really rattled. I heard about what happened at the hotel. That must have been unpleasant."

He kept his voice level, his tone neutral, reminding himself that he wasn't supposed to know the identity of the body.

The odd thing was, it felt surprisingly easy to distance himself from Mannering's death now. It was as though the death, the disposal of the body, had all involved someone else. Now it was done, Derek felt utterly separated from the event.

He heard Will take a deep breath and ask, "Has Fliss been in touch?"

"No, why should she be? We rarely speak these days; in fact I can't remember the last time."

"You know who it was?" Will asked. "The dead man?"

Derek sighed. "Will, how the hell could I know? The police are still trying to identify him, aren't they?"

"It was Jeff. Jeff Mannering. Derek, he's dead. Someone killed him, someone dumped his body at the Palisades."

Derek decided that the best response was a shocked silence. Truthfully, it didn't take much acting. Hearing Will say it out loud did shock him, but, oddly, it didn't shock him in any kind of 'I did that' manner. Rather, it felt as though he was acknowledging some dreadful thing that some other unknown and unknowable person had been responsible for.

"Derek, are you still there?"

"Yes, I'm . . . did you tell the police who he was? No, I don't suppose you did. They would have released his name by now."

"Fliss and I, we both said we had no idea. It was horrifying, seeing him like that."

"Well, I'm glad the bastard's dead."

Derek was surprised at the vehemence in his own voice, and it was Will's turn to lapse into silence.

"Look," Will said at last, "I just thought you should be told. Just in case, you know."

Derek had thanked him and hung up. Now he eyed his mobile as though it had become a guilty party in all of this, a conduit through which he could be discovered. He felt a sudden surge of anger at Will for having contacted him, even though Will had been at pains to say he had been careful.

Consciously, Derek slowed his breathing and regained his control. Leaving the phone on the table, he went out into his garden. There was some heavy digging to be done on his veg bed, and in Derek's experience, that was the cure for most ills.

* * *

Rina was gratified to find Fliss in the shop.

"Well, this is lovely," Rina said, looking around with genuine approval.

"Rina, what brings you here? Not that you aren't very welcome," Fliss added hastily.

"Well, I was in town, and I remembered James telling me about your costume hire business and I thought I'd come and take a look. I've an event coming up in spring next year, and I wondered what you might have here."

She could see Fliss debating whether or not to believe her and finally settle on cautious acceptance that this might be the truth. "Any idea of what you're looking for?"

"Something extravagant and elegant," Rina laughed. "I don't get to play dress-up very often. Lydia Marchant is quite conservative in the way she dresses, and I suppose I've fallen into that habit as well. It would be lovely to swan around in silks and velvets for a bit."

Fliss laughed. It was a relaxed sound, Rina thought, the wariness gone from her eyes and the little lines on her forehead easing. She was a very handsome woman.

For ten minutes or so, they flitted around the shop, examining Elizabethan and Stuart possibilities and Georgian brocade and panniers, giggling like little girls at the idea of Rina having to go sideways through doorways.

A peacock blue velvet caught Rina's eye and she pulled it from the rack. "Oh, now this is lovely."

"Isn't it? It's a very clever copy of a bohemian dress from about 1910. Everyone assumes the fashions were all about tight lacing and exaggerated curves, but actually this is more like the kind of things they were wearing in secessionist Vienna. Look, you can see it fastens at the front, it's pleated from the shoulders and all the shaping comes from the belt.

This one looks best with lightweight stays or a really simple corset, or even a supportive bra, just so you get the right line."

Rina eyed the beautiful fabric and the surprisingly simple styling. "I love this," she said sincerely. "I think this may well be what I go for."

They returned to the counter and Rina suggested when she might need the dress for, choosing a date in April by which time, she felt, she'd actually have organised an event to wear it to.

"You're looking a lot better," she said gently. "The weekend must have taken its toll."

"It did," Fliss admitted. "I've never seen anything like that. It was horrifying, if I'm honest. It knocked me for six for a while."

"I can imagine. Have you heard from Will?"

"He's called a couple of times, just to check I was OK. He was shaken up by it, too."

Rina nodded and glanced at her watch. Time to be off. "It would have been even worse if you'd known the man," she said. "You can imagine what a shock it's going to be for the family when they find out." She paused, looked thoughtfully at Fliss. "It's a pity no one seems to have seen him before. Even a casual sighting might give the police a lead."

The open, happy look on Fliss's face vanished, and Rina could feel the barriers coming up.

"Well, unfortunately, I can't help with that," she said. "Now, if there's nothing else, I've got costumes to pack for a client."

"Of course. Thank you, my dear," Rina said, and left the shop.

Fliss knew the dead man; Rina was certain now. And if she knew him, likely Will did, too. But who was he, and what was the association?

Rina glanced back at the shop. Fliss was watching her through the window. Rina waved.

You won't be able to keep your secret forever, **Rina thought.** *Mac will get it out of you and then you'll wish you'd been straight with him from the start. Mark my words you will.*

CHAPTER 15

But nothing did break. Christmas came and went. Rina, not religious but very partial to a carol concert, had attended three, accompanied by the Peters sisters and the Montmorencys, who all enjoyed a good sing-song.

Christmas in the Martin household was always a busy time, days filled with baking and cooking and gatherings of friends, and Rina had been left with little time to investigate. For a time, she had put the puzzle from her mind, content to spend precious time with those she loved, and for whom each passing festive season became more precious.

Now, watching the Lydia Marchant Christmas special at Peverill Lodge, on Boxing Day, surrounded by her family, she felt a degree of melancholy that had nothing to do with too much wine and a too-nice-to-resist brandy.

The investigation, she sensed, had stalled even before it had begun. The dead man's picture had been circulated in all the media, appeals had been made, the case featured on news bulletins and crime shows. Names had been suggested, been checked out, rejected, but for all the solid evidence that had emerged, he may as well have been dropped into the library by UFO. Mac had admitted to Rina that the police were flummoxed.

Tim had even taken a second and then a third look at the library to see if there might possibly, even though logic dictated otherwise, be a secret entrance, through which the killer had escaped. He had found nothing. Rina sensed that he was quite disappointed about that.

He was due to star in a big magical extravaganza at the hotel on New Year's Eve, and, so far as Rina could make out, having a murder on their premises had done the Blakes no real harm. Christmas and New Year had been booked up solidly and there was even a waiting list, in the off chance any guests should have to cancel. Rina knew Lily and James were both profoundly relieved, from a business point of view, though she felt they were also still very unsettled. Had a guest simply died of natural causes, that would have been unfortunate and sad. Had there been an incident where a fight had broken out and someone killed, that would have been catastrophic and, ironically, have hit trade harder, because their reputation might well have suffered. But it would at least have been comprehensible.

For someone to have murdered a so-far-unidentified man and then chosen their hotel as a dumping ground . . . well, that seemed beyond reason and therefore somehow even more distressing.

In the days that followed the incident, and particularly after her conversations with James Blake and Fliss Cameron, Rina had sought out information on the early days of William Toons's career and the founding of Fliss Cameron's theatre company. Her little family otherwise occupied with something on the television, she picked up her phone and reviewed what she had learned so far.

As Toons had suggested, the company had begun with the intention of earning the actors involved some cash while they worked their way up. There had been six founding members, two of whom had left within months, one for RADA and one for a touring company. They had been replaced, and the Cameron Players had found work at a mix of corporate training days, murder mystery weekends, small theatres and village halls. They'd even performed as ghosts and spirits at a Halloween extravaganza at some country pile Rina had never heard of, but which she gathered was prestigious.

Fliss also started a peripatetic theatre school which, it seemed, was still going. It had begun as an after-school enterprise, Fliss holding drama groups for establishments that did not run their own. So far as Rina could gather, she hired out the school halls and ran her drama class there. The kids — or their parents — paid a termly fee, non-refundable, even if they decided not to turn up. Rina had come across an old advert for one such group on the Wayback Machine. They seemed to have been successful, even if not particularly profitable, considering the hours she must have put in with travelling and organising performances and probably sourcing props and costumes, and all of this alongside the other work done by the Players and — if Fliss had been anything like most performers Rina knew — probably odd hours in casual jobs as well.

But Fliss Cameron had only been in her early twenties then and Rina knew from her own career how youthful exuberance and a hopeful attitude could carry you through.

William Toons was with the company for just over a year before his own career took off and took him away. Others came and went, and Rina was struck by just how many of the Players went on to get more sustainable and influential work. Whatever Fliss was doing, it was giving her people a good grounding in performance skills and confidence. It was no wonder that her after school drama clubs had morphed into a small but — from the notices Rina came across — very successful theatre school. From what she could gather, Fliss now oversaw the operation, but her teaching staff were freelance, making use of the accommodation and the Cameron School banner and presumably paying a fee for the privilege. She imagined they'd also be teaching or performing elsewhere alongside this commitment and have what she was bitterly amused to note was often referred to as a "portfolio" of work. That tended to be the way things went all across the creative industries, though the word "portfolio" was, she felt, gravely misleading. It sounded as appealing as, say, a portfolio of stocks and shares, or property might be, when what it really meant was a whole collection of part time jobs, none of which paid enough for anyone to actually live on.

The doorbell rang and reminded Rina that this was supposed to be a day of celebration, not a day for running over so-far-useless research. George and Ursula had spent the past few Christmases at Peverill Lodge, as had Tim and Joy. The last couple of years, Tim and Joy having moved into their cottage, they had decided they wanted to cook for themselves on Christmas Day and had come over to spend Boxing Day instead. The Montmorencys had responded by simply cooking Christmas twice. This year, they had done the same. George and Ursula, in their own little flat for their first Christmas as a proper couple, had taken a similar tack. From the number of texts that Rina and Matthew had received about timings and how to know if their chicken was cooked, she wasn't sure how well it had gone, but presumably well enough that no one suffered food poisoning. That was a plus.

Bethany had left to open the door. Tim and Joy and George and Ursula arrived together, with Mac and Miriam on the way. The scent of food floated through from the kitchen as Matthew and Steven set the table for their second Christmas.

Resolutely, Rina set all thoughts of murder aside and went to greet her guests.

* * *

Will Toons was not having a good time. He had been invited to spend Christmas day with friends, and that had been nice enough, but Boxing Day found him alone in his apartment. Alone and with far too much time to brood.

He had allowed himself to believe that his troubles were over, that he could now get on with his life with no one to interfere or cause him grief. But he had been wrong.

The Christmas Eve post had brought him a letter, and the world had once more come crashing down.

He had called Fliss.

No, she had received nothing, and she hadn't sounded all that sympathetic, either. "Will, let it go. It's just some bastard trying to spook you."

Well, they'd succeeded in that, Will thought. But this time he was going to try a different tack. He was going to do what he should have done all those years before and confess what he had been party to. One incident, but it had haunted the rest of his life. One major regret, and God alone knew how much he had paid for it.

Well, no more, Will thought, as he put a match to the offending letter, dropped it and the envelope into his kitchen sink and watched it burn. *No more.*

CHAPTER 16

The last person Rina expected to find on her doorstep, the day after Boxing Day, was William Toons. He was clutching the piece of paper she had given him, with her address and phone number written on it, and was looking doubtfully at the sign that declared that Peverill Lodge had No Vacancies.

There were never any vacancies at Peverill Lodge, and had not been since Rina came to own what had once been a holiday boarding house, but Rina, living in a street where tall, Victorian B&Bs proliferated, found it behoved her to keep the sign on display, especially during the summer months.

"William? What brings you here? Come along in." His car was parked across the road; she recognised it from the hotel.

William Toons hesitated on the doorstep. "Truthfully, I'm not sure. Maybe I shouldn't be bothering you."

Rina hustled him inside before he could change his mind and do a runner. This was a troubled man if ever she saw one. Hearing the bell, Matthew, the only member of the household currently at home, had come out of the living room. He assessed the situation immediately and announced he would make some coffee.

"In your room, Rina?"

"No," she said. "I think the living room will be more comfortable. The fire's lit in there."

Matthew nodded and went through to the kitchen. The fire was also lit in Rina's little sitting room at the front of the house, but that was a space reserved for friends and private conversations. For some reason, she wasn't comfortable inviting Toons into that sanctuary.

"Come and sit down," she said, "and tell me what's on your mind."

He was already regretting the impulse; Rina could tell that. She could see on his face that he was working up to making a bland excuse about having just been passing and thought he'd call in. Or of drinking his coffee and escaping as soon as he politely could. Well, he wasn't going to get away with that.

They settled themselves either side of the fire, Rina in her usual chair and Toons on the small sofa opposite. A much longer sofa occupied the space facing the fire. She watched as Toons assessed the long room, the dining table at the end closest to the kitchen, the old-fashioned serving hatch that Rina had kept because it was so useful. French windows looking out over the garden. This sociable area around the wood burner and another sofa and chairs clustered around the television.

"When I bought this place, this was the guest lounge and dining room," she said. "Most people who buy these old places tend to subdivide the space. Our next-door neighbours, the Friths, they got permission for change of use about the same time I moved in here. They have a lovely bifold panel door they can pull across, but for our purposes, the space is perfect. We can all be together when we want, but all doing different things. It's a nice, sociable space."

"My entire flat would fit into it," Toons said. He laughed, relaxing a little. Matthew brought coffee and set the tray on the table beside Rina. He nodded to Toons. "Nice to see you again," he said, before disappearing and leaving Toons and Rina alone. Rina noted Matthew had got the hint and the serving hatch was now just cracked open, so he could overhear.

"So," she said, as she poured coffee from the tall pot and offered cream and sugar. "Have you recovered from the weekend at the hotel? It must have been a terrible shock."

"It was," he agreed. "Not the kind of thing you expect, is it? To find a body in the library," he smiled at his own attempted joke, but Rina could see the strain. She decided to be direct.

"So where do you know him from?"

"I don't," he said quickly. "I told the police, I'd never seen him before."

"I'm not sure they believe you," she said quietly. "William—"

"Will, please. No one calls me William. Look, maybe I should—"

"Will, you've come here because you want to talk to someone. There are times when it's easier to talk about difficult things with a relative stranger. I promise, I'll give you a sympathetic hearing, and it seems to me that you do need to talk to someone."

He stared down into his coffee. For a moment she thought she would lose him; that he'd make his excuses, thank her for the coffee and that would be that.

"Whoever he was, you were glad he was dead," she said. "And you felt dreadful about that, but you're still relieved he's gone." She paused as Will Toons looked up at her, and the pain in his eyes told her that she was only half correct. "Or you were," she said. "What's happened since then?"

He slumped back in his chair, the coffee spilling unnoticed over his thumb and into the saucer. "Oh, Rina, I don't know what to do. I can't go to the police, I can't tell anyone, I can't—"

"You can tell me. Will, it's obviously taken a lot of effort and pain to get this far. You're here now; you've taken the first step. So talk to me. Let's see what can be done to sort this out."

112

"You really think the police don't believe me?"

She had no real notion of what the police thought, but she had watched young Andy talk to this man. Inexperienced and young he might be, but he had still had his doubts. She was pretty certain Mac had them, too. "How did you know him?" she said. "Who was he? The police still haven't released his name."

Toons sighed, but gave in. He was desperate to talk, she realised, and also terrified of doing so.

"His name was Jeffery Mannering," he said, "or at least that's the name I knew him by. I think he has others. And I know him because he was blackmailing me, had been for years. I thought it would stop, now he was dead. Rina, I didn't kill him, and I don't know who did, but I'm not sorry. That man made my life a misery for years. Mine and . . . and others. I thought now he was dead it would all be over. I was free. But it's not. Rina, I can't go on like this. I can't take any more of it."

He's broken, she thought. Then, *Mac should be here to listen to this*. But that wasn't going to happen. All she could do right now was listen to him, and then try and persuade him to speak to the police. "Tell me," she said gently. "Start at the beginning." And then when he didn't seem to know where that was: "What did you do that he was blackmailing you about?"

"I killed someone," he said. "It was an accident, but Rina, it was all my fault. Somehow, he found out, and he's been extorting money from me ever since."

* * *

"I was nineteen years old, stupid and irresponsible. Fliss had started the Cameron Players — she was in her early twenties then, but way more sensible and practical than the rest of us. Not that I'm making excuses," he added quickly. "I know what I did was terrible, but I couldn't undo it and I couldn't confess."

"So, what did you do?"

"I got in a car when I'd had far too much to drink. I drove roads I didn't know well, and I drove too fast, I suppose. I hit a woman, killed her — and Rina, the worst of it is, I didn't remember anything about it. I must have left the scene, and when I woke up the following morning with a stinking headache and the worst hangover you can imagine, I didn't even know what I'd done."

"So, how did you find out? Did you remember afterwards?"

He hesitated as though unwilling to tell her. Rina said, "You weren't alone, were you?"

He shook his head. "No, I had a friend with me. Well, not really a friend; more of a family friend. I knew his daughter. We were at school together, though she was a few years younger than me. He used to live near us."

"So how did you end up getting drunk with this man and then getting into a car with him? Was it your car?"

He shook his head again. "No, look, I just ran into him in the pub, and we got talking. My lift went off with friends, and he offered to drop me home. But we'd both had too much to drink, we were both . . . I don't know. Maybe I'd had less than him, Rina, I don't know, but I ended up driving his car and I killed a woman, and I don't even remember it happening."

"Are you even certain you were the one driving the car?"

"Derek said I was. But what difference does it make? I'm still culpable, aren't I?"

"Yes, I think you are."

He looked away, and she realised that he'd been looking for even a hint of absolution. "Rina, that was probably the worst day of my life, waking up and knowing something terrible had happened and then finding out what it was. She had a family. She was married and had two children."

"And did she have a name?" Rina struggled to keep her tone even.

"It was in the news the following day. Her name was Genevieve Atkins. She was only twenty-seven. She had two little kids."

"And why didn't you go to the police?"

"Because I was scared! Dammit, Rina, I was terrified. I thought they'd lock me up and throw the key away, and there was my friend to think about, too. His daughter was only about fourteen, and he was her only family. His wife had died, and he'd started drinking after that, I think. He was terrified social services would get involved and take his kid away. He begged me not to tell. There was nothing to connect us to the accident. Sure, the car had got banged up a bit, but nothing that couldn't be fixed, and, well, I suppose he wore me down. I suppose I thought it wouldn't do any good, making his daughter suffer just because of something I'd done."

"Or he'd done. Will, as far as I'm concerned and as far as the police would be concerned, you are still guilty, but do you really believe that you were the one driving the car? It sounds to me as though you might have passed out, that he might have been the one to have driven the car, and then persuaded you to take the blame."

He regarded her with eyes that were haunted by doubt, but also just a little hope. Did he think that let him off the hook?

No, she thought, he was horrified by what had happened, by what he had done. He'd never really forgive himself, even if it was proved definitively that he was not the driver. He would still be responsible.

"I've wondered about it, if he was lying about me being the driver, but it doesn't make it much better, either way."

"No," Rina told him. "You still compounded the error by not reporting the accident. As you say, a woman died, and her family had no answers as to how or why."

"Would they have felt better about it, knowing it was a drunk driver?"

"They would have seen you punished for it. Will, did you even check she was dead before driving off? Did this friend of yours tell you that?"

He nodded, but could not meet her gaze. "He said she was definitely dead. He said he'd have called for help if she hadn't been."

And you don't really know if you should believe him or not. Yes, he had only been a teenager, and she could imagine how scared he must have been. And if this friend of his had really convinced him that he'd been the driver, then all of that fear and guilt would have been compounded. Then, as more time passed, the harder it would have become to even think of making a confession.

"So how did the blackmail begin?"

He sighed. "It was because of the car. The car swerved to try and miss her, but the wing clipped her somehow and she was knocked down. There were dents and the headlamp was broken. If the police had seen the car . . . if anyone had seen the car, they might have—"

The *car* hadn't done anything, Rina thought. The driver had swerved, had caught the woman and knocked her down. She asked, "How do you know that's what happened if you can't recall anything of the event?" She didn't want to call it an accident. Accidents were unavoidable; if they'd not got into the car after having a skinful, then the young woman would not have been killed.

"I suppose he told me. I suppose I remember something. I don't know, Rina, not really, but sometimes when I'm half asleep I see it as vividly as I'm seeing you."

"And are you driving?"

"I don't know."

She let it go. "You were telling me how the blackmail began."

"We had to get the car repaired. My friend, he had a cousin or something that could get it done. He got the parts and pushed the worst of the dents out and fixed the headlamp. It wasn't perfect, but it was an old car. The odd dent, it wouldn't even be noticed. We'd cleaned and scrubbed and jet-washed everything. He said he'd skidded on some ice and clipped a gatepost, but—"

"And this cousin, he was this Jeffery Mannering?"

"Yes, unfortunately, he was. He put two and two together and figured it out. I found out later he was good at that, finding things out. And maybe D . . . my friend let something slip. When he drank, he could be stupid."

He seemed to have forgotten that he'd mentioned the friend by name earlier. The man was in bits, Rina thought. The past had caught up with him big time, and now he was existing in a state of shock. He'd been relieved when Mannering had died, so what had changed since then to upset him so much?

"You think this man blackmailed other people? People you know?"

He nodded.

"Who?"

"I can't tell you that. It wouldn't be right. At least not until I've spoken to them."

"You know you have to go to the police."

"Maybe. I thought I could ring that phone line they have."

"You need to speak to them properly. You know this."

Outside the clouds had thickened and shadows crept across the room, but she didn't want to reach to turn on the lamp. William Toons sat in the half dark, his cup with the untouched coffee still in his hands. She took it from him, set it back on the tray. "So what else has happened?" she asked. "Is someone else threatening you?"

He ignored her question, said, "It gets worse. I tried to break away once before. I told him, forget it. I'm not paying up anymore. Told him he'd had enough from me and that he could just fuck off. I was away, working in the States. I was doing well, had a house and a girlfriend and she'd moved in with me. I thought I was invincible. He told me I'd regret what I said, that I'd be crawling back, happy to pay up and to pay more than ever. That he'd show me just how much power he had, how easy it was to make me suffer. I just laughed, Rina; I laughed at him. I thought he was bluffing. But he wasn't, was he?"

"What happened?" But she thought she already knew. The girl that was attacked in his house. The girlfriend's sister.

"Gail decided she would throw a surprise party for me. I wasn't due home until after midnight, but friends came over from around ten. They brought other people with them; the house was full, and there were a lot of people she didn't even know. It wasn't the first time she'd thrown a party without telling me. She'd made a bit of a habit of it, using my credit card . . . I didn't know until I got the bill. But that wasn't the point, was it? This time, it all went wrong.

"Terri was fifteen. She'd been staying over, seeing the sights, shopping . . . it was a couple of weeks before Christmas. She shouldn't even have been at a party like that. Gail's parents would have gone spare if they'd know. As it was, it turned out worse than that.

"Terry had been drinking, Gail had sent her to bed to sleep it off and she was more or less passed out when a man came into her room, put a pillow over her face and . . . God, she must have been terrified. She thought it was me. I mean, like I'd ever do a thing like that."

"Why did she think it was you?"

"She said she smelt my aftershave, heard my voice, said I told her I was only dating Gail to get closer to her. Like I'd ever say that. Like I'd even think it. She was just a kid."

"And anyway, you were on a plane, flying in from America when it all happened."

He nodded. "Just coming in to land. Thankfully, I was miles away. He knew I would be. If he'd got me put in prison, he'd have lost his cash cow, wouldn't he? No, he knew how to twist the screws."

"And what happened to Terri?"

"She soon realised it couldn't have been me. Everyone said there were people at the party who no one knew. It was assumed it was one of them who realised she was drunk and incapable and followed her into her room. But *he* sent that man, or he did it himself, I don't know which, but he was responsible. She never saw him; he made sure of that. But he did it deliberately, just to prove he could get to me, just to turn the screw."

Rina felt she had to shock him into action. She said, "He got to you at the expense of a fifteen-year-old girl," she said sharply. "He had someone rape a child, just to prove a point. William, you need to talk to the police. Tell them all this. You need to do that now."

"I know. But Rina, I can't. I mean, I will, but I need time."

"Will, in coming here, you've made me complicit. If you don't go to the police and go now, then I will."

He looked away, she could see him gnawing his lip, angry at her words but knowing there was no argument against them. "It's not just about me," he said finally. "He's been blackmailing other people. If I go to the police, they'll be drawn into this too."

"They already are! Look, you can't fight people like that by hiding what you did. Not any of you. Yes, it will be hard, it will be terrible, but so is living with this. So is knowing that someone else could get hurt, just like poor young Terri."

"I've not had a relationship since," he told her, his voice sharp. "I've not got involved with anyone."

"Presumably you have family? Parents, siblings — do they have family? Friends? Colleagues? William, just avoiding having a partner doesn't deny you hostages to fortune."

"I know that! Believe me, I've been careful since then not to give him cause to do anything else. But I thought he was dead! I thought I could start again, and now—"

"Now someone else is threatening you."

"Not yet, but they plan to. I had a letter, Rina. Someone sent me a letter saying they know what I did and they know I was paying for it. Rina, even though he's dead, it's all going to begin again."

"A letter?" That sounded a tad old school.

"Just a note, a printed note, like anyone could do on a computer."

"You have it with you?"

"No, I chucked it in the bin, then I took it out and I burned it in the sink. I didn't want to believe it."

"You have to go to the police." Rina was careful now to take the sharpness out of her voice. "That's the only way this is going to stop."

He nodded, his face a picture of misery. "And I will. But not now, I have to talk to some other people first, people who are already caught up in this. Warn them, so they can prepare themselves."

"Fliss?"

He looked shocked, and she realised she had guessed right. "Will, you have to understand, whoever dumped Jeffery Mannering's body at the Palisades knows about not just you but most likely Fliss, too. They might have been telling you that this man was dead—"

"So they might be on our side. I mean, telling us that the threat was gone?" For a second or two he looked hopeful, then he remembered that this threat had been renewed.

"Or it could have been a threat, in itself," Rina told him. "You were both in one place, available. Vulnerable." She leaned towards him. "Will, let me call Mac. He's a good man; he'll listen to you."

"Will he?" He sighed. "Look, Rina, I know I'm to blame for a lot of this. I was young and stupid and someone else paid the price, and I know I have to confess up to that— But I have to speak to the others, tell them what I plan to do. They've got to prepare. Please, Rina, just give me until tomorrow, and in the morning, you can go with me to speak to the police?"

He made a question out of the last sentence. Reluctantly, Rina nodded.

"I'd better go," he said. "Thank you, Rina."

She closed the front door on him and then went to her little sitting room to fetch her phone. Matthew had come out of the kitchen.

"I'm assuming you heard all of that."

"I did. I must say I'm not totally impressed by his attitude, though I suppose he was little more than a child when it began, and couldn't see a way out. It's harder to excuse him for not taking action when that young girl was attacked, though." He held up his own phone. "It might not be terribly ethical, but I thought it best to record the conversation, just in case he decided to deny any of it."

Rina was already finding Mac's number on her contacts page.

"He asked you to wait," Matthew said, but there was no disapproval in his tone.

"And I didn't tell him I would. Matthew, I feel like he's made me into an accessory of sorts, and I don't like that one bit. Neither am I comfortable with risking letting this go on and others perhaps being hurt. If new threats are being made, who knows what other people might be dragged into this mess? So no, I'm not going to wait."

The front door opened, bringing with it a blast of frigid air. The Peters sisters and Steven blew in on the cold wind. They took one look at Rina's face and the questions began to form.

"I'll let Matthew fill you in," she said and retreated to her front room. She got through to Mac. "William Toons was just here," she said, without preamble. "And you are going to want to talk to him immediately. I think he might be on his way to the Palisades, or more likely to see Fliss Cameron. The dead man is called Jeffery Mannering, though that might not be his real name and he was a blackmailer. And now he's dead, it seems someone else has taken over his game."

CHAPTER 17

When William Toons left Rina's house, he wasn't entirely sure where he was going. His first instinct had been to go and speak to Fliss, but as he left Frantham, he changed his mind. He turned left instead of right and headed towards the home of the man whose actions had started it all. Who had demanded Will not go to the police, who had told him that as he was driving the car that he was responsible for the death of Genevieve Atkins.

Long ago, Will had come to the conclusion that Derek was lying; that *he* had been the driver and not Will, but what could he do about it? As time had passed, the possibility of confession had slipped further from his reach. How could he possibly explain why he had not come forward sooner?

True, it was in part because Derek was afraid of losing custody of his daughter, and at the time that had felt like a valid reason to keep silent. But had it been? Later, the weight of guilt had kept him from acting, that and the threats from his blackmailer that he could make him suffer in ways Will could not even imagine, if he cut off his funds. And what had happened to young Terri was proof of that.

It hadn't seemed like extortion in the beginning. He remembered how relieved they had felt when the car had been set to rights, how he had even been inclined to like Derek's younger cousin. Jeff was a cheerful soul, happy to help and seemingly content to believe Derek's version of events. Then, as time went on, he started asking for favours. Little things at first: a small loan — which never got repaid — which he needed to buy a car. Then other requests for money, accompanied by hints that he knew exactly what they had done that night, what had really happened to Derek's vehicle.

Then the envelope Jeff had given him one night, full of press clippings and printouts about the death of Genevieve Atkins and the impact this had on her family. The three of them had been having a drink in a local pub and trying to pretend this was an ordinary meeting of friends when it was anything but. This had been two years after the hit-and-run and Will's star was rising. Small but significant roles in television had started to come his way and he now had a steady income. Jeff had said nothing, just handed this envelope across the table and Will could remember the sense of utter dread that had clenched his gut. He had broken out in a sweat, his heart racing as he looked at the contents, Jeff already heading through the door and crossing the car park to collect his vehicle.

Will had made to go after him, but Derek put a hand on his arm.

"Nothing you can do," he said. "We're not the only ones he's screwing over either. He's always been a nasty piece of work."

"If you knew that, why ask him for help with the car? You must have realised he'd work out what really happened."

Shamefaced, Derek had looked away, and Will had understood, "he knew about it already. You told him?"

"He got it out of me. Came round a couple of nights after it happened. I suppose I'd had a drink or two and I was worried sick, just in case anyone might have seen the damage to the car and wondered about it."

"And you told him."

"He got it out of me."

"For fuck's sake, Derek!"

And then he had found out about Fliss — and, Will realised, probably from the same source. Had Derek fed her to the wolves, or at least this particular wolf, just to deflect from himself?

Who else had Jeffery Mannering targeted?

And he had bled them all over the years, not demanding so much that it might destroy them financially, that would have been counterproductive, but enough for the anxiety of it to dominate their lives.

Well, he was dead now, and Will wasn't going to let someone else, anyone else take over the game. It was time to come clean.

Will was glad he had spoken to Rina. He liked her, even though they'd barely spoken before. The truth was he had no one close that he could confide in. A side effect of Jeff Mannering's persecution had been that Will had kept everyone at arm's length over the years. Or at least since that nasty business with Terri. Occasionally he still crossed paths with Gail and her sister, but those meetings were difficult, fraught with guilt and, he sensed, everyone was glad that they happened rarely and were concluded as quickly as politeness allowed.

He was lonely, Will admitted to himself. Rina had seemed a friendly, neutral acquaintance, and at least he now had some idea of what he was going to say. A dress rehearsal. He now needed to give Derek a heads-up, reassure him that he wouldn't even mention his involvement in the death of Genevieve Atkins. If they wanted to know whose car he had been driving, he could lie; maybe even add taking without the owner's consent to his list of admissions.

As he turned down the first of a series of narrow B roads leading to Derek's house, he felt a slight worry that he had confessed to there being a second person in the car. Rina would be bound to mention it to her policeman friend, and no matter what Will said to deny that, they would be sure to believe her. He tried to recall if he had mentioned Derek by name, but could not remember. He decided that if he was challenged on this, he would say that he'd just made up the name, and refuse to tell who had actually been with him.

He could always tell the police that the man was long gone. Dead and buried. After more than a decade and a half, that was possible, wasn't it?

But he decided he would not tell Derek he'd spoken to anyone about it.

The road was rising now, and Will pulled into a passing place and gazed down onto the landscape spread out below him. There were more direct routes to Derek's house, but this view was why he had come this way. The view and that it had given him time to think. More time to delay the inevitable. Maybe even more time to change his mind?

He cut the engine, got out of the car and stood in the cold, gazing down into the valley, knowing that he could be doing this for the very last time. In the distance to his right, he could still glimpse the Cannington Viaduct that had once taken trains into Lyme Regis. Now topped by trees and ferns, it was still a spectacular sight. The landscape spread out below him was a mix of farmland and scrub that reminded him of family trips to Exmoor when he'd been a kid. On a clear day, he could have glimpsed the sea.

He closed his eyes, shutting out the grey of the heavy cloud, the sudden burst of sunlight raking across the greens and browns and russets and the kestrel turning into the wind, and he felt the tears pricking his eyelids. *What a waste.* All these years of worry and loneliness and anxiety, because of one man. He could not face the idea that he might be subjected to more years of persecution, that Jeff Mannering might have arranged for his little business — as he called it — to have been sold on, like an advertising company might sell on Will's email and phone number. It felt like the final nail in Will's coffin.

"I should have gone to the police, confessed what happened. I could have told them that I'd borrowed Derek's car.

I could have told them I was the only one involved. I could have paid my debt and been free of it all long ago. I should have done that back then."

Almost half a lifetime ago, he had made a decision, and it had haunted every day since then. He had made the decision to get into a car with a man who'd imbibed at least as much as he had, and Will had been so pissed he could barely open the car door. He could remember them both laughing as he tried to grab the handle for the third time and had missed again. Laughing so hard he almost collapsed onto the sodden ground of the pub car park. Sure, he had only been a kid, but when Derek had offered him a lift back to the house he was sharing with friends, he hadn't even thought to refuse.

Will opened his eyes. He didn't need them closed to remember the car swerving and the thump of the impact, and then Derek struggling to regain control as the vehicle skidded to a halt.

Everything beyond that continued to be a blur.

Will got back into his car, started the engine and drove on.

CHAPTER 18

Mac had called the Palisades and spoken to the Blakes, but they had neither seen nor heard from William Toons since the murder mystery weekend. He had also called Fliss Cameron, but she had told him the same. She had no idea where William Toons might be staying, either. She had assumed he had either returned to London or even left the country. He asked both the Blakes and Fliss to let him know if Toons did turn up and left the message that Mac would like to speak to him.

"Andy, can you ring round to local hotels, see if our man is staying at any of them?" He thought about contacting DI Kendall, then decided it could wait until he had something definite to tell him.

Mac had then gone to see what on earth Rina was on about.

Rina seemed unusually excited — and also unusually annoyed, Mac thought. She told him about Toons's visit, and then sat Mac down in her little sitting room. Matthew laid his phone on the table between them, switched to play.

Mac listened with increasing astonishment as the conversation unfolded.

"You do know this was technically illegal," he said, when the recording had finished. "You didn't have his permission to record the conversation."

"Good thing I took notes immediately after he'd gone, then," Rina said, and set a sheaf of papers beside the phone.

"And, of course, I couldn't help but overhear," Matthew added. "But my guess is he'll already be regretting this conversation. He asked Rina to wait until tomorrow until contacting you. He knew that she would have to speak to you, of course, but she was supposed to wait and then go with him in the morning. Rina — quite sensibly, I feel — decided that you needed to be informed straight away."

"I feel sorry for the man, he's obviously been through the mill, but I'd also feel like an accomplice if I didn't speak up now. All of this mess has gone on for long enough."

Mac raised an eyebrow. In the past, Rina had certainly delayed passing on information when she thought that was the right course of action, but evidently she felt that loyalty to Mac certainly trumped any interest of William Toons on this occasion.

"At least you now have a name for the dead man." Matthew said.

"That's certainly welcome," Mac admitted. "Always supposing Toons was telling the truth about that. And he seems to be suggesting that our man might have aliases."

"And you can perhaps let the family know what happened to Genevieve Atkins. I did a quick internet search and what he told me does seem to check out."

Mac nodded. "You have no idea where he was going?"

Rina shook her head. "As you heard, he said he had people to speak to. Others that were involved. I thought he might go straight to see Fliss, but obviously I was wrong. So, my guess is he'll have gone to speak with this Derek he mentioned."

"Derek what?" Mac wondered. "He seems to have regretted, or maybe even forgotten, mentioning him by name. Later in the conversation, he's careful not to use his name."

"I don't think he'd really thought anything through, apart from the need to get this off his chest," Matthew said. "And I'm not so sure he'd have even done that if it hadn't been for this new threat, implied in the letter he received."

"Which he'd destroyed," Rina added. "Which was a particularly stupid thing to do."

"Perhaps. I'm not so sure there would have been anything forensically useful. I wonder if he made it up, just to give himself an excuse to come and speak to you." Mac frowned. "Why did he come to talk to you anyway? You don't know the man well, do you?"

She shook her head. "Never met him before that weekend. But I was there just after he discovered the body, and he wouldn't speak to Andy unless I hung around. He even asked if I could go with him when he went off to make his formal statement."

"He was like a duckling imprinting on the first thing he saw," Matthew suggested. "He suffered a terrible shock and Rina's was the first sensible face. Fliss Cameron did nothing but scream."

"So, I think we can definitely assume that Fliss Cameron also knew this man," Mac said. "We all suspected they might, and in that case, they are both guilty of withholding evidence. Will Toons is going to be in deeper trouble than he can imagine, once we catch up with him. And Miss Cameron has a lot of explaining to do. Such as what our Mr Mannering had on her."

"I still think Lily recognised him. There was just something about her denial that didn't ring true." Rina said.

She sounded put out, and also worried. Mac knew that she liked Lily. Well, Mac thought, they would certainly be asking again. He got up. "I need to talk to Dave Kendall," he said. "Get the name out there and see what leads that generates. I'll also need to look into the Genevieve Atkins death. That was long before I came here, so I know nothing about it. Toons didn't mention where he was staying, I suppose?"

Rina shook her head. "I didn't think to ask. Once he'd started with his story, I didn't think to ask him about where he was staying or how long for or any of that ordinary stuff. Truthfully, Mac, I was just taken aback."

Mac had walked from the police station and as he trudged along the wet roads, back towards the promenade, he considered his next actions: Call DI Kendall and get more bodies on the search for Will Toons. Kendall was better placed to get a search of Toons's London flat in progress, and to have an alert put out at ports and airports.

Now they had a name for the dead man, and a narrative. They knew what the connections were between the dead man and William Toons — who, as a blackmail victim, would now have to be considered as an active suspect. And who the hell was this Derek character? Was that even his name? If Fliss Cameron and Toons had been friends for a long time, was she likely to recognise the name? Or admit to knowing it?

Still so many questions. But they were further on than they had been at any time since they had found the body in the library.

* * *

Will Toons had been to Derek's house many times in his younger days, but it was years since he had last visited. Derek had called him on occasion, had texted to ask for help, had sent Christmas cards from himself and Emily, and then separate cards from himself and from Emily and her family. Will had done his best to reciprocate, but that had been the sum total of their interactions in the past fifteen years. At first, what had happened on that night had bound them, but as time went on and the chains of memory grew heavier and tighter, Will's need to escape the guilt and fear had intensified. He was still a young man; he'd wanted to forget, so far as that was possible, put all this behind him and get on with his life.

Jeff Mannering had, of course, made that impossible, but he had tried despite that. Will had realised very quickly after the blackmail started that he blamed Derek utterly and completely for putting him in this position to start with, and that had exacerbated his need to get away from the man.

Who was Derek, anyway? Just someone his parents knew, and whose daughter had been a couple of years behind

Will at school. A man who had persuaded him to get into a car and drive, despite the fact that both of them were way over the limit.

As time went on and small flashes of memory returned, though, Will had become more and more certain that Derek had lied about that. Will had been a passenger, not the man driving the car that had killed the woman.

Did that make it any better? At first, it had. Later he had realised that he was just as culpable either way. Neither of them should have been anywhere near a vehicle that night. He had the vague memory of neither of them having the money for a taxi and Will's friends had gone on somewhere else by the time he and Derek left the pub. He should have gone with them. Why hadn't he gone with them?

The reason for that, Will recalled, was as petty as it was significant. He'd had a row with his then girlfriend. When she'd left with the others, he'd decided to stay, just to show her that he didn't care. That it was over between them. That he was the one calling the shots. Teenage stubbornness, he thought, as he pulled up outside of Derek's house. It meant you had to be the one to have the last word, even if you were then the one to lose out.

Derek must have known that Will had something important to say, maybe even anticipated the reason for his visit, but his manner was as easy and casual as if Will had been a neighbour popping in for a coffee.

Not, Will thought, that he had any close neighbours. The closest house was a holiday let, and that was a couple hundred yards away.

"I had a letter the other day," he said, as he cradled the mug of coffee between his hands. The mug was bright pink and covered in flowers; it seemed oddly out of place in this single, male household. He wondered, absently, if Emily had been responsible for this and the matching stack of four others sitting on the kitchen shelf.

Derek followed his gaze. "Local charity shop," he said. "Two quid for the lot." He smiled, briefly. "So, you got a letter."

"It said that Jeff might be dead but that didn't mean I was off the hook. I wondered if you'd had anything. Or if Fliss had."

"And has she?"

"No, she's received nothing. Have you?"

"Well, you could have given me a call and I'd have told you. You didn't have to come all the way out here. But no, I've not had anything like that."

It occurred to Will that Derek didn't seem particularly upset by the prospect. Maybe he hadn't fully understood. "Don't you understand?" he said. "Some other bastard plans to pick up where Jeff left off."

Derek nodded, then he smiled. "Jeff didn't exactly 'leave off' though, did he? You might say he was 'cut off'."

"What?"

Derek was laughing, presumably at his own joke. Will was infuriated. "I found the body, Derek, and believe me, it wasn't funny. I've never seen anything so horrific."

He was aware that Derek had stopped laughing and was looking at him thoughtfully. "No," he said, "I don't suppose you have. I was forgetting you didn't see *her* body. You were still in the car when I got out to look."

"I don't remember you doing that," Will admitted softly. "Derek, look, I can't face any more of this, so I've decided on something. I'm going to the police. I'm going to tell them what happened what we . . . what I did. And I'll take full responsibility. I won't mention you; I won't say there was anyone else in the car. It was all my fault that woman died. I'll tell them that, but Derek, I've had sixteen years of paying through the nose for what happened, and I can't take any more of it. And whoever this is, they might not have contacted you yet, but they will. You know that as well as I do. If it's all out in the open, then they can't get at any of us, and it'll all be over. You see that, don't you?"

Derek was regarding him solemnly, head on one side like an inquisitive dog. "One little fault with that reasoning," he said. "If you don't tell the police about me, then our new friend who's sending out these letters will still be able to come for me. For Fliss, too. She had nothing to do with our little business, did she? So as far as our new blackmailer is concerned, she's still fair game. What do you plan to do, confess on her behalf as well?"

Will hadn't thought of any of that. "No. I . . . Look, you've not been contacted and Fliss hasn't either. So maybe they don't know about you. Maybe Jeff just told them about me. Maybe he knows it's no good asking for anything more from you anyway."

"Because I'm broke, you mean?"

"I didn't say that."

Derek laughed. "No, you didn't have to." He held up a hand as though to fend off Will's protests. "But you're right. All I've got left is this house. I finally paid off the mortgage a couple of years ago, never let him know that, though. I let him believe I was still renting the place, moaned about the landlord not keeping up with the repairs, that sort of thing." He smiled grimly.

"I should go," Will said. He set down his coffee mug, the second he'd failed to drink that afternoon. "It's going to be dark soon, and I'd as soon not drive back in the dark. I just wanted to come over, let you know what I plan to do. And if the police come calling, just tell them you know nothing. I'll take full responsibility for everything."

Derek had not responded, but he seemed to accept Will's words. "You stopping down here?" he asked.

"Thought I might, just for a day or two. Emily and family, OK?"

"They're doing well. I'll be over there tomorrow. I'll give her your best."

"Do that. I'm glad things have worked out for her."

"Wouldn't have done though, not if you'd gone to the police back then."

"Which is why I agreed not to. I'll keep you out of this, I promise." He was aware of how hollow that promise sounded, how little good it was likely to be. How much Derek resented him even thinking about it. Suddenly, he wanted to be as far away as possible, from Derek, from everything. He was exhausted, worn out by it all. He just wanted to be away.

Derek was still sitting at the table when he left. Will started the car and drove away. He knew these roads well, even though he'd not driven them in years, and he decided that when he came to the crossroads about a mile from Derek's house that he'd turn back towards the major roads, instead of snaking back the way he'd come. He could find somewhere to stay in Axminster, or if not, then a services back on the motorway would do. Or maybe he should head back to Frantham and ask Rina to call her friend Mac before his nerves got the better of him and he ran again. It was already dusk, and in the hollow of the narrow lane, high hedges on one side and a low bank, topped with a stone wall on the other, it felt as though night was falling at twice the natural speed.

Will had reached the T junction and was about to make his turn when he heard the sound of a car coming up behind him. The engine was loud, revving hard, approaching far too fast. Looking into the mirror, Will could see a green estate car hurtling up the lane. With a jolt, he realised that he had seen that car parked by the side of Derek's house.

"What the—?"

Flustered, Will accelerated from the junction, turning automatically onto the more familiar road that led across the moor. He swore when he realised what he had done, but there was no choice in the matter now and whatever Derek intended to do, Will would have to stay ahead of him. He was driving a hire car; he rarely drove as living in London left him with little need to bother.

He accelerated, feeling the effort of the small engine dealing with the sudden climb. He shifted down, floored the accelerator. The larger, heavier vehicle was gaining on him, and a moment later, he felt the bump as the front of Derek's car rammed into the rear of his. Looking back through the mirror, he could see the man's face — he could barely recognise him as Derek — contorted with fury and, Will realised, with desperation. It had crossed his mind the day they had found the body that Derek might be responsible. But Fliss's reaction, derisive and dismissive, had encouraged him to dismiss the idea. Surely she had been right; Derek would not have had the guts to act against Mannering. The look on Derek's face now told a different story.

He accelerated again, taking the next bend at a speed that terrified him almost as much as the man driving behind him, but Derek wasn't finished yet. Will felt the bump as Derek nudged him again, and then, more terrifying still, the sudden realisation that his car was being pushed and that Derek was intent on going faster still, and Will no longer had any control over the situation.

Desperately he tried to swerve, but there was nowhere to go on the narrow road, no means of getting away from his pursuer, the high hedges, the ditches and the low wall conspired to hem him in and prevent any means of escape.

Up ahead was the crest of the hill and the passing point at which Will had stopped on the way to Derek's house. If he could just get ahead of his pursuer and perhaps swing his car around. And then what? Did he really have a chance of heading back down the hill and outstripping the bigger, more powerful car? Briefly it occurred to him that he could drive across the moor and perhaps outdistance Derek, but the thought of taking this little hatchback off road was, he realised, absurd. Though he was so desperate he found himself putting his doubts aside. It suddenly became imperative that he reached the lookout spot ahead of his pursuer so that perhaps he could turn the little car onto the rough ground and get away.

He began again to swing the steering wheel left and right, trying to shake himself free, but Derek was unstoppable. As they reached the passing place, Will swerved right diving into the shallow scoop as though it was sanctuary. Too late, he realised this was exactly what Derek had in mind. His car was now blocking Will's exit. Will started to get out of his car, looking for a place to run, then thought better of it. Perhaps he would be safer in the car. But it was too late, he realised, as his one-time friend flung open his door, something in his hand that Will could not immediately identify, but which looked large and heavy.

Will twisted away. "Derek, we can talk about this! I promised you I would never mention you were there. No one will ever know. I won't go to the police. I won't do any of that. We can carry on as normal, and I'll go away. I'm hardly ever in the country anyway. No one knows about you. No one will."

But it was too late for all of that. For a moment, he clung to the thought that as long as he remained inside the car, there was no room for Derek to swing for him. Then he saw the older man change his grip on the object he held in his hand. He swung not down, but forward, through the open car door and straight towards Will's face.

Will saw the blow coming and threw up an arm to defend himself. He felt a sickening pain as the bone broke under the force of the blow. His arm fell, Derek struck again, and then there was only darkness, no more thoughts, no more feelings, no more anything. Will Toons was gone.

CHAPTER 19

Fliss played with her mobile phone, fingers fiddling with the fastening on the case, repeatedly flicking the magnetic closure open and closed until Mac, irritated by the snap-click, snap-click, reached across the table and gently took it from her hand. She stared at him and then stared at her phone. "Sorry," she said, "I know that's annoying. People always tell me so, but when I'm tense—" She shrugged.

"I fiddle with my pen," he said. "It drives my sergeant mad."

She smiled tensely at him. "I've tried to call him loads of times since you called; I just can't get through. I thought maybe he was driving. He keeps his phone in his pocket, doesn't have a hands-free or anything. He doesn't like answering the phone when he's driving."

"It could be he's somewhere he can't get a signal," Mac said. There were still areas in Dorset that could be patchy and particularly if Will had driven into North Devon, signal dropouts were certainly not unknown. "You've no idea where he might have gone?" He had asked this question several times already, but it didn't hurt to ask again.

She shook her head, as she had done each time he had put the question to her. "I've only spoken to him a couple of times, since that weekend. As I've already told you, he called to check I was OK. I assumed he's gone back to the States. I know he was prepping for a role, some big legal action thing."

Mac nodded. "And this Derek. You don't know where he lives or even his second name. Miss Cameron, this is no time to be withholding information."

Her gaze flicked toward him and then she looked away. "I vaguely remember there being someone called Derek when we were young. Some friend of his parents, I think. Not someone I knew personally, and I definitely can't tell you where to find him."

"And this Jeffery Mannering. What can you tell me about him?"

"I've already told you. Nothing. I didn't know the man. The name means nothing to me."

Mac sighed. He had come to see her at home, hoping that the informal setting might encourage her to talk, especially as Will was now impossible to contact, and she was clearly concerned about that. They now sat either side of her small kitchen table, coffee growing cold between them. He leaned back in his chair and regarded her thoughtfully. He'd hoped that she might finally admit that she had recognised the dead man, that perhaps she was also one of his victims. Instead, she had taken refuge in flat denial. He'd have to have her brought in for questioning, see what a proper interrogation might shake loose, but still as a witness, there was nothing explicit she could be charged with as yet. He was certain she was deliberately obstructing the enquiry, but he had nothing the CPS would approve charges on. He had, in fact, nothing but a name and a story told to a woman Will Toons barely knew, and which he could still deny, should he feel so inclined.

"Did Will tell you about a letter he'd recently received?"

She shook her head.

"And when did you last speak to him?"

He saw her hesitate, then she said, "He called to wish me a happy Christmas. Christmas Eve, I think that was."

"Perhaps you could check your phone, just to be sure."

She scowled irritably, but did as he asked, then set it down. "Yes," she said. "Christmas Eve, just after seven in the evening."

"And he said nothing about a letter or about going to see Derek?"

"I told you. No. And I don't know who this Derek is, so why should he mention him?"

He tried a different question. "How long have you known the Blakes?"

Her gaze flicked at him again. Her fingers moved towards the phone again. She picked it up and looked at the screen as though hoping a message had arrived and she'd just not heard the alert. "Since before they bought the hotel. About fifteen years, I suppose. James was a property developer. He bought places, did them up, rented them out. He was my landlord for a while. Then when they bought the Palisades, they got in touch again. They knew about the Players and the Murder Mystery weekends. They wanted something tailored to the location. We've been very successful. Until now."

Mac nodded. "And they don't know Mr Toons, apart from through the mystery weekends?"

She shook her head.

"It seems an odd thing for a successful actor to do," he said. "To come back and take part in something like that."

She bristled. "Will is a friend. I helped him when he was just starting out. Some people are loyal to their friends. Besides, he enjoys them."

Mac let that pass. To his mind, it still seemed a little odd. "And when did you first meet Mr Toons?"

She sighed. She was getting bored with the questioning now, Mac could see that, which probably meant she was relaxing. She had decided that he'd done with the hard questions, the ones she didn't want to answer.

"We met when he was eighteen, nineteen, something like that. I must have been about twenty-two or -three. I was running these drama groups for kids and teens, and I was doing well, but I wanted to branch out. I'd gone on one of these mystery weekends with my aunt, she was into all that kind of stuff. I was living with her at the time. I remember thinking I could do better; I just needed the script and a team of actors capable of going off script when they needed to. I advertised, and Will replied to my advert."

Mac nodded. "You lived with your aunt?"

"My parents divorced when I was sixteen. I couldn't seem to settle with either of them. Aunt Margie offered me a place to stay. It was supposed to be temporary, but I never moved out. We got along well. She had no kids of her own, and I was far more comfortable with her than I was with my mother sniping about my dad and vice versa."

"Are you still close?"

"Sadly not. She died when I was twenty-four. She left me her house and a bit of money in her will. That got me off to a better start than most people. I'm very grateful for that."

Abruptly, she picked up her phone and Mac watched as she found the contacts page and tried to call Will Toons again. As before, it went to answerphone.

"Where the hell is he?"

She was really rattled, Mac thought, as though she suspected something serious had happened to her friend. Something specific.

"We'll find him," he said. But he was already experiencing that heavy, dreadful feeling that they would not be finding William Toons alive.

When he returned to his car, he called DI Kendall. "Anything?"

"Nothing useful," Dave Kendall said, sounding tired. "His neighbours back in Camden reckon they saw him about a week ago, and think he was at home up until the day before yesterday, on account of seeing his curtains open and close and his lights on. Local police have done a preliminary sweep of the flat but found nothing obviously significant. They're attempting to track down friends and relatives, but it's all going to take the usual time. Anything useful from Miss Cameron?"

"She's denying all knowledge of Jeffery Mannering, blackmail and anything else she can think of distancing herself from. She vaguely remembers that someone called Derek was a friend of the Toons family but will admit to no more than that. She knows a lot more than she's willing to say, but she's genuinely afraid that something serious has happened to William Toons."

"More than the general worry of someone who can't get hold of a friend?"

"I would say so, yes."

Kendall considered. "Well, best get off home. We can't do much more tonight. I've applied for Toons' financials and, if he's not turned up by morning, I'll ask for a forensic search of his flat. His agent is sorting out a list of professional contacts. Fortunately, a quick stroll via Google was all it took to find her. She reckons there's been no significant other since that business with Terri Murray. We got hold of the ex-girlfriend, Gail, but she denies seeing him since the breakup, apart from the odd occasion they happened to be at the same social event. It seems they still have acquaintances in common. She seemed distinctly miffed to even be hearing his name again. Apparently she's made a life for herself since and doesn't want the past raked up again."

"And the sister? Though I don't suppose he'd have made contact with someone who accused him of rape."

"I asked. Got very short shrift. Apparently the sister is now living with the mother in Portugal, which is where she came from before her marriage. After the divorce, and not long before the events that happened in Will Toons's house, she went back home. Terri stayed on with the dad so she could finish her exams. From what Gail told me, the mother blamed both father and sister for what happened to her youngest child and hasn't been on good terms with them since."

"Ok," Mac said. "And still nothing on this Jeffery Mannering?"

"There are a number of Jeffery Mannerings in the system, with a variety of different spellings, but no match to our dead man. But we knew that back before Christmas, when we couldn't get a match on his prints. So no, we're no further ahead on finding where he came from or who he was. Having a name is good, but with nothing more than that to go on, it's a case of trawling through electoral rolls and other equally scintillating levels of bureaucracy, then the legwork of checking addresses to see if anyone has lost a husband or father or brother and not troubled to report it."

"There can be good reasons for not reporting," Mac said. "Marriage breakup, domestic violence, temporary accommodation . . ."

"Don't start," Kendall laughed humourlessly. "Get some rest and start again in the morning. Hopefully our man will have surfaced by then."

CHAPTER 20

Will Toons might have lain by the roadside for several days, so little used was the narrow road on which he had travelled. In high summer, tourists might end up travelling that way, directed by their satnavs via the shortest route, though a proportion of that number had gained unwanted experience of reversing over a lengthy distance, when they'd encountered a tractor coming along in the opposite direction.

There were passing places at intervals, and verges that just allowed for two cars to squeeze by, albeit risking the loss of their wing mirrors, but this late in the year, between Christmas and the end of December, even the locals avoided it. There were better routes, less prone to icing up.

Will Toons might have been left to the crows and the foxes had it not been for April Balman and her two boys, bringing their dogs for a winter walk and heading for the one reliable parking spot. The passing place was so little used as such that folk who knew about it tended to take advantage, pulling their cars onto the verge and out of the way, just in case it was required. For those that knew about it, the passing place providing an easy access point for long walks over what was still wild land. For April and her boys, this back road, parking spot and walk was their special, secret adventuring spot, where they could run around and make noise, accompanied by two large and boisterous dogs.

"There's someone parked in our place," eleven-year-old Lex said, as they drew closer. "The car door's open. Do you think they've broken down?"

April's first thought, when she spotted the car, had been wild campers or van dwellers, needing a quiet and safe place to overnight. But as she got closer, she realised that this was just a little hatchback, the kind of car that didn't fit either of those categories.

She stopped her own vehicle a few yards from the passing point. The dogs, recognising where they were, yelped in the back of the four-by-four and Finn, her seven-year-old, did his best to hush them. The sight of the car, with its open door, uneased her.

"Lexy, see if you can get a signal on my phone." There was usually a weak one at this high point. "Dial in two nines, just in case someone's hurt and we have to call an ambulance."

Lex nodded, angling his mother's phone to get the best signal. April left the car engine running and her own door open. If someone needed help, then she would help them, but with her two boys in the car she was taking few chances. There were some crazy people about. You just never knew. But she had already spotted the crows, perched in the scrubby, wind-bent trees, before she got out, and she sensed that Lex had, too. Something or someone was hurt . . . or worse.

April shivered, zipped her fleece, and approached cautiously, calling out to whoever might still be with the car. "Hello? Are you OK? Have you broken down?"

She circled warily around the front of the car, glancing back at her own. Finn had now pushed his way between the seats and was leaning forward to see what she was doing. She could see Lex, eyes fixed on her, his arm up to prevent his little brother from squeezing all the way to the front. She could see the driver's door of the little hatchback was open, and this initially blocked her view of what was beyond. As she moved round, first she saw a foot, twisted at an awkward angle, the heel dug into the mud and grass. Another step and she saw the rest of him, lying partly on his back, but with his upper body twisted away and his arm thrown up as though to ward off a blow.

"Oh, my God." She ran back towards the car. "Lex, call an ambulance and the police, give them the What Three Words location, I think he's dead but I'm going to make sure. Finn, give me that blanket."

April had never been more proud of her boys as they hastened to do as they were told without questions or arguments. Lex dialled in the final nine and Finn handed her the blanket through the gap between the seats. At this time of year, April never travelled without blankets, a folding shovel, snacks . . . drinks. She ran back to the body beside the car and knelt down. The defensive arm was clearly broken and a messy head wound had bled profusely. She spread the blanket over the man's body, glancing around nervously, fearful in case the assailant should come back. The blood on the man's head still oozed slightly from between the lips of a wound that had spilt to the bone.

It took April a moment to understand what that meant. She touched his hand. Cold and limp. Touched his face and then felt for a pulse. Was she imagining it? No, it was there. Faint and uneven, but definitely there.

April raced back to the car. Lex was explaining where they were. "Mum's here," he said and handed her the phone. The relief in his eyes that he could now hand this task over to an adult, stabbed at her painfully. She took the phone, smiling as reassuringly as she could at her young son.

"Hello, yes. No, he's still alive. There's a pulse. I've covered him with a blanket. Yes, thank you."

A few more questions followed, and the location was confirmed. Then she flopped gratefully into the driver's seat and turned to look at her boys. "You're both brilliant; you know that. Lex, you dealt with that so well. Thank you."

"Someone's hurt?" Finn asked.

145

"A man, yes. But he's not dead. Finn, can you give me that other blanket? He's freezing cold, but the ambulance is on the way. He should be OK."

In the rear of the car, the dogs were making a fuss. They couldn't understand why they had been denied their walk. "If I put the leads on them, can the two of you take them onto the moor? Don't go out of sight of the car, OK?"

Moments later, she watched from beside the hedge as they took the now very excitable hounds onto the rabbit-cropped, still half-frozen grass. From where she stood, she could keep the man and her boys in view and look out for the ambulance and any other traffic that might come by.

It still worried her that whoever had attacked the man might still be around. She had taken the jack handle from the space beside the spare tyre and now held it at the ready. The dogs, on their extendible leads, bounced excitedly, barking their joy at the freezing cold but brightly lit winter's day. Large dogs, they were both soft as tripe, but April knew that they could look intimidating, a fact she was glad of in this instance. Lex, having caught her anxiety, was being careful to keep dogs and little brother within a short dashing distance to the car. She had left the car unlocked and the keys were in the other hand — the hand not occupied by the jack handle.

April knew she could take care of herself in most circumstances, and the man lying prone by his car was no danger to her, and the sense of being watched was probably just her imagination, coupled with the gaze of a dozen or so corvids, their hoarse cries from the treetops presently a little unnerving, even for a country woman. The fear that whoever had attacked the man might return remained. She could not quite shake any of these things.

She was profoundly relieved when she heard the sound of the ambulance making its way up the narrow lane, a police car following on behind. Quickly, she went over and crouched down beside the injured, unconscious man. "It's going to be all right," she told him, even though she knew he couldn't hear. "The ambulance has arrived. You're going to be all right now."

CHAPTER 21

The news reached Mac just after midday, when Dave Kendall called him.

"Our man's turned up, but someone did their best to bash his brains out," Kendall said.

"He's dead?"

"Not yet. By some miracle he's still breathing, and he's now being prepped for surgery. A young woman and her kids found him this morning when they were taking the dogs for a walk. They called an ambulance and the police. It was pretty obvious that foul play was involved." Briefly, Kendall filled Mac in on what he knew.

"His name's not been released yet; there's been a delay in notifying next of kin. The media release just talks about a man and his car being found at the lookout point and emergency services being called."

"Perhaps advise the press office that we want to keep things vague for the moment," Mac suggested. "Chances are whoever attacked him thought they'd finished the job. Once we release the information that he's still alive, it might shake things up."

"I've already suggested that. There's only so long we can keep the lid on it, though. If our attempted murderer is local, then word will get around that April Balman, who found our man, called the ambulance and that the injured party was still alive at that point. Though from what I'm told, it's not looking good.

"Anyway, in view of your prior involvement, I've arranged for you to go up and speak with the SIO, view the scene. They're expecting you this afternoon."

Mac could now hear an odd reticence in Kendall's voice. "Who's the SIO?" he asked.

"Well, DCI Munroe is in overall charge, but the SIO is DI Clive Anning," Kendall's tone was cautious. "He seemed to recognise your name."

He would have done, Mac thought. Anning. That was all he needed. "We've crossed paths."

"Anything I should know about?"

"You know him?" Mac asked.

"I've run across him. Mac, if this is going to be a problem for you . . ."

"No problem," Mac said. "I'll take Andy with me; the experience will be useful for him."

"Good idea." Kendall was all businesslike now. "One other thing: the place where Will Toons and his car were found is not two miles, as the crow flies, from where the accident with Genevieve Atkins occurred. If Toons really was involved in that, and if there was a second person . . . this mysterious Derek . . . it's not beyond the realms of possibility that he might be responsible for this incident as well."

"You've mentioned this to Anning?"

"I have, yes. The records, such as they are, are being scanned as we speak. You'll get your set later, and I'm getting copies sent through to Anning."

"Best get off then," Mac said.

After the call, he sat staring at his phone for a moment or so, thinking about the consequences of all this. So, Will Toons might or might not survive. Whoever he had been to see may well have been responsible. And all this complication was about to bring Mac into contact with a man he disliked intensely. He rarely bothered with the effort of hating anyone — it took far too much time for one thing, and past experience had taught him that being the hater often had a more negative effect on him that it did on the hated. Though that was probably a consequence of Mac rarely letting the other person know how he actually felt about them. That would have been far too impolite. Anning had a way of needling him that Mac resented, even while he acknowledged that he really should not let the man get to him as much as he did.

Mac went through to the front office and primed Andy for their trip. Sergeant Frank Baker would be left to hold the fort. Then he returned to his office and did what he so often had done these past few years: he called Rina Martin.

* * *

"How badly hurt is he?" Rina asked.

"I'm not sure. It's likely he was lying exposed to the elements for a long time, so it's a miracle he's survived at all. Hopefully, he's due another one. His name's not been released yet, so—"

"Keep it under my hat. Well, while there's life and all that. So, you're off Axminster way."

"The incident room's been set up at a local farm, just down the road from where he was found. The woman who found the body, she's letting them use her yard to park the mobile on."

"Well, it's a lovely day and should be a nice drive. So what else is bothering you?"

She heard Mac laugh. "I'm that transparent?"

"Well, yes," Rina admitted. "You are. But that's fine between friends."

"My problem is with someone who is definitely not a friend." She could hear the discomfort and anxiety in his voice as he admitted, "I feel like a small child complaining to his mother."

"I'm about the right age," Rina told him. "What's the name of this miscreant? I'll get Eliza to put a hex on him."

"Is she any good at that kind of thing?"

"You know Eliza. She'll try anything once."

"The mind boggles. Anyway, his name is Clive Anning and, let's say, we don't get on. But I'll be fine. I just thought you might want to know about Will Toons. Funny thing is, he was found not far from where Genevieve Atkins was killed. I think I might take a look at that location too, if I've still got enough light. Now I'd better tell Miriam I'm going to be late home."

"Well, good luck with it all," Rina said.

She was thoughtful as she wandered into the kitchen and made herself a cup of hot chocolate. This was definitely hot chocolate weather. She'd not heard that level of uncertainty in Mac's voice for years. When he'd first come to Frantham, it was fair to say that he'd been a broken man. He'd been involved in a kidnap case that had ended in the death of the child involved. Mac had been a witness to her murder, unable to prevent it and then, because he had gone to the child and not chased after the man, her killer had escaped.

Later, Mac had got his man, but her friend's healing had taken time. She wondered if this DI Anning had been among those who had despised Mac for what they saw as weakness, or blamed him for the killer getting away. It was not going to be an easy day for him.

Hot chocolate in hand, she retreated to her little sanctuary and fired up her computer. As Mac had told her, William Toons's name had not yet been released, and reports spoke of emergency services being called to a remote lane crossing Dartmoor, to a single vehicle RTA. It was clear that most news agencies, citing previous accidents nearby, were assuming someone had been driving too fast and had skidded off the road. There was no mention of the death of Genevieve Atkins, but then, Rina thought, that had been a long time ago, and had certainly not been her fault. The implication of the reports seemed, judging by the other incidents mentioned, that this accident might well have been down to driver error.

Rina opened another tab and called up the map she had previously examined, and on which she had marked where Genevieve Atkins had been killed. Mac was right. It was very close by.

She switched to a satellite view and followed the road from one location to the other, marking the distance. Less than three miles. The narrow lane on which Will Toons had been found was at a higher elevation, and the passing point could be seen clearly in the satellite image. It seemed to also sit at a natural lookout point across the farmland. The image showed a summer view; she found herself wishing the location had been mapped in winter, so the hedges and trees were not so much in the way. Hedges, mostly, she noted, and what trees she did spot looked stunted and wind-blown. She knew this to be a beautiful part of the country, having walked there many times with Bethany or with Matthew, both of whom appreciated a good yomp — their twins being less keen, Steven because of the increasing pain in his knees and Eliza because she really didn't like walking boots. Rina smiled at the thought; the Peters sisters were so alike in so many ways, that it always felt odd when the differences were highlighted. It was as though one half of a single body suddenly decided that it didn't like cake.

So, she thought, where had he been coming from? Coming *from*, she considered, was most likely. He had been on his way to speak to someone — that much he had told her — and had, given the time that had passed, most likely driven to see this person, spoken to them and left before meeting with his injuries.

Damn, she should have pressed him harder to give her more details. She should have asked if he was staying down here. Should not have made assumptions about the person he had been going to see being Fliss Cameron.

But then, she reminded herself, he might have been in the mood to unburden himself, but he wasn't so unguarded that he actually wanted her to know anything really usable. She had been the audience for his dress rehearsal, not his full performance. Rina — naively as it turned out — had assumed he was saving that for the police. She had evidently been wrong. He'd gone to tell someone else that he was going to the police, that secrets were about to be revealed. On balance, Rina felt, that had probably led to his death.

She examined the map again, following the road back down the hill in both directions. She had no way of knowing from which direction Will Toons had been travelling. If she imagined herself standing in the passing place, with the road travelling to right and left, Rina found that the right-hand lane led down past a farm and a scatter of houses, and then to a larger road. Going left, she found a T junction. A left turn there would have taken Will back to that same, larger road; a left turn passed a bungalow, then a row of four houses and then odd dwellings set back from the road before reaching that bend where Genevieve Atkins had been killed some decade and a half before. Onward to the village of Tilling Howe and the pub where Will and this mysterious Derek had probably been drinking that night. A little Googling told her that the pub, The Pony, was still in business, had been recently refurbished and now had holiday lets in what had been a small barn and stable complex. Curious, Rina took a look. She found they were advertising winter breaks and blazing log fires, with a warm welcome in The Pony after those long winter rambles through stunning scenery.

Rina agreed with the bit about the stunning scenery, and she was partial to a log fire, but how many people actually came to the middle of rural Dorset for a winter break?

A quick look at The Pony's availability for January and February informed her that it was quite a substantial number. Judging by the pictures, the one-bedroom apartments did look inviting.

Well, good for them, Rina thought.

So, logic dictated that Will may well have been visiting someone along the road between the village and the T junction. Had it been Rina, she'd probably have continued along until she'd intersected with Cannington Lane and eventually back to the A 3052, rather than the scenic route along the back lane. That would be lovely in summer, but at this time of year, with the temperatures falling fast from mid-afternoon, she'd have preferred the safer route.

She went back to the map, examining the scatter of housing along the lane. Will had visited one of these houses. She was certain of that.

The sound of the front door opening and the voices of the Peters sisters and the Montmorencys drew her away from her research. They had all been out for lunch with friends, at the marina in Old Frantham. She'd not heard a taxi pull up, so guessed they'd taken advantage of the clear day to walk back round the headland. From experience, Rina knew that this was probably the last chance they'd get to do that for a while. January and February were not months when this was either possible or desirable, the sea usually being too wild, whipping the waves right over the section of wooden walkway that joined the two sections of undercliff path. On still, bright winter days like this though, it was a lovely stroll. Steven must be having a good day, or have taken extra pain killers, or both. It was a walk he loved and missed sorely now he was not always up to it.

She went out into the hallway to greet them as they unbundled from scarves and hats and padded coats. Eliza and Bethany were positively glowing, cheeks pink from exercise and biting winds. Steven looked tired but triumphant, and Matthew regarded his ersatz brother with such pride and affection that Rina's throat tightened.

"I've just had a hot chocolate," she said. "I'll make some more for all of us."

I'm so lucky, she thought as she went through to the kitchen. *I'm loved and I have people to love in return.* She suspected it had been a long time since Will Toons had been able to say that much, and she wondered, sadly, if he would ever get the opportunity now.

CHAPTER 22

PC Andy Nevins had also been studying the maps and had come to much the same conclusion as Rina. "The passing place where he was found, it's on what looks like just a narrow lane I imagine visitors use it in the summer, especially if there are holiday cottages round there. But if you're going to travel that way in winter, most likely you're local, and most likely you know the road or you're visiting someone who lives locally. So, my guess is that he was visiting somewhere along this little road here or at one of the farms. Or possibly in the village of—" Mac saw him squint and then enlarge the map on his mobile phone — "Tilling Howe."

"Which is close to where Genevieve Atkins was killed. Andy, how much of a detour would we have to make to go and take a look at that scene before we go on to the other?"

Andy fiddled with his map again, calculating. Mac was glad his constable was with him. Young he might be, but Mac had known him since his probationary year and had watched Andy Nevins develop into a thoughtful and insightful officer. He knew that Andy was aware of Mac's unease, even if he didn't understand the cause of it, and that he sensed his boss needed to be distracted — preferably by something useful.

Mac was glad of that. Had Andy not been present, he would have spent the entire trip brooding.

"Guesstimating, it'll add about twenty minutes or a half hour to the journey, depending on how bad the roads are. Theoretically, we can go straight from the scene of the Atkins hit-and-run and cut back up to the new crime scene. It'll be cordoned, but they'll probably let us through. If not, it's back down the hill and a big loop back to the farm where the incident room is."

"And that could add considerably to our journey time." Mac considered. Was he just delaying the moment he met Clive Anning? Probably. But at the same time, he didn't want to look unprofessional or give the man further ammunition if he looked like he was dragging his feet. He sighed. "No, we'll go straight to the farm, see what DI Anning and his team have to say, make sure we get to see this latest scene before it gets dark. Then we go and have a quick peek at the scene of the RTA. Is there a pub in Tilling Howe? We may as well get a bite to eat before we drive back."

Andy agreed enthusiastically.

And a stiff drink for me, if it's gone badly with Anning, Mac thought sourly. Andy could always drive them back.

He thrust that idea aside almost as quickly as it formed. When he had first come to Frantham, he had been self-medicating all too readily. Not heavily in real terms, perhaps, but enough to have a discouraging number of empty bottles to put into the recycling box at the end of the week. He wasn't going to fall into that trap again.

A constable opened the gate into the farm yard. Like every farm Mac had ever visited, it was muddy and smelt of cows, even though no bovines were visible in the fields beyond. The farm house was long and low, reminding Mac of the longhouses that had once dotted the west country, settled into the landscape and extended organically as and when the families increased in size. He wondered what it was like to live somewhere that seemed to him to be at the back of beyond, even though it was only around a half hour's drive from the coast. But then, he'd seen Frantham in much the same light when he'd first moved there.

As he got out of the car, he was struck by the quiet of the place. There seemed to be nothing but the sound of crows and sheep, and then a familiar, raised voice coming from the mobile incident room parked up at the edge of the yard.

Andy raised an eyebrow.

"That'll be DI Anning," Mac told him. "He likes to be heard."

"Right," Andy said noncommittally, and took a box of paperwork from the back seat of the car.

Actually, if Mac was honest with himself, Anning was a damned good detective with an enviable clear-up rate and a reputation for being so straight the Romans might have used him as a surveyor's pole. Unfortunately, he was just as unbending as a Roman road. There was Anning's way or no way, and, Mac knew, he struggled to understand why anyone should even want to take a different route. He got results, didn't he? This, Mac knew, was at the heart of the problem between them. When Mac had seen six-year-old Cara Evans struck down on the beach, even though every bit of reason in his head told him she was already beyond help, he had run to her. Just too far away to have prevented her murder, guilt, despair, the horror of it all had compelled him to go to her, to cradle her body until help arrived. That moment had all but destroyed him.

He had known backup was on the way. He had known that if he pursued the killer, he might not have caught him, but he'd have known where he had gone and how he'd left. As it was, the investigation had floundered and, for a while, failed, because Mac had not acted like a responsible officer. He had, in the eyes of some — and Anning was not alone in this — fallen apart. Failed in his duty.

And you know what? I've no regrets about that. Not anymore.

He and Andy headed towards the sound of the shouting and opened the door to the mobile. Inside it was stuffy and crowded, a half dozen officers still setting up computers and pinning relevant information to the walls. Mac noted the pictures of Will Toons in better times, probably downloaded from the internet, and then the two images that looked as though they had been taken in the hospital. Mac winced. How had the man even survived such a brutal attack?

Anning had come across to greet them, hand extended, firm handshake presented. Mac saw him assessing young Andy before turning his attention to Mac. "DI McGregor. You're looking better than the last time we met up."

Mac managed a smile. "That wouldn't be difficult."

"No, indeed it would not. From what I hear, you've at least managed to find your feet again since moving down here. I expected you to have taken the pension and retired long since."

Out of the corner of his eye Mac saw Andy frown, puzzled more by the tone than the words. "I hope you're not too disappointed," he said.

"Too soon to tell. But you can be sure I'll let you know."

The portacabin door opened again and three more officers came inside.

"Right," Anning said, nodding a greeting. "Now the gang's all here, you can tell us your side of the story. What's your involvement with our victim?"

In short order, Mac found himself at one end of the cabin, his notes on a table, a cup of coffee in his hand and Andy distributing the material they had brought with them. Silently, Mac blessed the fact that his constable had copied, collated and bound everything they had from the murder at the Palisades and the subsequent enquiry. He now stood by, ready to answer any questions about his own involvement in the investigation.

Andy was relaxed now, Mac noted. This might be a room full of strangers, but he was well prepared and confident in his own abilities. A couple of years ago he might have been fazed, but he'd been involved in too many high-level investigations for that to be the case now.

Mac told them about the murder mystery weekend, the finding of the body in the library — pausing until the ripple of amusement died down — and the subsequent failure to identify the body until Will Toons revealed it to Rina Martin. That she had immediately called Mac, but that no one had known where Toons had gone when he left her house.

"So that was remiss of her," Anning said cheerfully. "Considering she fancies herself as something of a sleuth, from what I understand." He paused, glancing round at his team. "She's a bloody TV detective, isn't she?"

Again that ripple of laughter in the room.

"But even given that, why should our victim decide to visit some old woman and make some half-assed sort of confession, eh?"

Some. Old. Woman. You could tell this man had never actually met Rina. He saw Andy's jaw drop. Because, Mac thought, that was what tended to happen around Rina. People tended to tell her things.

Instead, he said, "I think we should see it as a trial run before he felt confident enough to speak to the police." Mac continued, "William Toons and Mrs Martin got along. It was William Toons who found the body and Mrs Martin who initially took control of the situation at the hotel, who calmed Mr Toons down enough that he could make his statement—"

"A statement that turned out to be inaccurate, if this so-called confession is to be believed."

"That's true," Mac agreed. "And if we'd been in possession of this information earlier, our own investigation would have progressed and Will Toons might not be fighting for his life in hospital. But," he continued quickly, before Anning could interject, "he didn't tell us. He delayed. In the end, he decided to go to Mrs Martin and explain matters to her. From what she told me, he then planned to come and speak to me."

"He didn't though, did he? He fucked off somewhere else. Your Mrs Martin got it wrong."

"No," Mac said, "She didn't get it wrong. He made it clear he felt the need to speak to other people first. The assumption was that it may have been other blackmail victims who needed to be warned that their secrets were about to come out. Mrs Martin could hardly prevent Mr Toons from leaving her house. She notified me about the visit immediately and made contemporaneous notes detailing the conversation."

"But she didn't call you while he was there."

"No, she did not. Had she tried, I believe he would simply have left."

"Like I say, fancies herself as an amateur sleuth. She should learn that it's a bit different when you don't have a scriptwriter providing the solutions, don't you reckon?"

"Mrs Martin acted responsibly," Mac said calmly, though inside his guts were twisting with impatience and annoyance. "The important detail in all of this is that William Toons came here, and it's probably safe to assume that whoever he planned to see is local to the area. It's also worth noting that Genevieve Atkins, the woman killed in the hit and run RTA that it seems Toons was involved in, was killed only a couple of miles away."

"Unless he was spinning her a yarn."

"To what end?"

"Who knows with these theatrical types? Well, you can be sure we'll take all of this under advisement." He flicked through the notes Andy had prepared. "Nice to see someone has the paperwork under control, at any rate," he said.

Mac stood. "We're losing the light," he said. "I'd like a look at the crime scene before it gets too dark to see."

Anning looked quizzically at him. "I can't see what use that would be to you," he said. "Seeing as you've done your duty." He tapped the notes. "Or at least, some bugger has. But if you want to go and take a gander, then feel free. If I've any more questions for you, I know where to find you, don't I?"

"What's his problem?" Andy asked indignantly, when they were back in the car. "And Mrs Martin doesn't think like that, anyway."

"No, she doesn't," Mac agreed, though he could recall a time, when he had first come to Frantham, when he had regarded her interference as utterly inappropriate. He had since learnt better. "But believe me, Rina can take it. She'll have heard worse, and if they ever meet face to face, I know who my money will be on."

"Too right," Andy agreed. He fell silent as they drove up the hill towards the point where Will Toons had been found. Around them the dusk fell, shadows deepening the enclosed lane until they reached the crest of the hill. From there, the evening shades of purples and grey, lit by a faint orange glow on the horizon, gathered across the landscape. Artificial light illuminated the pull-in where the injured man had been lying, and two officers got out of a car as they pulled up.

"Boss phoned, said you wanted to view the scene," one of them said. He smiled, his manner friendly and interested as he regarded Andy and Mac. The other officer repositioned the lamps and handed Mac a sheaf of photographs. "We managed to grab a couple of pics while the paramedics were doing their thing," he said. "Just so the body position was recorded, in case this becomes a murder investigation. CSI took the rest when they got here. DI Anning called through to expect you, said to give you a set."

Mac studied the pictures showing the wounded man. His finger traced the outline of the wound.

"Tyre iron, I reckon," the officer said. "Frankly, I don't give much for his chances."

He sounded genuinely saddened by that. Mac nodded. "Whoever attacked him certainly wanted him dead," he agreed. "They made a right mess of him."

He looked around at this isolated spot. Beyond the lights, the darkness seemed to have intensified and Mac had the sudden vertiginous sense of the four of them being contained inside some kind of bubble of light. Of there being nothing beyond. "It's amazing he was found."

"April and the kids come up here a lot," the second officer said. "We're assigned to the rural crime squad, so we check in regularly with the local farmers. She's managing that place on her own since her husband passed. Her in-laws help out, but it's still a tough ask. She's doing a good job though."

"Must be tough," Mac agreed.

Shortly after, they took their leave and continued on, down the hill again, turning left towards the village of Tilling Howe.

"So," Mac said, as he made the turn. "You want to know why Anning despises me. Though that won't stop him cooperating. Hence, the instruction to give us the additional photos."

Andy had looked a little shocked as his boss's directness. "I never," he said. "I mean . . ."

"It's natural to be curious. Truth is, he sees me as something of a weak-minded wimp and compared to him, I probably am. He thinks I made the wrong judgement call when Cara Evans was killed and that he'd never have fallen apart like I did afterwards. He's probably right — about the falling apart, anyway.

"Sending me to Frantham, a place where apparently nothing ever happened, was meant to be a punishment of sorts. Or, to look at it another way, it was an alternative solution to the problem of DI Sebastian McGregor, when he refused to retire early on medical grounds. So, you and Sergeant Baker got stuck with me. Everyone thought I'd last six months and then request a medical review and retirement. And that might well have happened. But it didn't turn out that way, did it?"

Andy nodded. "I'm glad," he said. They had been driving slowly, hedges and the occasional house picked out in the beam of the headlights. They saw a sign for a humpback bridge. "The bend where it happened is just up ahead, just before we get to the bridge."

Mac slowed even more, creeping up on the location, and, there being no sign of other traffic, examining it in the lights of the high beam. "Of course, we're coming from the wrong direction," he said. "On the way back, we can get a better sense of what might have happened on that night."

"Dinner now?" Andy said hopefully.

"Sounds sensible," Mac agreed. They drove on into the village of Tilling Howe and parked outside of The Pony. Had Will Toons been here since Genevieve Atkins died? Mac wondered. That night that had taken a young woman's life and changed two others irrevocably.

CHAPTER 23

The vehicle Derek had driven when he went to visit his daughter and her family, late that same afternoon, was not the one he had used to ram Will Toons' car. The four-by-four he had driven for that had belonged to Jeff Mannering, and Derek had in fact made no attempt to dispose of the car when he had got rid of Jeff's body. He had left it parked on the grass verge near his cottage, but no one had enquired as to who the car belonged to or even taken notice of it, so far as Derek was aware.

His immediate neighbours were both intermittent residents, the small, whitewashed house a couple of hundred yards in one direction being a holiday let and the house in the other direction owned by a young couple, Harry and Milly Bright, who were slowly renovating what had been a wreck of a place. They showed up most weekends, and on odd occasions had asked Derek to keep an eye open for deliveries of building materials. He had a spare key for the solidly built side gates, (the first thing the Brights had attended to had been to make the house and garden more secure) and could be relied upon to make sure the pallets of bricks and the bundles of timber were dropped into that space and then covered with a tarpaulin.

After he had killed Jeff, Derek had thought long and hard about what to do. He could dump the car somewhere, but that would have led to two complications. One being how he was going to get back home. The second that an abandoned car would attract attention and the police would then have reason to look for the owner. Left outside his house, it simply looked as though it belonged to him, or that he had a visitor. Had anyone asked, he'd say that a friend asked to leave it there when he went on holiday. Something of that sort, anyway. If anyone asked, he could quite reasonably say that he'd not expected to hear from that friend, so no, he definitely hadn't realised he was missing — or, in this case, dead. But the car as it was now, with a smashed in front end, missing paint, a broken light that might be matched to fragments of glass found at the scene — now that was a different thing entirely.

So, Derek had thought about it and come up with a temporary solution. The Brights, the young couple who owned the house, had told him they would not be coming down until mid-January. They were taking a well-earned break with family over Christmas, and their weekend forays would be temporarily curtailed by other long-planned family events. Jeff Mannering's car was now parked right at the bottom of their garden and covered with a tarpaulin, the big gate locked and the vehicle for the moment out of sight and out of mind.

Derek knew he'd have to find a better solution for the long term, but frankly, he didn't feel he had the mental energy to work it out just yet. The rage he had felt when he had killed Jeff Mannering had wiped him out, leaving him exhausted and bewildered for quite some time. He'd eventually built up enough energy to remove the body from the freezer and take it to the Palisades, an idea that had occurred to him when Fliss had told him about the pre-Christmas event she was doing there, and let slip that Will would be taking part. The idea of them finding the body, of it becoming a kind of joke that they should find it in the library, had come to him in an epiphanic flash. Hadn't Agatha Christie done something of the sort, as a way of misdirecting an investigation?

Over the next several days, the idea had coalesced and solidified into something resembling a plan, but moving the body had been more of a trial than he had expected. Just opening the old freezer and coming face to face with the man he had killed had nearly floored him. Mannering's body was frosted, his face pallid and blue with tiny ice flakes decorating his eyelashes and hair. It was somehow ghostlike and uncanny; Derek had stumbled back from the sight of him, suddenly appalled by what he had done.

But it's done now, he had told himself as he downed his second gin, the glass chattering against his teeth, his hand was shaking so much. *Time to stop dithering and do something about it.*

Quite how he had got the body back out of the freezer, Derek was never sure afterwards. He had struggled with it, stiff and cold and unwieldy . . . and then the horror of waiting for it to defrost enough to be picked up and manoeuvred into plastic sheeting and shoved into the massive boot of Jeff Mannering's BMW X5, that being far more practical than his old Ford. All through the waiting time, he had lived in dread of someone coming to his cottage, going into the outhouse and seeing the dead man lying on the floor.

Afterwards, he had asked himself why he had done this. What had he hoped to gain by placing the body where Fliss and Will would be sure to see it? Or at least, where he hoped they would. It occurred to him, as he drove away, that someone else might find the dead man. Someone else might be the recipient of this dreadful, almost existential shock. Well, that couldn't be helped now.

Had he wanted to punish Fliss and Will in some way? Had he intended to cry out for help, tell them, "Look, this is what I've been driven to?"

Perhaps both of those things. Derek could no longer be certain of his own mind. But it had worked out badly, hadn't it? And now Will was dead, and Derek could not, in all honesty, say that he was sorry.

All these thoughts he mulled over while driving to his daughter's house, but as he turned the corner into the short cul-de-sac, harsh street lights illuminating small, modern, semi-detached houses, he pushed all of them aside. He would not contaminate his time with his family with memories, regrets, horrors like this. Derek found himself encountering a sense of panic; what if the things he had done, the things he had thought, the feelings of rage and shame and elation and despair should somehow leak out and contaminate his child, her husband, his beloved grandchildren? He should turn back now, ring them and say he was feeling ill, didn't want to risk passing anything on — and wasn't that the truth of it? That he feared contagion? That he might somehow contaminate those he loved with what he had done?

But it was too late for that now. They had been looking out for his car and the children were in the open doorway, waving and smiling at him as he, knowing that to turn away now would invite far too many questions, pulled up outside their house.

He gathered Olivia and Ryan into his arms, hugging them close as his daughter kissed him on the cheek.

"Get along inside, it's bitter out. I'll get the kettle on." She smiled at him and that smile wiped all his doubts away. He'd crossed a line and now he could never cross back, but he'd had no option really, had he? Not after Jeff Mannering had mentioned his family in that way, had implied they could be threatened as well. He'd taken that man out of his life, and then Will too, when he had threatened Derek with exposure. Sad but necessary. And if whoever had sent that letter to Will, demanding more payment, then he'd deal with that too. A man had to protect his own. Now that he had crossed that line, Derek had no doubts about what he could and would do in pursuit of that.

CHAPTER 24

Both Mac and Kendall had led the press conference the following morning, explaining that they now had a name for their mystery victim and needed the help of the public in finding his family.

"This is an unusual step," Kendall said. "We would obviously prefer to speak to the family first. The idea of them finding out that their son or brother, husband or father is dead by seeing it on the television is abhorrent. But we've had no response to his picture; no one has come forward to identify our murder victim, and so we feel that we have no choice. We've reason to believe that our dead man was Jeffery Mannering, though it's possible he also used other names on occasion. And once more we appeal to the public for assistance in making a positive identification and in tracing his next of kin."

Mac took over. "We have reason to believe that Jeffery Mannering might have lived, or even still be living, in the local area. It's possible he moved away and perhaps returned on a visit. It's possible he lost contact with friends and family and they were unaware he had returned." He went on to give out the phone numbers, email, and social media contacts, and he and Kendall went on to field questions from representatives of the gathered media.

"The trouble is," he said sourly, as he and Kendall left, "this Jeff Mannering, if that was his real name, isn't going to start a fire under anyone in the press." No one liked to admit it, but there was a hierarchy to victimhood: children at the top, followed by attractive teens and old ladies. "Men in their forties or fifties who get themselves killed are somehow assumed to be less innocent, less appealing in a media sense, less interesting to the general public and somehow more likely to have been responsible for their own demise."

Kendall laughed at him. "Who get themselves killed?"

Mac smiled wryly as he realised he'd just made that exact judgement himself. "OK, so maybe finding out he was probably a blackmailer makes me a tad less sympathetic."

"Well, some bugger killed him," Kendall said, "and the likelihood is that it was one of his victims. That is, if we can believe what Toons told your Mrs Martin. Even so, a murder is a murder."

Mac nodded. *My* Mrs Martin, he thought. Kendall was still not a convert, though he did now admit that Rina had sometimes proved useful.

"I think the fact that Will Toons is now lying in the ITU gives credence to his story," he said.

"True. How did it go with DI Anning?"

"Well, he was a great admirer of Andy's organisational skills," Mac said. "But it was fine. He knows it's in everyone's interest that we all cooperate. I also took a look at where Genevieve Atkins was killed. The paperwork for that arrived this morning, but I've not had a chance to go through it yet, just glanced at the summary."

"What did you make of the scene?"

Mac thought for a moment. "Well, it was dark, and this is about the same time of year as when the RTI happened. Coming out of the village there's a straight bit of road, long enough to pick up some speed if you were so inclined. Then there's a hump-backed bridge and a sudden blind bend about ten yards before that. When you are driving into the village, the bridge isn't visible until you come off the bend. Going back the other way — the way the car was travelling when it hit her — if they'd picked up speed on the straight and then taken the bridge too fast, there'd be little or no time for correction before they hit the bend where she died."

"According to the report, she was walking towards the village when she was killed. Walking towards oncoming traffic, had a reflective band on her sleeve . . . she did everything right."

"And on this occasion, would probably have been better not following the standard advice," Mac said. "Had she been on the other side of the road, the driver might have seen her or she might have had a chance to throw herself out of the way."

They had reached Kendall's office. Kendall shed his coat and slumped down in his office chair and motioned to Mac to take the one opposite. Mac shrugged out of his own overcoat and sat down.

"Why didn't she hear the car coming and take evasive action when she realised it was being driven much too fast?" Kendall mused.

"Because there was nowhere for her to go," Mac told him. "On the other side of the road, there's a decent width of grass verge. On the side of the road she was walking on, the verge peters out after the bridge and doesn't reappear until you pass the farm gate about a hundred yards down the road. On that bend, there's effectively nowhere for a pedestrian to be apart from in the road, unless they cross to the other side. She'd have stood no chance."

"Poor woman," Kendall said. "And all these years, if Will Toons's story is correct, he and this mysterious Derek have been quite literally paying for it. The irony is, it would have been over and done years since if they'd stopped at the scene and admitted to what they'd done."

"Well, if Toons had gone to visit this Derek, and we're right about him being local to the area where Toons was found, it shouldn't take long to track him down. I don't think we passed more than a dozen houses between the crime scene and the village. Even if they extend their house-to-house as far as Tilling Howe, it's not going to take more than a morning."

"So, I'll be sure to tell Anning to get his finger out, if he happens to call," Kendall said.

Mac grimaced and Kendall laughed.

"I'd best be off," Mac said. "Let's hope the release of the name gets us further with Jeffery Mannering."

"Unless William Toons lied about his name," Kendall said.

"Unless that," Mac agreed.

* * *

Derek had stayed overnight at his daughter's house, babysitting while the parents went to a party. They had arrived home late and were still asleep when Derek got breakfast ready. Emily came into the kitchen just as the kids finished eating and disappeared into the living room to watch something on the telly.

"Thanks, Dad, you know how much we appreciate it."

"I don't mind; you know that. It reminds me of when you were little. We had some good times, didn't we?"

She nodded. "Yeah, we did. You remember when you used to take me sledging? We'd go up the back lane and park in that little cutaway. There was a run I liked to make down into the valley. I could only do it if the snow was deep enough. It was all hills and hollows otherwise."

"I remember that," he said. "I remember there was that one time you misjudged it and came a real cropper. You swerved, disappeared, next thing all I could see is a pair of red wellies sticking up in the air." He paused; that had been a place with such good memories. They'd taken the children up there a couple of times, but in the pandemic year, they'd not been sure they were allowed. Then the following two, there'd not been enough snow during the Christmas holidays, and now the place was tainted.

As though catching his thought, she said, "That's where they found that crashed car, isn't it? It's an odd place for anyone to come off the road; accidents usually happen down the hill when some idiot takes the bend too fast."

"Ice, maybe. Or mud left by a farm vehicle," he said. "I'd best be off, then you can enjoy your day. Anything nice planned?"

"Lunch somewhere, if I can get Luke out of bed. He was asleep before his head hit the pillow last night. We're not so good at staying out late these days."

As he drove home, he filled his thoughts with those happy memories. After her mum had died, he had been everything to Emily, mother, father, confidant — at least until she'd got older and discovered boys, and developed her tight-knit group of best friends and felt obliged to rebel. Not, he thought, that she'd been any good at it, not really. They'd had a row one day, no doubt over something really stupid and she'd told him in a fit of temper that she hated him, that he'd no right to tell her what to do, that he didn't understand her. She'd then burst into tears and asked for a hug. But that was about as bad as it got. He was more grateful for that than he could put into words.

They had, of course, drifted apart when she went off to university, but that was to be expected. When she had met Luke and moved in with him, it seemed as though she'd needed the reassurance of her dad being around — or at least the usefulness of his DIY skills. And once the kids had come along, their previous closeness had reasserted itself. He even got along well with his son-in-law, though he'd never in a million years expected Emily would marry an accountant.

Despite the predations of Jeff Mannering that had often made life financially difficult, he had been happy. He had felt, somehow, that by paying the man off and being a good father and an even better grandfather, he was compensating for the dreadful thing he and Will had done that night. That dreadful but totally unintentional act. That he had balanced the books, somehow.

Then it had all gone so terribly wrong. "Oh, God," he whispered softly. "This is not the way it should be. None of this is the way it should be."

He was almost at his cottage when he saw the police car, parked along the lane outside of the house owned by the young couple — and where he had hidden Jeff Mannering's car. He panicked, almost — he could drive on, stay away for a couple of days until the fuss died down.

But how would that look? He sighed heavily and instead of driving on, he slowed down, pulled up alongside the police car. The young officer, hearing the car, turned from the door to look at him.

"You'll not find anyone there," Derek told him. "They're doing the place up, not moved in yet."

"Oh. And you know when they were last here?"

"Couple of weeks ago. I've got the key to the gate, in case of deliveries. I've got their mobile numbers if you need them?" He pointed down the road. "I live down there, the white cottage with the green door." He grinned at the young officer. "I'll get the kettle on. You look like you could do with a brew."

A few minutes later, Derek was playing host to the policeman, now sitting in the same chair that Jeff and then Will had occupied and drinking from the same mug, listening to the same comment about Derek picking up the set of mugs for two quid at the local charity shop. Confirming that his name, as per the electoral register, was David Eric Ayre, and commiserating on the thankless task of knocking on the doors of empty houses.

"I assume this is about the accident up the road," he said. "From off, was he? Even the locals don't use that high lane much this time of year."

"I believe he was, yes. Nasty business, though. It's amazing he lasted so long. It gets bitter cold up there at night."

Lasted so long. What did that mean? "I thought the driver must have been killed in the accident," he said, hoping that the shocked tone he caught in his own voice would merely be taken for surprise.

"Thankfully, he was still alive when they found him. In a poor way, mind."

"I can imagine," Derek said.

Will was still alive? Oh, God, Will was still alive.

CHAPTER 25

Rina had managed to catch Mac on the phone just after lunch. She had seen the press conference on the local news and had been wondering if there was any news about Will Toons.

"No change, as yet, but the hospital reckon the fact that he's stable is a good thing. We're still trying to contact his family. Kendall finally got hold of his agent, but she was vague about family. Fliss Cameron reckons they were estranged, but, I don't know, even if that's true, they'll want to know he's in hospital, won't they?"

"Probably," Rina said. "I don't know. Families can be complicated, and he did say he'd tried to keep everyone at arm's length since that terrible business with the ex-girlfriend and her sister." She paused. "I wondered how it all went yesterday. With DI Anning?"

"Better than I'd expected. He was still trying to provoke, but I think I've grown thicker skin since we last met. He seemed to take a fancy to young Andy, though. Commended him on his organisational skills."

"Well, he can't have him," Rina said.

Mac laughed. "OK, I'd best be off. All good with the family?"

"We're all fine, thanks. But before you go, I wanted to tell you that I'm off to see Lily Blake in a few minutes."

"Oh?"

She could hear the sudden caution in his tone: *What is Rina up to now?*

"Oh, I plan to behave," she said. "But Mac, I know she recognised that man, even if she didn't know his name was Jeffery Mannering. I just thought she might be willing to say something, now his name has been released."

"Then maybe I should speak to her." She could hear the mischief in his tone. "That is my job, after all. To ask the questions."

"So it is, but sometimes a woman will talk to another woman when she won't talk to a police officer, even one as nice as you."

He was still laughing when she rang off and gathered up her coat and bag. She had no doubt that speaking to Lily again was already on Mac's list, whether or not Rina got anything out of her in the meantime. Her taxi had arrived; she shouted her goodbyes to the Montmorencys. They were in the lounge catching up with films they had recorded over the Christmas break and looked to be ensconced for the afternoon. Eliza and Bethany had caught the bus into Bridport to see if there was anything interesting in the sales. Rina could remember when the post-Christmas sales really did begin in January and not in the space between.

No doubt they would come home with another pair of shoes for Bethany and yet another silky scarf for Eliza, and probably yet more of those chocolate Christmas tree decorations that everyone seemed to like so much. *We're all just big kids really*, Rina thought.

Lily was surprised to see her and, Rina thought, a little flustered. They'd spoken on the phone, but not met up since that shocking weekend, and Rina thought she detected a degree of embarrassment in Lily that things had gone so wrong. There was no need for that, Rina thought. It was hardly her fault that someone had decided to dump a body in her library.

She wondered what Lily would have done had she been first on the scene. An image came unbidden of Lily being annoyed at the mess and clearing it away before it upset the guests.

Lily took her through to her little office and Rina recalled the last time she had been in here. Of Will Toons shaking and distressed, and Andy's gentle but firm interrogation.

"Tea would be lovely," Rina replied to Lily's query. "It's bitter cold out there. And far colder up here than it is in town."

Lily nodded. "We've had a week of really heavy frosts, despite being so close to the sea. I suppose it's because we're in a little dip." She was looking at Rina with a quizzical expression, and Rina was not surprised when Lily said, "Lovely as it is to see you, Rina, I don't think you've come up here to discuss the weather."

"I don't suppose I have," Rina admitted. "Lily, why didn't you tell the police you recognised that man?"

Lily turned away. The kettle had boiled and Lily took her time dabbling tea bags in large blue mugs. Rina, who always made her tea in a proper pot, frowned, but she let it pass and accepted the brew with good grace, setting it on the windowsill as Lily brought her chair closer to hers.

"You're right," she said finally. "I should have said something, but I wasn't sure, and it wasn't as if I knew anything about him or his name . . . or that I was even completely certain. And, Rina, it was all so awful and I had this thought going through my head that this was all going to ruin us, just when we're really starting to get on our feet, and . . . and then the moment passed and I just told myself that it was nothing, that it didn't matter. Anyway, I could hardly call Mac days later and say, 'look, I'm sorry, but I think I've seen him before, but I didn't like to say'."

The words had tumbled over one another. Rina waited to see if there were more to come and then said gently, "So tell me now, and then I'll help you to tell Mac. He'll understand that you were distressed and confused and not sure at the time. That sometimes it can be hard to know what's important and what's not."

Lily nodded, and Rina could see that she was grateful to have been given excuses she could use when the inevitable happened. And it was inevitable that she would talk now, as Rina had guessed it would be. She had just been waiting for the opportunity.

"So, the name 'Jeffery Mannering' means nothing to you," she said.

Lily shook her head. "No. And when I saw him, or rather, when I saw his picture, it didn't really look like the man I remembered. Or at least. not exactly. Maybe it was the expression, maybe because he was wearing glasses . . . Oh, I don't know, Rina, maybe I'm still mistaken and I felt like if I said something and I was wrong I'd be making unnecessary trouble for people. I talked to James about it, and he said to let it go. He said we'd got enough trouble as it was without bringing more to our door, and that I was probably wrong anyway."

That sounded like James. "But in your own mind, you've just become more certain, is that it?" Rina asked.

Lily nodded, and Rina could see the unhappiness in her expression. "I mean, surely Fliss would have said something if the dead man was the one I saw her with," she said.

Oh, Rina thought. *So that was it.* "Have you asked her?"

Lily shook her head. "I can't. She was so shocked. Anyway, if he was the man I saw her with, wouldn't she have said something?"

You'd have thought so. Rina considered her response. "I suppose shock does strange things to people," she said. "But, Lily, she might have felt she had a reason for denying she knew this man. Where did you see him with her?"

"If it *was* him."

Rina could see Lily was starting to doubt herself again, and also starting to remember her husband's judgement, that they could do without more trouble.

"If it wasn't, no harm done," Rina said briskly. "If Fliss is in some kind of trouble and that led her to deny knowing this man, then by bringing it out into the open, you'd be helping her as well."

Lily blinked. Rina held her breath. She could practically see the cogs whirring in Lily's brain, and hoped they would click into the right formation.

A small change in Lily's expression told her that they had. "All right," she said. "I'll tell you. It was about a week before the . . . event. Fliss had called to say she was having car troubles and might be a bit late. She was coming to discuss the final details for the weekend. Anyway, I told her I'd expect her when I saw her and left it at that. About an hour later, she turns up in a car I didn't recognise. That man, or someone like him, was driving it. He was wearing heavy, dark-rimmed glasses. You know the old-fashioned sort that seem to be making a come-back?" She shuddered. "Horrible things. You'd have to be a young Michael Caine to look good in something like that."

"Like in the Ipcress Files?" Rina asked.

"Yes! Exactly like that. Anyway, they pulled up outside and sat taking for a minute or so. I saw them from the office window and I was heading into the reception to greet her, but then, well, I saw she wasn't getting out of the car, that she was still talking to the man." Lily pointed out of the window. "He'd pulled up there, at the edge of the grass, so I got a good look at them both."

Rina looked to where she had indicated. The entrance to the drive was over towards the left of the frontage. A round lawn sat at the centre of an in-out driveway and Lily had pointed at the right-hand side of the curve. Yes, if the car had stopped where Lily said, then she'd have got a very good face-on look at the driver.

"And you assumed a friend had given her a lift?"

"I did, but they seemed very friendly, if you know what I mean. She gave him a kiss before getting out, and it wasn't just a peck on the cheek. I'm afraid I kind of backed away from the window as she got out. I didn't want Fliss to see me and think I was spying on her. I asked her, 'so you got a lift over?' and she said she'd have to get a taxi back. James drove her in the end. I just assumed she must have a new man in her life, but that the relationship was too fresh for her to want to talk about it."

"And did she mention him again?"

Lily shook her head. "And I didn't ask. I like Fliss; we've known her for a long time . . . but it's a professional relationship, really, not a friend thing. Fliss has — how can I say it? — boundaries, I suppose. She's always friendly enough, but she's not keen on people getting too close."

Rina nodded. From what she'd seen of Fliss, she could imagine that to be the case. Though if the dead man had been someone Fliss was actually close to, that probably explained her need to attempt to drink herself into a stupor, as she had that night. She'd really been putting it away — though she'd also still seemed fairly lucid, which squared with what she'd heard about Fliss having an intimate and ongoing relationship with alcohol.

"Look," Lily said, getting to her feet. "Lovely as it is to see you, I've got heaps to do. New Year's Eve is only a couple of days away and you've really no idea how much this has set us back. Shall I call a taxi for you?"

Rina's tea still sat untouched on the windowsill, but she was content to leave it there. She'd learnt what she had hoped to learn, and now Lily was, almost inevitably, regretting her confession. "You'll have to tell Mac," Rina reminded her.

"Yes, yes, of course. But not just now. I'll give him a ring later. Now, about that taxi?"

Rina assured Lily that she could walk back. She had donned her good boots in preparation, and the day was cold but bright, ideal for the two-mile walk back. She could take the cliff path part of the way and then cut back towards the town.

Lily regarded her as though she thought this was a mad idea, but Rina could see she was also relieved not to have her hanging around waiting for a taxi to arrive.

As she went through the gate onto the cliff path, Rina fetched her mobile out of her pocket and attempted to call Mac. The phone went straight to voicemail. She then tried the tiny police station in Frantham and got through to Andy Nevins.

"He's not here, Mrs Martin. He and Sergeant Baker are likely to be gone all afternoon. Anything I can do?"

"Thanks, Andy. If you just tell Mac that I've spoken to Lily and she confirmed that she thinks she had seen the dead man before but didn't immediately recognise him. She thinks he's a man who gave Fliss Cameron a lift to the hotel one day. Andy, I think that's all she knows, but if you can pass that on?"

"Of course I will, Mrs Martin. Soon as I can get hold of him."

Rina walked on. The view from the cliff path was stunning. The sea was almost unnaturally still today. She had found that people who did not live close to the coast assumed that as soon as you hit November, it was nothing but storms and crashing waves. Rina herself had assumed that before she'd moved down to Frantham. In part, of course, that was true. Storms could be brewing out beyond the horizon and the only warning you got of their impending arrival might be a slight darkening of the horizon before suddenly they hurtled in with full force, sea darkening as you looked at it, and waves roiling and boiling as though the kraken was about to appear. Rina could well understand why people believed in sea monsters. No chance of that today, though. The sky was a bright Meissen blue and the ocean flat calm.

So, where might Mac have gone to? If he'd taken Frank Baker, then chances were it was to see someone who would need sympathy and careful handling.

CHAPTER 26

Mac had indeed gone to see someone in need of sympathy and careful handling. Jeff Mannering's sister had called the police information line that morning, in shock at discovering that her brother was dead. She was by turns furious that this was how she'd found out and angry with herself that she'd not even realised her brother was missing. She'd been away on a winter break with her husband and a couple of friends. They had needed two weeks of sun — or at least, not persistent rain — and had gone to southern Spain. No, she'd not seen the pictures, but after hearing his name announced, she'd gone online in search of the previous appeal for information and seen the artist impression of him.

"It doesn't even look like him! I'd never have known even if I had seen it. How do you expect anyone to recognise him from that picture?"

Now, having seen several pictures of the living Jeff Mannering, Mac could see she had a point. It wasn't that the artist had got it wrong, he thought, just that she had not been in possession of all the facts. And also, perhaps, because she'd been drawing from photographs of a previously frozen Jeff Mannering. What might the freezing and defrosting process have done to his features? And then there was the fact that he seemed to have lost a considerable amount of weight since his sister had last met with, or photographed, him.

"When did you last see you brother?" Sergeant Frank Baker asked gently, as they looked at the array of pictures of a younger, round-faced man wearing heavy, dark-rimmed glasses. Mac was reminded of Clark Kent specs, before he took off his glasses and turned into Superman. It was obviously the same man, and DNA comparison with his sister would satisfy any niggling doubts, but he had changed his appearance enough that Mac could understand that she'd not believed she would have made the connection solely on the basis of the artist's impression.

Sally Frith, previously Sally Mannering, shrugged. "We'd not been close for years. There's a ten-year age gap; he'd left home by the time I was eight or nine, so I suppose we never really established a grown-up relationship, not like siblings usually do. He didn't come home much, either. Mum had remarried, so Jeff and I we were only half-siblings anyway, and I think he took his dad's side when they got divorced. Whatever, Jeff and my dad, they didn't really get along. He'd go off and stay with his father for a bit, but his dad wasn't what you'd have called organised. He'd have to fend for himself most of the time. When he got sick of not getting three meals a day or getting lifts to school, he'd come back home. For a while it would be OK, then something would happen, and he'd blow up at Mum or at my dad, and they'd row and he'd go off again for a bit. Jeff never seemed as though he could be settled anywhere for long."

"How long since these pictures were taken?" Mac asked.

"Not so long ago," she said sharply, as though resenting the implication that it was a while since the two of them had got together.

"He's lost quite a bit of weight since they were taken," Frank Baker observed. "So, a little while then?"

Mac saw her glare at Frank, but no one could resist the older man for long.

She sighed. "About three years ago," she said, pointing to one of the pictures. Sally and her brother standing on what looked like a beach promenade, outside of a shop selling buckets and spades and brightly coloured pin wheels. "We'd met for a birthday lunch. My birthday is April and his is September. We always tried to meet up for those, and to see one another at Christmas. Of course, this year, we were away, so we'd planned to meet up just after New Year."

The tears were starting now. Mac could see that despite their differences in age, in parent, in experiences growing up, despite what Sally had said about them not being as close as siblings usually were, that she had loved her big brother and was genuinely mourning his loss. How would she feel when she found out what her brother had been involved in? Mac wondered.

"Did he always wear glasses?" In one of the pictures he was sporting a pair of wraparound sunglasses, but in the rest the heavy, dark-framed spectacles were much in evidence.

She nodded. "He tried contacts for a bit but couldn't get on with them. And he always seemed to go for the same style of glasses. Si, my husband, he used to joke that Jeff was hiding behind them. That no one would know him with his glasses off." She realised what she had just said and burst into tears. Mac was relieved when the sound of a key in the front door announced the arrival of said Simon. Sally had called him when he and Sergeant Baker had arrived and he'd promised to leave work and come straight home.

The door opened and Mac observed as Si took in the scene, dropped his briefcase onto the floor and then swept his wife into his arms. He looked accusingly at the two officers. "Couldn't you have waited until I was here?"

And do what in the meantime? Mac wondered. All sit around and stare at one another, across the expanse of low coffee table set between the two sofas?

"It's all right." Sally freed herself gently from his embrace and sat down again, Simon now beside her, holding her hand tightly. "The officers have been very kind. It's just upsetting, that's all."

"Mr Frith," Frank Baker said, "we realise how much of a shock this must be and that you need time to come to terms with it, so if you could provide us with a few details, we can be on our way. We may well need to speak to you both again, of course, but we do understand the two of you just need some time just now."

Mac could see the relief in Simon Frith's eyes. These intruders would soon be gone, and he could comfort his wife and talk about who the hell would want to murder his brother-in-law. He would cooperate in every way possible, just so they would go.

By the time they left, almost forty minutes later, they were armed with Jeff Mannering's address, his employer's name and address, and a list of friends and places he liked to visit. They also had copies of several photographs, scanned and printed for them by Simon, and a whole clutch of random information about Jeff Mannering's taste in food and films and girlfriends — none of which seemed to have lasted very long. Finally, they had the address and contacts for Sally's mother and her second husband.

"Mum's devastated," Sally told them. "She's not seen or heard from him in years. I used to call and tell her about him when we'd met up, and the last years or so, I persuaded him to send her Christmas and birthday cards. I'd hoped they might—" she broke off, unable to hold back the tears.

As Simon Frith was seeing them out, Mac asked, "Your wife mentioned meeting up with her brother for birthday lunches. So, April and September?"

"That's right, yes."

"Your brother-in-law had lost quite a bit of weight, changed his appearance. That would probably have happened over quite some time. Did you notice that when you met in September?"

Simon Frith looked suddenly awkward. He glanced back towards the living room door, as though to check that it was closed. "Look," he said. "He was Sally's brother and I don't like to speak ill of the dead, but Jeff was an asshole. Always

184

out for what he could get. Yes, we'd meet for lunch, which we would always pay for, and he always . . . always seemed to need a loan for something or other or have some sob story that led him to being short that month. Oh, it wasn't like he wanted a lot in the scheme of things. Most times, I ended up stumping up fifty quid, a hundred, maybe. It was . . . it was like it wasn't that he wanted the money, so much as he wanted to prove he could get it, if you see what I mean. And it wasn't as though he was short, not really. Always had a decent car, nice flat, expensive suit, flashy watch. And genuine, not a knockoff; I know my watches. It wasn't that he needed to tap anyone for the cash; it was more that he liked the fact he could. Frankly, I was sick of it. This September, I managed to wangle things so we were busy on the birthday weekend and the ones on either side. It took a bit of organising, but we were free of him for once. Sal felt guilty as hell, and then when I booked the Christmas break as a surprise, she was reluctant at first, because we'd be missing our Christmas lunch with big brother. In the end, I had to arrange something for just after New Year."

He seemed, Mac thought, to brighten when it occurred to him that was an appointment he would not have to keep.

Simon Frith glanced back again at the living room door. "Look, I'd better get back to her. If I think of anything useful, I've got your card and I'll give you a call."

"He's very relieved Jeff Mannering is dead and gone," Mac said as they got back into the car.

"Understandable, perhaps," Sergeant Baker agreed. "You think Jeff Mannering tapped the husband for money at other times?"

"Possibly. I'll talk to Kendall see if there's a possibility of looking into their financial records. He's in the process of getting Mannering's and that should move things forward. First though, Mannering's employer. You start driving in their direction and I'll make the calls."

* * *

Rina was enjoying an afternoon snack of tea and cake with Steven and Matthew when the Peters sisters arrived back home. She could see at once that all was not well; for one thing, they had taken a taxi all the way from Bridport instead of getting the bus. For another, Eliza refused tea and announced that she was going for a lie down.

Bethany collapsed into a chair at the scrubbed pine kitchen table and gratefully accepted the mug that Matthew placed into her hands.

"What's wrong?" Rina asked, as Steven slipped an arm around Bethany's shoulders.

Rina was shocked to see tears spring into Bethany's eyes. "Oh, Rina, it was so frightening. We were having a lovely time, and then Eliza suddenly just had a moment, you know? She stopped dead. We were outside of the gallery café in Sladers Yard, and she just looked around like she was lost and just couldn't remember where she was. Then she looked at me and — oh, it was horrible, but just for a split second it was like she didn't know who I was either. And she was so distressed. She wanted to know where we were and what we were doing, and then she wanted to come home. She was so pale, Rina, and so frightened. I took her into the café, that was where we'd been heading anyway, and I think the familiar atmosphere helped to settle her nerves and she was much better. But she still wanted to come home and it was more than an hour until the next bus, so we had to find a taxi. Thankfully, I had enough money on me, or I'd have had to make it wait outside while I came in and got some. Oh, it was just so expensive, but what could I do?"

"Take it out of the jar," Rina said, referring to the jar she kept in the hall sideboard and which she kept like a petty cash fund, just in case of domestic emergency. "Are you all right now?"

Bethany nodded. "Thank you. I'm fine. It's all fine now we're home. She just has these moments; you all know that. Then they pass." She took a deep breath. "I'll take her some tea. She'll probably feel like a cup now."

Matthew poured tea into the yellow Shelley cup that Eliza was particularly fond of and set that on a small tray, beside Bethany's blue mug. Yes, she assured him, she could manage.

Once she had gone up the stairs, Rina, Matthew and Steven looked at one another.

"Matthew, you and I will take a trip to the DeBeers garage and ask Ed to find us a little car," Rina said. She had bought a little hatchback a few years before, but it had seen little use and when, during the pandemic, the clutch had failed, she'd not bothered replacing it. Now, however—

Matthew nodded, "You'll have to put me on the insurance; that way there'll be cover for when you're away filming. And we'll make sure that we all have emergency taxi fare, just in case. We could both do with some driving practice," he added. "Perhaps Joy could help us out there."

"I'm sure she would." She was grateful that she was in a position to provide even a partial solution to the problem. A gentle ringfencing of this most vulnerable member of the family was something they could all help out with. But nevertheless, it did worry her.

We're all getting older, she thought. But the Peters sisters were considerably older than Rina and the potential problems suddenly much more acute.

* * *

After a bit of a runaround, Mac had finally been put through to the personnel department of Marris and Moore PharmaSolutions, the pharmaceutical company Jeff Mannering had worked for. He had been a sales rep, Sally Frith had told them, travelling around the country talking about the latest developments in treatment for the elderly. Gerontology was big business, apparently and, according to his sister, most of Mannering's customer base had been private nursing homes and clinics.

They were, according to the satnav, only fifteen minutes away from the company when Mac finally got put through to someone helpful. She introduced herself as Margie Jones, personnel manager, and seemed very puzzled at his enquiry.

"I'm sorry you've been passed around so much," she said, "but my colleagues couldn't find his records and now I see why. Mr Mannering left us, just over two years ago. So he's not on our current list of employees."

"I see," Mac said. "Ms Jones, I'm sure you've seen on the news that—"

"Oh, my God, *that* Mr Mannering? The murdered one?"

"I'm afraid so, yes. So, we're trying to establish some background and—"

"But he left here, two years ago. I don't see what I can tell you."

She sounded really anxious now, Mac thought, and was no doubt wondering how much further up the food chain she could now pass him.

"Miss Jones, we're literally ten minutes away from you. Could you spare us some time to take a look at his employee records?"

Her discomfort was now so profound he could almost hear it.

"You do still have his employee records, I suppose?"

"Of course. Yes, but now is not—"

"Good," Mac said. "Thank you for being so helpful. We'll be with you in just a few minutes." With that he rang off.

"So, he's no longer working there," Frank Baker mused. "So, did he go to another job or was he making enough from his side hustles?"

"I get the feeling that the blackmail was no longer any-thing on the side," Mac said. "I'm guessing it had become a full-time occupation."

The personnel manager kept them waiting. She sent an assistant to tell them she was digging out the records and would be about fifteen minutes. She sent another, some twenty minutes later, to offer them refreshments and apol-ogies. It seemed that upper management was now involved, and so her meeting with the officers had been delayed.

Another fifteen minutes passed and, typically, when Mac had just gone off to find the toilets, she finally appeared. Mac returned to find her making effusive apologies to Sergeant Baker for having kept them waiting. She led them down a corridor, up a flight of stairs and into an office that, to Mac's eyes looked too large and posh to be that of a personnel manager, even one for such a major company. At an antique desk sat an older man in an expensive suit, confirming Mac's suspicions. Another man whose demeanour screamed *corporate lawyer* was seated at a small table to one side of the room. Both men rose to shake hands with the officers and as Mac had suspected, the second man, Mitchell, was indeed a member of their legal department. The personnel manager took a seat beside him.

"I understand you're enquiring about a previous employee," Mitchell said.

"Actually, I'm conducting a murder enquiry," Mac corrected him. "I was led to believe that the murdered man, Mr Jeffery Mannering, worked for your company. I'm told that's no longer the case?"

Mitchell tapped on a stack of paper sitting in front of him on the table. "I'm sure you understand that I'm here to protect the interests of this company. Mr Mannering left the company twenty-two months ago. He left, and we've had no dealings with him since, so it's hard to see how his employment record could impact on your murder enquiry."

He had a point, Mac thought, but if it was all as simple as that, why did anyone consider this meeting necessary? He could have simply had an informal chat with the manager and that would have been that. He said as much and saw the look of annoyance that crossed Mitchell's face as it occurred to him they may have overplayed their hand.

"Mr Mitchell," Mac said. "The fact that you've become so defensive over a simple enquiry makes me wonder if Mr Mannering might have left under a cloud? If he'd done something that might indeed threaten the good name of the company?"

He let that question hang for a moment before continuing. "According to Mr Mannering's family, he worked for you as a pharmaceutical rep, the main focus of his business being elder life care. The majority of his clients, then, were private clinics and nursing homes that specialise in the problems of later life. Would that be correct?"

Mitchell glanced at his boss, and then back at Mac and Sergeant Baker. "That sums up his employment with us, yes."

"And the reason he left? Mr Mitchell, it might help you to reply if I tell you that we suspect Mannering might have been involved in criminal activities, probably while he was still in your employment. We've yet to assess the scope of those activities, but they seem to include extortion."

Once more, Mitchell and his boss exchanged a glance. The personnel manager looked distinctly uncomfortable. Mac felt a little sorry for her. At length, Mitchell nodded as though making up his mind. "Inspector McGregor," he said, "I'm sure I don't have to explain to you that a company like ours depends on its good reputation. Ours is an industry in which trust and honesty are valued above all else."

I thought it was profit.

"So, when we find out that a rep is obtaining personal advantage from our good name, we have to act swiftly. And we did. Mr Mannering was dismissed immediately."

"And the police were not involved," Frank Baker asked.

Mac stifled the urge to laugh at the horrified look on Mitchell's face.

"I take it that's a no, then," Sergeant Baker continued. "Gentlemen, I understand that this might have caused your business some short-term embarrassment, but surely your publicity people could have put a positive spin on that? Made it plain that you really are a company for which, what was it, honesty and fair dealing are of central importance?"

"As it is," Mac continued quietly, "the fact that you failed to report Mannering's actions meant that while you'd rid yourself of a problem, he continued with his actions elsewhere. We've reason to believe that not only did this eventually lead

to his own murder, but to the attempted murder of an innocent party. If that man dies, which seems likely, then it could
be argued that two deaths can be laid squarely at your door,
simply because you failed to report criminal activity."

"We had no idea that Mannering's activities extended
outside of the company." It was the first time the man behind
the desk had spoken since introducing himself as Director of
Operations, whatever that might mean.

"Would you have acted differently if you had?" He
doubted it. "You've not explained exactly how Mr Mannering
was — how did you put it? — turning your good name to
personal advantage."

The man glanced at his watch, ostentatiously informing
everyone in the room that this had taken up enough of his
time.

"We'll cooperate fully with your enquiries," he said. As
though, Mac thought, he really had a choice. Kendall could
have pulled strings, threatened the company with a much
broader range of enquiries and the Director knew that. As
did his lawyer.

He stood. "I have meetings to attend. Mr Mitchell will
provide the information you require. I'm sure that will be the
end of the matter."

"If I have further questions, then, I'll direct them towards
him," Mac said pointedly. "I'm sure he'll do his best to assist
my investigation in any way he can."

They left a few minutes later with a folder full of printouts, an ID photo of Mannering to add to their collection
and a business card from Mitchell, the legal eagle.

"Well, something of an eventful day," Frank Baker said.
"It makes me hungry, all this investigating." He grinned at
his boss.

Mac returned the smile. His stomach seemed to have
been listening in to the conversation, because it rumbled
loudly. He glanced at his watch. It was five fifteen.

"I think we should find somewhere to eat," he said. "Let
the rush hour traffic ease."

Over fish and chips and mushy peas, well sprinkled with salt and vinegar, Mac checked his messages, finding the one from Andy that told him that Mrs Martin had wrung a confession from Mrs Blake. Mac laughed, read the rest of the message, which was couched in more professional language.

"Lily Blake told Rina she thinks she saw our dead man on a previous occasion," he told Sergeant Baker. "She's certain he was a man who gave Fliss Cameron a lift to the hotel one day and that they seemed very friendly. Lily assumed this was a new man in Miss Cameron's life, though apparently she never mentioned him to the Blakes."

"Mrs Martin strikes again," Frank Baker said.

CHAPTER 27

29 December

Jeff Mannering's flat was in a modern block. A security code allowed entry into the lobby, a series of lockers provided means for the post to be dispersed to the different flats and the flat itself was opened by a standard Yale lock.

Mac had been on his way there early the next morning when he'd had a call from Kendall telling him that DI Anning would be present for the search of Mannering's flat. Mac had been surprised and not a little irritated, but as Kendall reminded him, it was highly likely their two cases were linked.

"Sure, but does he have to show up in person?" Mac complained, when the call had ended. He was alone in the car, so had no one to complain to, but still felt it was something that had to be said out loud.

Now he stood in the lobby waiting for the door to the flat to be opened, Anning at his side, eyeing the place with interest.

"It's just the sort of block where you're guaranteed never to meet your neighbours," he said. "You come in, collect your post, go upstairs to your insulated box, shut out the world."

Despite himself, Mac was amused. "Sounds like you'd be happy here," he said.

Anning nodded. "A bit of peace and quiet wouldn't go amiss," he said. In response to Mac's raised eyebrow, he added, "The lad and his wife and kids are staying for a few weeks. They're moving house and there was an unexpected delay. They'd given notice on their flat and their new house still hadn't got a roof on it."

"That sounds . . . .serious," Mac said.

"Damned right it is. Don't get me wrong; I love my kids, and I like my son's wife and she's a good mother to those two kids. But you get to realise that you're past wanting the noise, not to mention the mess. The wife and I 'downsized', isn't that what they called it? Sold our old house and bought a little bungalow. Two bedrooms. Thought that would be that, enough room for the occasional visit, but for the rest of the time just the two of us. And very nice it's been, too. Three weeks they've been there, and to be honest, it feels like we've been invaded. If I could bribe the builders to get a move on, I bloody would."

Mac found himself laughing. To see Anning so put out was genuinely funny.

Footsteps on the stairs announced the arrival of a constable. Entry had been gained. It was time to go up.

Was Anning trying to be friendly, Mac wondered, talking about what might be classified as personal stuff? Or was he trying to catch Mac off guard, put him at his ease before delivering another Anning blow?

"I hear you and Miriam Hastings are an item," Anning said.

"We are, yes."

Anning nodded and there was something that looked suspiciously like approval in his expression. "Sensible woman, she is. Worth hanging onto. Got a level head."

Mac wasn't sure how to respond to that, but he was saved the need to by their arrival at Mannerings flat.

Jeffery Mannering's apartment was . . . Mac sought for the right word. Bland. That was probably it. The walls were

194

beige, the carpet a darker shade of beige. The sofa and chair a peculiar shade of muddy brown that almost matched the curtains. Shelves and dining set were utilitarian flat pack: they did their job, but Mac got the impression that little thought had gone into the choosing of them.

"Definitely got a girlfriend, though," Anning said, as though following Mac's train of thought. He jabbed a fat finger at the sofa, at the bland, laminate-covered shelves. "Tried to make something of the place, by the look of it. The lass, whoever she is, was fighting a losing battle, though."

Mac nodded, noting now as Anning had done the three bright scatter cushions piled on the floor at the end of the sofa, as though Mannering tolerated their presence but had no actual use for them. A cute toy lion had been stuffed into a corner of one of the shelves atop a stack of box files. It was unexpectedly pink with a looping mane and oversized eyes. Anning had picked it up and was examining the pink paisley body with interest.

"Looks like something a kid would buy," he said.

"Mannering's sister didn't mention any children in his life, and she doesn't have any, so no nieces or nephews." He frowned, thinking back to the house he and Sergeant Baker had visited the previous day. "She might have given it to him, though. It's the kind of thing you might buy as a joke for a serious older brother?"

Anning shrugged and shoved the toy back. "Who the hell needs that many box files?"

Mac had been wondering the same thing. Two of the shelves were stacked with a half dozen identical, bland black and grey files. They were identical apart from the letters neatly printed in white on the black spines. A-B on the top shelf, working their way through the alphabet.

"More bloody paperwork," Anning said. "Where are we taking them? Your place or mine? Be a bit cramped if we try and get all this lot into your tiny shed in Frantham."

"Neither," Mac said. "DI Kendall has organised an incident room over in Dorchester. I'll get everything shipped out there."

Anning nodded, glancing around. "No computer."

"I'll try the bedroom."

Mac moved through the door that led from the living area into the only bedroom. The flat was small, impeccably neat, smelt clean though not in any overworked-bleach-bottle way, just in the nature of a space that was regularly maintained — and this, despite the fact that Mannering could not have been in the flat for quite some time. He'd been killed, dumped in someone's freezer, thawed, left in the Palisades library and yet . . . In the bedroom the faint scent of fabric conditioner hung in the air, the source easily identifiable as the sheets and duvet cover. The computer sat on a small desk set against the wall and no dust had settled on either it or the desk.

"Are these serviced apartments?" he asked suddenly.

"You mean, does our dead man have a cleaning lady?" Anning's eyes narrowed as he absorbed what Mac meant. "You're right, the place is far too clean, considering our man got himself killed a while back."

And we're still not sure how long that while was, Mac thought, as Anning ducked back into the main room and instructed one of the constables to go and knock on doors, find out about domestics.

He turned his attention to where a laptop computer, small printer, mouse and mat sat on the desk. With gloved hands he tried the drawers and found them locked, though the desk, like the rest of the furnishings, was cheap flatpack and wasn't likely to put up much resistance. The lock was there to deflect idle curiosity, not to resist, for example, a determined constable armed with a table knife.

"If you were a blackmailer and an extortionist," he said, "would you risk leaving anything around for a curious cleaning lady to stumble upon? Surely you'd want to keep everyone out? And look at this place. It's functional, sparse — he comes here to eat and sleep and use it more like an office than a home. It doesn't exactly scream 'friendly and sociable', does it?"

Anning nodded, taking his point on board. "So, you reckon whoever's responsible for the scatter cushions and the kid's toy also comes in to keep the place tidy."

"And do his washing," Mac said. "You can still smell the fabric softener on the sheets, and I don't care what the adverts say, it's not going to be that strong maybe weeks after our man died. Someone's been in here recently to clean, change the sheets—"

"And maybe have a bit of a forage about for incriminating evidence," Anning agreed.

Mac followed him back through to the living room and watched as he removed one of the box files from the shelf. Anning swore. The file was empty, as was the next and the one after that.

"So," Anning said. "Who tidied up after him? The killer or the woman with the fancy cushions? Unless they're one and the same, of course."

Mac reached for his phone and called Kendall. He had nothing solid on which to base the assumption, beyond Lily's revelation that she recognised Mannering as the man who had come to the hotel with Fliss Cameron . . . but nevertheless, he was certain. Fliss Cameron had been the person who had come here, set the apartments to rights, taken whatever was in those files. He'd lay money on it.

* * *

"The computer's been sent to the tech unit," Mac said. He was back in Bridport with Kendall, bringing his colleague up to speed. "The contents of the desk drawers are in those boxes over there and hopefully whoever emptied the filing boxes left us something behind in the desk, but I'm not hopeful."

"So, what makes you suspect our Miss Cameron?" Kendall asked.

Mac had been thinking this through on the drive back. "We're now pretty sure they are — or were — an item."

"Lily Blake *thinks* she recognised him. Thought they were together. Fliss Cameron didn't mention having a new man in her life—"

"Unless he's not a new man. What if . . . look, if you're in a new relationship, do you go buying throw pillows for the other person's flat? I don't know, it seems like a personal touch. Like you spend enough time in their home that you feel you've got a right to impose some of your own taste. Or you'd like that to be the case."

"Maybe," Kendall agreed, "As it happens, I'm the one to choose the soft furnishings in our place. My other half thinks they're unnecessary faff. But I agree, it's worth getting Fliss Cameron in for a formal interview, see if we can get her to admit to knowing our dead man. Suggest we have witnesses that can prove it. Though my guess is Lily will backpedal as hard as she can. I can't see her or her husband wanting the trouble."

Probably true, Mac thought. "Which is why I've got Andy and Yolanda on the case," he said. "Going door-to-door to speak to Fliss Cameron's neighbours, to see if they recognise our man. In the meantime, she's coming in this morning for some follow-up questions."

"And how does she feel about that?" Kendall asked.

Mac recalled his phone conversation with Fliss that morning. "She told me I was wasting time with her when I should have better things to do."

"Well, we've had preliminary findings from the forensic search of Mannering's apartment. Whoever cleaned up in there ought to start an agency."

"Any prints at all?"

"Three and two partials, which for a flat even of that size is—"

"Beyond unusual," Mac agreed, "however efficient your cleaner is. And we did double check — the flats are not serviced accommodation, and no one knew about Mannering employing a cleaner. The neighbours all agree he had few visitors, though as Anning pointed out yesterday, the layout of the block makes it ideal for anyone who wants to avoid their fellow humans. Now, if one of those fingerprints could turn out to be Miss Cameron's, that would help us out immensely."

"Well, it would prove she went to Mannering's flat. Which yes, would prove she knew him. But would it get us any further?"

"It would prove that she was lying to us."

"Which hopefully Andy and Yolanda will be able to do anyway. If anyone can worm information out of the neighbours, it will be those two. The question is, *why* did she lie? All she had to do was admit to knowing who he was, and chances are we'd have pushed no further. She could have said, 'yes, I know this man, his name is Jeffery Mannering and we were an item for a while', or, 'he was an acquaintance'. We'd have asked a few questions, still been wondering why the hell his killer chose to dump the body at the hotel, and would probably have done some digging around to see if they might have done it to scare the blazes out of Miss Cameron, but . . . what did she hope to gain by denying even recognising him?"

"Hoping to avoid that bit of digging, I expect," Mac said. "We'd have looked for reasons someone hated Fliss Cameron enough that they'd dump the body of her boyfriend or even her ex-boyfriend or casual acquaintance where she was almost bound to find him. Or to see him, even if she didn't find the body. Maybe she thought that we wouldn't have had to dig very deep. We've also got to wonder why Will Toons didn't own up to knowing him. He and Fliss Cameron have known one another for a long time, move in the same circles — or at least they did — so if one of them knew him, chances are the other did, too."

"I suppose you don't want to own up to knowing your blackmailer," Kendall said. "The fear would be that any digging into the man's background might turn up something that implicated you."

"And if, as we've done now, we've begun to find those connections anyway, then not admitting to knowing the man might just add to our suspicions."

"You're making the mistake of looking for rational behaviour," Kendall said. "Two people in shock from recognising the body of a man who's been persecuting them all this time are likely not going to be in their right senses."

Mac supposed he had a point.

"Are you doing the interview?"

"I thought I might, or I can sit in while you do the honours?" Mac glanced at his watch. "I offered to send a car for her. She was quick to decline. She should be here by now."

As if on cue, the internal phone began to ring. Fliss Cameron had indeed arrived and was sitting in reception.

"Time for another coffee," Kendall said. "See how she responds to being kept waiting for a little while."

CHAPTER 28

Andy had not spent long at the Palisades. Just enough time to write out Lily's statement and get her to sign it, and then he was on his way to meet Yolanda. Lily had been oddly short with him. He guessed it was because she was having second thoughts about getting so involved.

James Blake had been hanging around in the lobby all the time Andy had been speaking to his wife, as though he was planning to charge into the office and challenge the constable's right to be there. It was clear that he was irritated by the visit and, Andy gathered, even more irritated at his wife and Mrs Martin for having further dragged the Palisades into the mire. Or so Andy had overheard him saying when he had entered the lobby.

The Blakes had been cordial enough, Andy supposed, but had definitely not displayed their usual easy friendliness.

He spotted Yolanda's car parked up and managed to find a space for his own a little further along the road. Parking was always tight on Mayfield Road; in the evening, it was packed tight with residents' cars and when they left for work in the morning, their places were taken by workers looking for somewhere to lodge their vehicles for the day. It was an arrangement that was predicated on everyone arriving and leaving at set times. He was glad he was only driving a little hatchback and could worm his way into the smallish gap.

Yolanda was standing beside his car as he opened the door. She glanced around and then, noting that the street was empty, dived in for a quick kiss. Andy found himself blushing, but then, Yolanda often had him blushing — and grinning like some red-haired, freckled Cheshire cat.

They had worked out their story over pizza the night before. Making use of copies of the most recent photo, one of those borrowed from Mannering's sister, they would spin a yarn about a missing person who'd been spotted in the area.

"You reckon there'll be anyone home?" Andy asked.

Yolanda shrugged. "Got to hope so. There's a nursery and primary school in the next street. I figure any stay-at-home mums will just have got back from the school run, and there's a couple of student houses at the end — they'll not be up yet." She grinned at him.

"Or they'll be out at lectures. Students never notice a damn thing anyway."

She ignored his pessimism. "And there are still a fair few older people on this road and the next, and a newsagent and a corner shop."

"OK, so let's make a start. You take this side; I'll take that."

She handed him three copies of the photo, one to use and two spare, in case the first got creased from too much handling. It made him smile; he loved how organised Yolanda was. It chimed with his own love of efficiency.

Then they were off, knocking on doors, reassuring smiles at the ready, photo in hand, cover story ready to tell.

"Do you happen to have seen this man? His family are worried. Any information . . ."

This was not, Andy thought, his favourite part of police work: the tedious foot slog that most times didn't turn up anything of use. Yolanda, after three no-replies, had finally got a resident on the doorstep. *Oh well, onward and upward*, Andy thought, though he'd much rather have been sitting in on the interview his boss had arranged for that morning. Much rather be hearing what Fliss Cameron had to say.

* * *

At that moment, Fliss Cameron wasn't saying very much. She was sitting across the table from Mac and DI Kendall, a cup of cold and now scummy tea on the table before her. She was looking very annoyed.

"I told you then and I'm telling you now, I didn't know this man."

"And I can produce witnesses who saw you with him."

"Then they must be mistaken, or lying. Anyway, what witnesses? Am I a suspect or something? You've dragged me all the way here to throw accusations my way, and I think, quite frankly, that I've cooperated enough. Poor Will may have found the body, but I saw it too and I never want to see anything like that again. And I'm certainly not prepared to answer any more of your questions."

She stood, plucked her coat from the back of the chair and hoisted her bag onto her shoulder. "I'm going now, Inspector MacGregor, and I'll be making a complaint about you and about this enquiry."

Mac sighed. "If you ask the desk sergeant on the way out, I'm sure he'll be able to advise you how to do that." "But I know he was no stranger to you, Miss Cameron. You knew Mr Mannering and quite likely you knew what he was doing. You knew about the blackmail. It would be in your own interest to tell us what you know now. Withholding evidence is a serious offence."

"And you *did* know about the blackmail," Kendall said.

The sudden change of subject seemed to throw her. For a split second, Mac saw her self-assurance falter.

He pressed that slight advantage home. "Will Toons told you that he was being blackmailed. He implied that Jeff Mannering had something on you, too? What was that, Miss Cameron? Though it does seem that your relationship with

Mr Mannering was more intimate than Will Toons could have possibly known. How would he have felt, do you think, if he'd known you were involved with the man who'd been making his life hell for all these years?"

"A man I did not know," she hissed at him. The mask of annoyance was back in place, and she had a hand on the door. The set of her shoulders suggested that she was expecting to be called back or at least for him to have more to say, but Mac held his peace. Fliss Cameron was rattled. That would have to be enough until they had firmer evidence. Mac hoped that would not be long coming.

"Have a good rest of your day," Kendall said cheerfully.

Fliss Cameron glanced back at him with an expression designed to chill blood and freeze bone. Then she was gone, the enraged tapping of her heels echoing down the hall.

"Well, I think you've shaken the tree," Kendall observed. "Let's just hope a few witnesses fall out, willing to testify to Fliss Cameron and Jeff Mannering actually knowing one another."

Mac nodded. "Though that won't prove she knew anything about the blackmail," he said. And so far, they only had Lily's reluctant testimony to any kind of relationship. Hopefully, Andy and Yolanda would come back with a prize or two — or better still, one of the three fingerprints found at Mannering's flat would be a match to Miss Cameron.

CHAPTER 29

Rina had begun her morning with a trip to the shops and a walk along the promenade. Once home, she settled in front of her computer, with a large cup of coffee and continued her research into the early days of the Cameron Players.

It wasn't an easy search. Fliss Cameron wasn't famous; her Fliss Cameron Theatre Company had been a peripatetic enterprise to begin with, and although it now had an official base, was still focussed on providing afterschool and evening sessions to local people. Only, so far as Rina could tell, her incarnation as The Players, who specialised in murder mystery weekends and corporate training, employed professional actors. Not unexpectedly, that company was a flexible and fluid amalgam of whoever happened to be available for particular dates. Presumably her pool of actors participated when they did not have contracts elsewhere.

Looking at her previous performances — well-advertised, Rina noted, and at several local hotels and some further afield — a few names cropped up regularly and presumably formed the core of the company. Crosschecking suggested that they were either semi-retired from their fully professional lives or just starting out, rather as Will had been back in the day. It seemed to Rina, however, that Fliss Cameon engendered a certain loyalty in the minds of those who had worked with her. Will Toons's name was not the only one she recognised as having success elsewhere while also returning to the Cameron fold from time to time.

No doubt that earned Fliss a big slice of the kudos cake.

Rina, having a mildly suspicious mind, wondered if they really came back because of a fondness for Fliss, or if something more sinister was going on. A weekend of murder mystery, plus time for rehearsal, would not provide much in the way of financial incentive, she didn't think. In fact, most of the small companies running such weekends were, in Rina's experience, keen amateurs who also had day jobs.

Draining the last of her coffee, she sat back and thought about where to probe next. Fliss had mentioned an aunt who had left her a house and some money, Rina remembered. Now, how could she find out about that? She didn't even know the aunt's name.

Rina made a rough guess as to when this might have been. Perhaps, she thought, around a decade ago. She searched for Cameron obituaries from the time, but of course couldn't even be sure if the aunt had been a Cameron, or if there had been a public obit. Not everyone advertised funeral details in the papers anymore — which was a shame, from Rina's point of view — and in these days of social media, it was far more likely that friends and extended family might receive the details that way.

Fliss Cameron, The Players and Will Toons all had a social media presence, of course. Will's was currently filled with shock and grief and well-wishers. Fliss Cameron used her pages mainly for advertising and posting images of past performances and good reviews, none of which was helpful to Rina.

She tried another tack, looking instead at the other businesses Lily had talked about, the costume hire and the Fliss Cameron Theatre Company, widening her search from local news to more national sources and focusing at first on the theatrical and trade papers that she'd once read so avidly.

Ah, Rina thought, as she came across an article. Now she might be getting somewhere.

* * *

Derek had spent the past hour sitting at his kitchen table and staring into space. He'd barely slept the night before. Talking to the police officer after he'd returned from his daughter's house had put him thoroughly on edge. What if Will woke up and told the police what had happened? He would have to do something, but he didn't know what. Only thing certain was that Will would have to be silenced once and for all. He would ruin everything, and Derek could not bear that.

His mobile phone rang. He didn't recognise the number and almost didn't answer, expecting it to be an advertising call for a product he didn't want, or from a claim-line for an accident he'd never had.

In the end, as the caller showed no signs of ringing off, he replied. The idea of hearing another human voice seemed better than sitting in the increasingly dense silence of his kitchen, silence broken only by the faint tick-tick as the hands moved on his electric clock. He'd not registered before just how loud that was.

The speaker made no effort at a preamble: "Have the police spoken to you? I had to go and talk to them this morning, about Will Toons. They seemed to think he might have been coming to see me. They talked about him being blackmailed. Did he come to see you? Where his car was crashed, that was near your place, wasn't it?"

There was no chance of missing the accusation and impatience in her tone. He hesitated, then said, "Yes, there was an officer going door-to-door yesterday asking if anyone had seen anything. Seen his car, or the car that—"

"I'm assuming you were responsible. I'm assuming you were responsible for Jeff Mannering, too? I told him I didn't believe you'd have the nerve. Was I wrong?"

Derek said nothing.

"You've made a bloody great mess of everything, Derek. It's just like you to do that. You always were a waste of skin."

The words stung. "What else was I supposed to do? Jeff came here, making threats. I just . . . I just decided I'd had enough."

"*You'd* had enough. Derek, we'd *all* had enough, but surely even you know that if you murder someone, you get rid of the body someplace it can't be found. You don't dump it in some hotel. You don't bring the police down on the rest of us."

It was, he had to concede, a stupid thing to have done. But really, had part of him wanted to implicate the others? Had part of him wanted payback for . . . for what? The truth was Derek knew he had brought Jeff Mannering's avarice and cruelty down on his own head, and it had not stopped there. It was his fault that Will and this very angry woman had been dragged into the mess.

"I'm sorry," he said at last. "You're right. It was a stupid thing to do."

"You could always be counted on to get it wrong," she said. "Always be counted on to throw your friends to the wolves. Well, I suppose at least Jeff's out of the picture now. If we can just keep the police off our backs. They know about the blackmail. They know Jeff was blackmailing Will."

"They know! How? Do they know about us? How can they know? He hadn't been to see them yet."

"How the hell should I know that? But they talked about it this morning, about Jeff blackmailing Will. I told them I knew nothing about it and that's the story we stick to, Derek. You know nothing, never did. Are we clear about that?"

He remembered, with a sense of dread, what Will had told him that day he had come over, sat at the very kitchen table where Derek sat now. "Will said he got a letter," he said reluctantly.

"A letter from someone who said they knew he was being blackmailed. That just because Jeff was gone, it wasn't over."

She was silent for so long he wondered if she'd rung off. He strained to hear the faint sound of her breathing. At

208

last she said, "He phoned me and told me that. Have you received anything?"

"No, nothing. Have . . . have you?"

"No."

"Will said he couldn't cope with more trouble. That he wanted to tell the police what had happened. That he couldn't go on the way he had. He said he'd not tell them about me, but . . . well, that wasn't going to happen, was it? I had to do something."

"So, you tried to kill him, too." She laughed harshly. "Couldn't even get that right, could you?"

Derek was still holding the phone when it rang again. This time it was his daughter. He stared at the screen for a moment, knowing he would have to answer, but not knowing what he could say. He tried hard to keep his voice steady as he said, "Hello, darling. How are you today?"

"Dad, I just saw the news. The crash up on the back road near you . . . it was Will Toons."

His head reeled. Of course, he realised, the earlier bulletins had just mentioned a male driver. The police officer who had come to the house had only told him that the man was seriously injured but alive; he'd not given a name. Derek had not seen the lunchtime news — had that been the first time Will's name was mentioned? Surely it must have been.

"Dad? Dad, are you there? Sorry, I didn't mean to shock you. I thought you might have heard it on the radio."

Usually, he listened to the radio while making lunch. She knew that. "Um, no, I was in the garden, lost track. Will, my God . . . a police officer came by yesterday, just as I got home, was talking about the accident, but I had no idea."

"Dad, what was he doing out there? Do you think he was coming to see you? I mean, what else would he be doing out that way?"

"I have no idea. Surely not. Why would he?"

"I don't know, but why else would he be out there? You didn't see him?"

"I'd have told you if I had. No, love, it's been years. He's so busy and . . ."

"Dad, you need to tell the police. Tell them you think he was coming to see you. It might be important."

"Important how? Darling, I've no idea if that was even the truth. He could have been out this way for a whole host of reasons. No need to bother the police with something that probably isn't true."

"But what if it is? What if that changes the route they think he took? What if they're looking in the wrong place for witnesses?"

Derek sighed. "All right," he agreed. "I'll let them know. But I can't think what he'd have wanted, coming out to see me."

She rang off shortly after, satisfied that he would do what she had asked.

Derek went through to his sitting room at the front of the house and switched the television on, found the lunchtime news was about to start. Will Toons's crash was the fourth item on the main bulletin. The fact that he was a famous actor made him worthy of national interest. The local news that followed included more details. His injuries were severe, and police were appealing for possible witnesses — though the newsreader stressed the remoteness of the location. Will Toons was in an induced coma, following surgery.

Derek listened as the bulleting reprised his life and career, skimming over the scandal involving the sister of his then-girlfriend and including a statement from his agent that everyone who knew him was deeply shocked.

And that was all.

What should he do? Derek had tried to make things better, but had only made them worse. What was he to do now?

CHAPTER 30

Mac had his phone on speaker so Kendall could listen in.

"We worked our way along her street and then two streets either side. There was nothing useful until we reached the newsagents," Yolanda told them. "It's run by an old couple, Mr and Mrs Fincher. They told me they'd been there thirty years and they seemed like they knew everyone. Anyway, I showed them the photo and asked if they recognised him, and they did. He came into the shop fairly regularly to pick up a newspaper and milk and sometimes magazines. Women's magazines. And guess who they saw with him on more than one occasion?"

"Fliss Cameron. Are they sure?"

"Better than that." Yolanda sounded positively triumphant. "They described him as 'Fliss's young man'. I asked, did they recognise him, and they said, 'oh yes, that's Fliss's young man' and wanted to know if something had happened to him."

"They made no connection with the dead man at the hotel?"

"No, but then neither did anyone else, and in the photo, he still has a round face. In the drawing, he's much thinner."

"That's true," Kendall commented. "Even his sister didn't recognise him from the artist's sketch. Can you arrange for one of them to come and make a formal statement?"

"Mrs Fincher's coming back with me," Yolanda told him. "I think she's quite excited about it all."

"Well, be sure to tell them not to get too excited if they happen to see Miss Cameron," Mac warned. "She's likely to be back home by now and was not in the best of moods."

"So," Kendall said, when Yolanda had ended the call. "That's a step in the right direction. If we can get forensics to come up with a decent result on one of those fingerprints, we'll be quids in."

Mac nodded, but cautioned, "All this indicates is that they knew one another. It still doesn't prove they were in a relationship or that she knew about the blackmail."

"No, but if one part of the story begins to break down, if we can chip away at the cracks, it might lead us onto something more relevant. Those filing boxes in Matthew's apartment must have held something of importance, otherwise why would anyone empty them? That apartment was scrubbed clean. They're still working on the computer, but someone went in there and took away possible evidence. If she and Mannering really were an item, it might well have been Fliss Cameron. Which suggests she knew what was in the files and what it all meant."

Mac nodded. He knew all that; he just wished they had something a little more solid to work on. "I suppose what's bothering me," he said, "is that Mannering wouldn't have stopped with Will Toons. There were a half dozen box files in that flat. Potentially, that's a lot of victims."

Kendall nodded. "By the end of day, we should have financials for Mannering and Cameron," he said. "What did you discover about why Mannering got fired?"

"Ah, well as far as I can make out, Mannering's job involved selling pharmaceutical and elder care packages to upmarket homes and clinics. The main charges were obviously for the latest cutting-edge medication, though as a sweetener, the pharmaceutical company cut deals with providers of other services — massage, alternative therapies, trips

212

for employees and residents, that sort of thing. These were offered at a reduced initial price. It looks like Mannering was taking cash to push certain interests and promote some of these businesses to the detriment of others.

"It's hard to know how much extra he was making, but his employers obviously took a dim view."

"How did he get found out?"

"Well, that's a bit vague. It's down as 'information received from an anonymous source'. My guess is someone gossiped over a round of golf. Isn't that usually what happens?"

"I rather like a round of golf," Kendall said, somewhat wistfully. "So, the picture we're building up is of a man who was always looking for a deal. Who would even play his brother-in-law if he thought he could get away with it."

"And for whom targets like Will Toons were probably just the tip of the iceberg."

Kendall nodded, and they both fell silent for a moment.

"What do you make of this Caydhill Trust business?" Kendall asked, meaning something interesting that had come up when looking at Will Toons's financial records. He had been paying over a thousand pounds a month to the Caydhill Trust, and occasional payments of considerably more.

"Well, it's got a nicely produced webpage," Mac said. "But as we now know, it's not registered at Companies House and it's not a registered charity. Though how many small donors would even bother to check on that?"

"If there are any other donors. Though I reckon what was working to screw Will Toons out of his cash likely came in useful to con other people, too."

The Caydhill Trust appeared to be a charity supporting young people looking for a career in the arts. Another hint that Fliss Cameron was involved. It looked authentic and had a nice line in merchandise — mugs, notebooks, scarves and the like, apparently designed by beneficiaries of the trust and which, it seemed, could actually be bought. An added touch, Mac supposed, of authenticity.

"So, the next question is, who benefits from this?" Mac asked. "I don't for one minute imagine it's any of the kids."

* * *

Derek had searched the news channels for more information, and then gone online to see if there was anything he'd missed. He was distraught. He should have made certain that Will was dead.

No, he should have just let Will walk away and, had the police come, denied everything. Will had been his friend, had helped him out more than once, had taken the blame for something Derek had done. And Derek was pretty certain that, as time had gone by, Will had recalled enough about that night to be certain he had not been driving the car that killed Genevieve Atkins.

He had never said a word. He'd sent him money when Derek needed it. He'd been a friend.

What had he been thinking, when he'd got into that car and chased after his friend, then dragged him from the car and killed him?

Not killed him. As good as killed him. He'd intended to kill him.

So, what could he do now? He should have trusted Will to keep his silence, to blag it so the police believed he was alone in that car. Will had promised; he would have kept his promise.

Wouldn't he?

What if he broke down under interrogation? What if he told everything? If Derek's daughter ever found out, how could he look her in the eye ever again? If the police found out, they'd lock him up and he'd never see his grandchildren again.

The enormity of what he had done escalated as he thought about it. He was a murderer, not of Genevieve Atkins or, really, of Will. Even if he died that had been . . . what . . . a moment of panic, of uncontrolled desperation.

But the fact remained that he had planned to do away with Jeff Mannering. It had just been a matter of when. Every time the man had shown up at his house, Derek had promised himself that it would be the last. Each time he had made his demands, Derek had promised himself that he'd not let that bastard drain any more from him. He was a leech, a bloodsucker, a vampire. He'd deserved to be put down.

And then, finally, Derek had found the nerve to do it. Mannering had pushed that bit too far; he didn't deserve to even speak his daughter's name! Derek was sure as hell not going to put up with the implied threat either to tell her or to somehow make her pay for her father's mistakes.

And so, Derek had finally plucked up the nerve to carry through the plan he'd rehearsed over and over and over across the years since Mannering had started to bleed him dry.

To bleed them all. Derek and Will and Fliss and Lord knew who else. Well, Derek had done what had to be done and they should all be grateful to him. He was a hero, if you really thought about it.

Derek slumped back in his chair and closed his eyes. He had no regrets about killing Jeff Mannering. He was an execrable man, a blot on humanity. The only thing Derek regretted about Mannering's death was that he had made such a massive misjudgement when he had taken the body to the hotel.

He was still in shock, he told himself. Not in his right mind. In fact, if the police did come for him over Jeff Mannering's death, wouldn't that be what he could tell them? That he'd been pushed beyond the bounds of reason, killed the man because he felt threatened — that in fact, he'd feared for his life. He'd just been defending himself. Then he'd had the crazy idea of dumping the body in the middle of a murder mystery weekend. A body in the library. Ha, ha, ha. Didn't that just prove he wasn't in his right senses? That he was — what did they call it? — suffering from diminished responsibility?

And Will . . . that had just been a big mistake. A moment of panic. What could he do about it now?

He glanced at his watch, was surprised to find that it was now after three. Had he dozed in the chair after he had completed his search for news? Or had he merely sat there, staring into space, while the thoughts and memories, the excuses and reprisals, ran around in the maze of his brain, like trapped rats trying to gnaw their way out?

Will could wake up at any moment. Will could accuse him, could reveal all the lies that they had told, all the years of maintaining those lies, all the monetary atonement for sins that had taken a split second to commit.

No, Derek wasn't having that. Things had gone too far now.

He got to his feet, collected his coat from the hall and car keys from the hook by the kitchen door, then carefully locked up the house, wondering if he'd ever see it again. Then he got into his car and he drove away.

CHAPTER 31

Mac parked as he usually did on the cliff top car park above Old Frantham and walked down to the converted boathouse where he and Miriam had lived for the past few years. The streets were dark, the fragmentary street lighting supplemented only by the illumination leaking through partly drawn curtains or lamps outside of the shops and pubs.

Mac habitually carried a torch in the winter months. Old Frantham was strictly pedestrian, the narrow streets and network of little alleyways being totally unsuitable for anything more modern than feet, the occasional brave cyclists and well-trained ponies could manage. More recently, there had been an initiative to provide access for disabled visitors. Now, if they made use of the newly paved Cable Street, an odd little thoroughfare that zigzagged back and forth down the hill, it was possible to get to almost all of Old Frantham in a wheelchair or on a mobility scooter. He'd spotted a couple of kids attempting it on skateboards, with mixed results.

He was very fond of the Old Town and extremely fond of the home he and Miriam had made in the boathouse. Their apartment was small but cozy and it had sea views that Mac adored. They had recently been putting out feelers regarding the possibility of buying the building, and it was this, rather than the case, that was occupying Mac's mind as he made his way down the steep hill. He'd got into the habit of leaving work behind at the cliff car park, or at least attempting to. Inevitably he and Miriam would talk to one another about their current jobs, but he had come to treasure that brief respite that occurred after he'd locked the car door and usually held until after they'd cooked dinner together.

This being the case, he was slightly miffed to find Rina Martin in his living room, chatting to Miriam. From the look on her face and the bundle of printouts on the coffee table, she was about to break his brief peace.

Mac sighed, then put his irritation aside. It was always good to see his friend, and she'd not have come over if there had not been something important to report.

"I won't keep you," Rina said. "I've promised to pick up fish and chips on the way home. It was my turn to cook, but I got a little involved in chasing Fliss Cameron down the internet rabbit hole."

Fish and chips sounded like a nice idea. "And where did you chase her to?" Mac asked.

Rina tapped the sheaf of paper on the coffee table. "Well, she'd mentioned that her aunt had left her a house and some money, and she used that to set up her business. It took me a while to chase that down. Her aunt wasn't called Cameron. So I called Lily, who I have to say was not best pleased to have to answer yet more questions, but I also remembered that Lily had mentioned that they had met Fliss when she rented from them."

Memory like an elephant, Mac thought.

"Well, I'd assumed she meant a house, but it wasn't. The Blakes bought what had been a church hall on the out-skirts of Bridport. They had plans to convert it, but planning permission took a while. In the meantime various groups, including Fliss's drama group, rented spaces from them. I think in the end, the planning problem was too much and they sold it on. I understand it became some kind of com-munity arts hub, but that's not what's interesting. When Fliss started hiring it out, her aunt was paying. When the aunt died, Lily remembers wondering if Fliss would be able to keep up payments and she had a chat with her to find out what her financial position was. The Blakes are nice people, but they are businesspeople, first and foremost, so no surprise there."

She paused for breath, and Mac said, "And? Rina, I'm not sure what—"

"So, listen," Miriam told him, handing him a mug of coffee. She smiled, a twitch of amusement at the corner of her mouth that told him she knew all this already, and that it was worth a little more patience than he was showing.

"Fliss assured her that it was all fine. That her aunt had left her the house — which she sold and bought the smaller place she lives in now — and some money, and that if it was all right with Lily, payment would continue to come from her aunt's old account for the next couple of months or so, until she could get her finances organised and a new direct debit set up."

"It sounds slightly irregular," Mac said, "but I suppose I can see how she might want to do that until she'd made other arrangements." Then he stopped, looked at the two women as the meaning behind Rina's words sank in. He said, "But wouldn't she have to inform the bank that her aunt was dead? Wouldn't she have to close the account pretty much immediately?"

"Well, in theory, yes. I did some phoning round and a bit more digging, and it seems that as long as a bank account is operating normally, it's unlikely that anyone is going to twig that the account holder is no longer around to be servicing it. And I just wondered . . . if Fliss Cameron was involved in blackmailing Will, and no doubt other people, too, could she be using her aunt's old account to hide the money?"

It was a thought. But . . . "What makes you suspect Miss Cameron of doing anything of the sort?" he asked. After all, he and Kendall had only just begun to have their suspicions. What had put Rina onto her?

"Oh, Mac, she knew who she was looking at from the moment she saw the body. I saw the way she looked at the dead man and then at Will. There was a moment when they were both in a panic, in case the other said something. I felt it at the time, but couldn't make sense of it. Later, I put it down to being a reaction to the pure horror of the moment. But I was wrong; I should have stuck with my first impression. Also, if you look through the stuff I've printed out for you, you'll see that Miss Cameron has set up a number of Ltd companies over the past few years, and several of them have gone to the wall owing money."

"Owing money to—?"

"No one big enough or important enough to have the resources to challenge her. On a couple of occasions she had a business running summer schools for would-be actors. Young people who paid a few hundred pounds each to attend. Some of them seem to have received bursaries from arts organisations; some had funded themselves. All was fine for a couple of years. Then all of a sudden, when the whole summer programme was booked up — and we're talking week-long bookings for almost three months here — the whole lot was cancelled due to illness and the company declared bankruptcy. Being a Limited company, Fliss was protected. She never paid the money back and the youngsters lost out all ways."

Mac thought about the charity he and Kendall had found.

"Then there were the showcases she set up, using a big name like Will Toons to front the enterprise and attract punters, and which were also cancelled suddenly. I managed to track down a half dozen incidents over the past ten years."

"But nothing local," Miriam added. "She'd use her connections, her good reputation and her successful friends to set these programmes up elsewhere. When they fell through, she'd no doubt be so distraught that it would be passed off as just one of those unfortunate chains of events."

"You think Will was involved?" Mac asked.

Rina shook her head. "I've found absolutely nothing to suggest that. I suspect that maybe the big names she invoked to get her foot through the door knew little or nothing about what Fliss was doing. Yes, she knew them quite legitimately. Some of them have performed in her company — a few, like Will, continue to do so. It seems, like a lot of con artists, Fliss Cameron is an excellent actor and perfectly capable of invoking loyalty in those she has a use for. She and this Jeff Mannering probably made a very effective team."

CHAPTER 32

Derek had driven past the hospital three times, looping back round the block and finally parking up in a side road where he was lucky enough to find a vacant spot. The hospital car park had CCTV, and he was wary of being caught on camera, though he told himself that the hospital itself would have cameras, so the additional caution was in fact pretty meaningless.

Perhaps, he thought, he was afraid that if he was spotted on camera coming into the hospital, someone would stop him. He knew this was a stupid thought; why on earth would anyone take any notice of a sixty-year-old man in black trousers and a winter jacket walking into a hospital? Especially as now it seemed to be visiting time.

He didn't even know where Will might be.

Almost, he gave up and went home, the idea that he could just deny everything becoming more and more attractive. Then his daughter called him again. Had he been to the police? Had he told them that Will might have been coming to see him? Her obvious concern that he should do the right thing almost broke him, as did her obvious distress that there was no positive news coming from the hospital regarding this man who had been a big part of her life when she'd been younger.

222

The two families had been close, back then.

It was her call that made up his mind. He had started this. He would just have to finish it. He could not bear the thought that Will might regain consciousness and tell the world what he had done. For his Emily to find out what he had done.

"I've been a bit busy," he told her. "I'll give them a ring in the morning."

Then he did something he had never before done. He hung up on her and switched off his phone.

Think, Derek, think. Of course, Will would be in the intensive care unit in the hospital. That's where he should go.

With no more than that single step in his plan, Derek got out of the car and retrieved his coat from the back seat. Now that he had a course of action, he felt oddly calm. He would go to the hospital, find where Will Toons was and work it all out from there.

He found himself thinking about Fliss Cameron. Now there had been a lovely girl. Older than Will and his own child, but he had come to know her when Will had started to work with the Cameron Players. A pretty young woman, always a kind word and a bright smile, though she had changed a lot over the years.

He remembered the phone call and the tones of bitterness and recrimination. How she had blamed him for what had happened. Yes, she had a point about what he'd done with the body, but twice now he'd helped her out. She should have been grateful for that.

"Grateful," he said out loud.

A woman walking her dog cast him a curious glance. Derek scowled at her and she hurried on.

"Grateful," he said again, more quietly this time. Everything she had was really down to him.

She had been in her early twenties when her aunt had died. She'd not been a well woman for quite some time, Derek remembered. Had been glad of her niece living with her, genuinely fond of the girl Fliss had been — and why not? She was different then.

Fliss had turned up one day in a panic. "Girl was in a muck sweat," Derek murmured. "White as a sheet."

Her aunt had always said she was going to leave Fliss the house and the bit of money she had in the bank. The will had been drawn up and her aunt had signed it. One of the neighbours having witnessed the signature. Now she had been rushed into hospital and was not expected to last the night.

"But I need two signatures, Derek. Two witnesses. I need two; I don't think Auntie realised that," she had told him when she turned up on his doorstep, tears flooding down her cheeks. Distraught, he thought. "Absolutely in bits."

And so he'd helped her out; of course he had. He knew the old lady — who could say he hadn't witnessed her signature? If her aunt died and the will hadn't been properly attested to, Fliss would lose her home and her future. He had considered it a good deed.

It was only later that he realised he'd probably broken the law. But then, he'd broken it already, hadn't he? And in a much worse way. And then, more fool him, he never could hold his tongue when he'd had a bit to drink and Jeff had wormed her story out of him too.

Not that Fliss would be doing with that excuse. Blamed him, didn't she, for the pressure Jeff Mannering put her under? For the money he'd made her pay?

He had reached the hospital reception now and looked for a sign to direct him to where Will might be. High Dependency Unit. Was that it? Was that what they called the intensive care unit these days?

Derek followed the signs, riding the lift to the second floor, down a corridor and round a corner. He paused, suddenly confused by the presence of a police officer by the nurses' station and another along the hall, sitting outside a room.

"Can I help you, Sir?" a woman asked. Derek turned to see a nurse. He was horribly aware that the uniformed officer turned to look his way.

For a moment, Derek was at a loss. "Ah, no. I think I'm just confused," he said. "I think I got off at the wrong floor."

Her look was quizzical. The police officer's suspicious.

"If you tell me what you're looking for, I can direct you," she said.

"I—" Derek began. *I what?* He took to his heels and ran.

* * *

Mac got the call at 9.25, just when he was assuring himself that the evening would bring no more surprises. He had spent the past hours going through Rina's notes and following up her public domain research with some of his own.

The caller was Anning. They had the mysterious Derek in custody and Mac might like to sit in on the interview.

"He was spoken to by an officer canvassing the area," Anning said. "His full name is actually David Eric Ayre, but he usually goes by Derek. Anyway, he turns up at the hospital acting suspiciously. Then he tries to run away." He sniffed contemptuously. "Didn't get very far. PC Knightly plays rugby, knows how to tackle."

"And is he talking?"

"Well, the words are coming out. Not sure they're making any sense."

Mac gathered Rina's notes and his own and got his coat, then explained to Miriam what was going on.

"I won't wait up for you," she said. "Probably see you tomorrow night. Call me in the morning if you get the chance."

He left the boathouse, feeling in his pocket for the torch and made his way back up the steep hill.

* * *

Fliss's garden was small and the metal wastepaper bin she had found in which to set her bonfire was now scorching the ground beneath it and threatening to set fire to the grass. Regardless, Fliss plunged another bundle of paper into the flames. Acrid smoke rose to fill her eyes and choke her; who knew paper took so damned long to burn, or produced so much thick smoke? Impatiently she shoved another bundle into the metal bin, catching her hand painfully on the rim as she did so. Fliss swore.

Smoke was billowing out now, filling her garden and drifting into those beyond. She looked up as someone shouted at her from an upstairs window, demanding to know what the hell she was playing at. It was the second time a neighbour had objected.

Ignoring him, Fliss pushed yet more paper into the flames, noticing with annoyance that the flames were not able to keep up with her impatience. The fire was actually going out.

"Dammit!" Fliss kicked at the now red-hot bin. Immediately regretted her impulse, wiped her hot foot on the damp grass.

The shouts of her neighbour came again, this time threatening to call the police, the fire brigade, the "bloody loony bin".

Fliss shouted back at him, a string of invective peppered with obscenities. She looked back at the fire. She had smothered the flames, she realised. Only thick smoke rose from the half-burned pages now.

Fliss sighed impatiently. *Oh well*, she thought, *did it really matter anyway?* After all, this was only Jeff's stuff.

She went back inside, suddenly uncomfortably aware that she stank of smoke. But somehow that didn't seem to matter either. Her bags were packed, she had travelling money . . . in her head she was already gone.

Fliss Cameron loaded her suitcases into her car and drove away.

* * *

Mac studied the screen, looking at the man in the interview room. He was average height, had thinning sandy brown hair and pale eyes. Mac could not make out the colour. He was strongly built, like a man who kept himself in shape, but from being physically active, not from hours in the gym. From gardening, maybe, Mac wondered, thinking about the cultivator. According to his details, the man was almost sixty-one years old.

"D. Eric Ayre," he said. "We'd never have found him, just looking for someone called Derek."

"Probably not," Anning agreed.

"So, what's he had to say for himself so far?"

"Mostly he keeps on about his daughter and about Will Toons waking up and telling her things. We're waiting for the go-ahead from the shrink before we conduct the interview. Hopefully, he won't keep us hanging around for too long."

Mac nodded agreement. What if this man was considered unfit to be interviewed? he wondered. That could prove very frustrating indeed.

It was another hour before they got the go-ahead. The duty solicitor had arrived, and the duty psychiatrist would hang around for a while in case he was needed, but the assessment was that Mr Ayres was determined to talk. That he almost seemed relieved to have been arrested.

That he wanted to confess to a murder.

Mac took a seat directly opposite and Anning perched his too-big bum on a too-small chair slightly off to one side. He leaned back at what Mac judged to be a dangerous angle, arms crossed over his barrel chest. It had been agreed that Mac should take the lead.

The recording began. The participants were noted.

"I understand you want to tell us about what happened with Mr Jeffery Mannering," Mac said. "He came to visit you?"

"Yes, he came. Turned up one day unannounced, just like always."

"And when was this? Can you remember the date?"

Derek squinted, thinking back. "November," he said. "Twenty third or twenty fourth, I think. It was a Wednesday."

"And what was the purpose of his visit?"

Derek laughed shortly. "Same as it always was. To gloat, to make me suffer. To demand more money so he'd keep quiet. He was a bastard and he deserved what was coming to him." Derek leaned forward slightly, his gaze fixed on Mac. "You know how many times I'd rehearsed it in my head? Killing him, I mean? How many times I thought I could do it, but I chickened out? But not this time. No, not this time. He went too far."

"Why was this time different?"

"Because he threatened to tell my Emily. He said how much she'd hate me when she knew. But he said she might be willing to pay up to keep it quiet, reckoned her husband was good for it. He was so . . . I hated him. I couldn't take it anymore. So I did what I'd been wanting to do for such a long, long time. I picked up the knife I'd left on the counter, and I stabbed him with it. I stuck him as hard as I could." He laughed, weakly. "Trouble was, I couldn't get the knife out and he still wasn't dead. He staggered back and out the door, and I was scared then, really scared, in case he got away. So, I got another knife from the block, and I followed him and I stabbed him again and again, not so deep this time, but still hard enough, until he fell over onto the ground."

"I see," Mac said, keeping his tone almost conversational. "And then what did you do?"

"I wanted to make sure he was dead. I'd been working in the garden, getting the raised beds near the door ready for planting. I'd been to the garden centre, got some winter bedding. It can look grim when there's no colour in the garden, you know?"

"It can, yes."

Beside him, Anning shifted his weight. Mac willed him to keep his mouth shut.

"I'd been using the cultivator to get rid of the weeds. It was still on the side of the bed, so I picked that up and I—" He paused, clawed his raised hand as though in imitation of the implement and then slashed downward. "I hacked at him with it. Once, twice, I don't know. I was in such a fury. I don't know where I got the strength from."

"Why did you do that?" Mac asked.

"Because I wanted to be sure the bastard was dead." This was said with such fierceness that Mac felt himself flinch as Derek almost spat the words. "Do you know how he made me suffer all this time? How he made all of us suffer?"

"All of us? Who are you referring to?"

Derek shrugged. "Me, Will, Fliss. Other people too, I suppose. People like him, they can't stop themselves, can they?"

"We know about the car accident involving you and Will Toons," Mac said, "but what was Mannering holding over Miss Cameron?"

Derek shook his head, and for a moment, Mac wondered if he would respond, but it seemed his train of thought had just gone elsewhere. "Will promised he wouldn't tell. He promised me he hadn't told you lot what had happened and that when he did, he would say it was his fault. He lied to me."

"Mr Toons didn't confess to the police," Mac said. "Our knowledge of the incident came from another source."

"From where?" It was clear Derek was genuinely puzzled. "Did Fliss tell you? No one else knew."

"Fliss Cameron knew?"

He smiled slightly. "Made it her business to know everything, didn't she? I reckon Jeff told her when he got it out of me. But she knew."

"And was Jeff Mannering blackmailing her too?"

Derek nodded. "About the will, of course," he said, as though it was obvious.

"Her aunt's will?" Out of the corner of his eye, Mac caught Anning glance at him and remembered that he knew nothing about this side of things.

Derek nodded. "Yes. Her aunt was taken to the hospital. Just before she died. Stood to reason she wanted everything to go to Fliss. She'd had the will drawn up and all, but not got the second witness to sign. So, I did it for her. I suppose it was wrong, but what was I to do? Poor lass would have been homeless. I knew her auntie wouldn't have wanted that."

Mac paused, not quite sure what he should make of this. He decided to leave it for the moment. He asked instead, "So what happened after you had killed Jeff Mannering?"

"I put him in the old chest freezer and I scrubbed the slabs clean. Tell the truth, once he was dead, I was at a bit of a loss. I mean, I'd gone through killing him in my head so many times, but I'd never thought about getting rid of the body." He sounded suddenly amused as he added, "I suppose I never reckoned I'd really get up the nerve to do it. But I did, didn't I?"

Derek smiled suddenly, but Mac could see that his eyes filled with tears, as though the man did not know how he felt or how to think about what he had done. Relief fought with regret, Mac thought, but regret only for the consequences, not for the act itself.

"So, what made you think of taking Mr Mannering's body to the hotel?"

Derek blinked as though trying to recall his train of thought. "Will happened to tell me he was going to take part in one of Fliss's things. That's what he always called them, 'Fliss's things'. I had a look on the website and I found out the dates. I thought, why not? They'd both be there, and I knew I could go the back way into the hotel. I thought it might be . . . I don't know. I thought it might be funny."

"Funny?" Anning demanded. "You've got an odd sense of humour."

Derek seemed to consider. "I suppose I have," he said. "Look, I know it seems like it was a stupid thing to do. I should have just buried him somewhere and had done, but in that moment, knowing they'd both be there and they didn't know he was dead. I suppose, I suppose it just appealed to me. I wished I could see their faces when they found him."

"How could you know it would be Miss Cameron or Mr Toons that would find him," Mac asked.

Derek looked confused. He shook his head. "I suppose I just assumed it would be."

"It could have been anyone. Any of the guests."

"I didn't think about that," Derek said. "Anyway, I was right, wasn't I? Will found the body and Fliss saw it next. I thought they'd be happy he was gone. All the trouble. It would all stop."

"But then Will got a letter, telling him that it wasn't over," Mac said.

Derek's face clouded. "Yes. That's why he came to see me. He said he couldn't take any more, that he was about to do what we should have done all those years ago and go to the police. He was going to tell you lot what had happened. How Genevieve Atkins died. I couldn't have him doing that, not after all this time."

"So, when he left your house, what did you do?"

"I followed him. He turned back up the hill. I wanted to run him off the road, but he pulled into the passing place. I don't know why. Maybe he thought he could talk to me. But it had all gone too far for that. I couldn't back down, could I? I didn't know how."

Mac was silent for a moment, shocked and oddly sorry for this man who had well and truly painted himself into a corner.

Anning filled the gap. "So you killed your friend?"

Derek looked as though he had been slapped. He glared at the detective and then swung his attention back to Mac. "What else could I do?" he demanded. "He was going to tell! After all we'd been through after all these years of keeping quiet, of living with the terror that it might come out, he was Going. To. Tell!"

"So, what did you do?" Mac kept his tone calm and level.

Derek slumped back in his chair. "I opened the door. I'd taken the tyre iron from the boot of the car before I went after him. I couldn't take a proper swing, not with him sitting in the seat. He knew that. He leaned back, away from me and he tried to talk to me, tell me he'd keep quiet after all, but it was too late for that. I took a step away, like I was considering, but he was a lying bastard, made a grab for the door. So

I jabbed him a couple of times with the iron, stunned him enough to undo the seatbelt and drag him from the car and then I hit him. I hit him hard. I thought I'd killed him."

He looked at Anning and then back at Mac. "He should have died."

"He still might," Anning told him.

Derek seemed almost relieved about that, Mac thought. Even though he'd already confessed, would soon be charged. It was as though he still didn't want Will Toons to betray him by telling anyone what they had done.

"The night when Genevieve Atkins was killed," he said, "who was driving?"

"Will always believed it was him."

"But it wasn't, was it?"

Derek shook his head. "I . . . we never meant to hurt anyone. It was stupid, a stupid thing to do."

"And it cost a young woman her life," Anning said harshly. "She had a young family. Your stupidity cost a young woman her life and two children their mother. Not to mention the pain it caused to her husband and the rest of the family."

"You think I don't know that? We've been paying for that mistake all these years!"

"Then you've been paying the wrong person," Anning told him bluntly. "Yes, you'd have been arrested, gone to court, maybe even done a short spell in prison."

Shorter than you deserved, Mac thought. That was the message in Anning's tone.

"Instead, you drove away and left that young woman in the road. Did you even think of calling for help?"

"She was dead!" Derek shouted at him. "I made certain she was dead."

Mac exchanged a glance with Anning. Did Derek mean . . . ?

He was about to ask, but the solicitor intervened, having no doubt also caught the possible implication. "I think I'd like to speak with my client alone," he said. Mac and Anning had no option but to terminate the interview and leave the room.

"You think he might have finished her off?" Anning asked bluntly.

"He might have just misspoke," Mac said, but he felt a chill crawl up his spine. He shook his head, as though trying to shake the thought away. "So, while the solicitor's consulting," he said, "we should send a car to bring Miss Cameron in, see what she has to say to all of this. It's pretty clear that she knew what was going on. At the very least, she impeded our investigation into Mannering's death."

"Which will do for starters," Anning said. He glanced at his watch. It was three fifteen. "Since we'll be disturbing her beauty sleep, best be a familiar face that wakes her up. I'll drive."

On the way to Fliss Cameron's house, Mac brought Anning up to speed on the payments Will Toons had been making the Caydhill Trust and the information Rina had dug up on Fliss Cameron's past business failures. He refrained from mentioning Rina as the source of much of this. "Once we get a look at their financials, I'm betting we can follow the trail back to Jeff Mannering."

"And our Miss Cameron, she's a con artist as well," Anning said.

"Albeit keeping just this side of legal," Mac said. He took his phone from his pocket and began to check for messages. There were two from Andy.

"Well, what she did with the will was *definitely* dodgy. Interesting about the bank account, though. You've contacted the bank?"

"We've left messages, and Andy Nevins was still trying to get hold of the branch manager when I left home. His wife said he was out at some function somewhere, but she'd try and get a message to him. That was the best we could do, considering the hour." He paused to read the texts Andy had sent. "And it looks as though he's managed to talk to him and set things in motion. If the account is still active, it should be possible to put a freeze on it before she tries to take any money out."

"He's a good lad, that PC Nevins. Looking for promotion, is he?"

"I expect so," Mac said cautiously.

Anning laughed. They were in Fliss Cameron's street now and Anning pulled up in a gap only just large enough to accommodate the small car he was driving. His reverse parking was sound, anyway, Mac thought, and was quite glad they had not driven over in his ageing Volvo estate.

The night was cold and still, and the air chill in his nostrils threatened frost. He sniffed again. "Smells like someone's had a bonfire," he said.

"And we can make a guess who that might have been," Anning said bitterly.

Moments later they were knocking on Fliss Cameron's door. Mac was unsurprised to find that there was no one home.

CHAPTER 33

Mac arrived home just after six in the morning. He showered and changed and snatched some breakfast with Miriam before driving to the branch of the bank that Fliss Cameron most often used.

Yes, he was told, the account was still active. Her aunt, Elizabeth Terry, had banked with them for years. Had still been doing so long after her death, clearly unbeknownst to the bankers.

"It's a fairly active account," the bank manager told him. "Money going in several times a month and some then being transferred out, some withdrawn in cash." He turned the screen so that Mac could see the statements. "A new cash-point card was issued only a few months ago." He sounded slightly embarrassed about that. "And as you can see, eight thousand pounds was transferred out of the account last night. That could have been done online or via the app . . ." He trailed off. "Of course, the account was frozen as soon as we got word. And Miss Cameron's other accounts with us now have a block on them, too. "

Mac nodded. Fliss Cameron had been ahead of them. "The account the money was transferred to?"

"Not one of ours, I'm afraid."

"Previous to this, of course, there had been no unusual activity. In fact, as you can see, several of these transactions seem to be interest from investments." He pointed to the transactions in question.

"Kipling Financial. What would they be?"

"Well, on the face of it, they could be brokers. Inspector, believe me when I say there was nothing in the operation of this account that would have raised any red flags."

It was too much to hope, Mac thought, that Fliss Cameron would show up at the branch in person that morning, but as he drove back to meet Anning, a phone call from the manager told him that an attempt had been made to transfer more money, this time to a different account. That had been unsuccessful.

Anning met him at the front desk. He too had been home to shower and change though, he looked as exhausted as Mac felt.

"I asked for the post-mortem report on Genevieve Atkins," he said. "I've just had a quick squint at it."

"He killed her, didn't he? I mean, he—"

"Made certain, as he put it. Yes. It looks that way. The post-mortem turned up all the signs of an oblique impact. Broken leg and hip, probably from how she landed. Internal injuries that suggest she was hit at speed and spun into the air. But there was more."

"He drove over her, didn't he?" Mac said.

"It certainly looks that way," Anning said.

In the interview room, Derek was waiting for them. He looked rested, Mac thought somewhat jealously. The duty solicitor who'd been with them previously had handed over to another. Derek didn't seem to mind.

"I want to talk," he said. "You've no idea how much of a relief it is to get this off my chest after all this time. How much it's weighed on me." He paused. "I'm not a bad man. Not an evil man. I'm not a murderer. I did what I had to do to protect myself. It was self-defence."

"Derek," Mac said, "two people are dead because of your actions, and a third might not survive. Whatever your intentions were, these are the facts. We're glad you want to talk. It's important to get everything down so we know what we're dealing with, you know that, don't you?"

The solicitor frowned at him and seemed about to intervene. Derek must have noticed that, because he said, "it's all right. I can't do any more damage. I just wish my family didn't have to know. I wish—"

The self-confidence he had demonstrated only moments before seemed to vanish. "Oh, God," Derek said. "I'm in it up to my neck, aren't I?"

"So, the night Genevieve Atkins died," Mac said. "You were driving the car. Did you see her?"

Derek nodded, but he would no longer meet Mac's gaze.

"You convinced Mr Toons that he was the one driving the car."

"When we got back to my place, I gave him a few more drinks and when he woke up in the morning he couldn't remember a thing. Not clearly. He knew something had happened and I told him . . . I told him I thought we'd hit someone."

"You thought?" Anning interrupted.

Derek ignored him. "I told him that he was behind the wheel, and that if anyone found out, he could say goodbye to any hope he had of a career or anything else. He was just a kid," Derek admitted. "Only a couple of years older than my Emily. It didn't really take much to convince him. He was scared and shocked and, well, I suppose I took advantage of that. I told him I couldn't risk anyone knowing because of my kid. They'd take her away from me. After her mum died, I raised her. It was just the two of us. In the end, he agreed.

"We went out to look at the car and cleaned it up the best we could. There was less damage than I'd thought. I'd swerved and just clipped her; she'd been thrown in the air and gone tumbling over. I'll never forget seeing her in that headlamp beam. Then she hit the ground and—"

"And you ran over her," Mac said flatly.

He saw the shock on the solicitor's face, and the impulse towards denial on Derek's as he glanced up at Mac and then looked away again. He continued as though Mac had not spoken.

"I went to check on her, but she was dead. How could she not have been dead? That following morning, we cleaned the car, washed it down, got a pressure washer underneath, and when I was satisfied, I called my cousin, Jeff. Told him I'd skidded on a patch of ice and hit a gatepost. He got me a new headlamp shell, repaired the damage to the wing. It was an old car, so no one was going to remark on the odd dent he couldn't get out. That should have been that."

"But it wasn't."

"No. Jeff was always sharp. He knew there was something up. Eventually, I suppose, he must have got it out of me."

"And how did he do that?"

"I suppose, one night, I'd had too much to drink and he started in on the questions. You don't understand. I thought I could trust him!"

"And then the blackmail started."

Derek shrugged. "It was just a few favours at first, then it got serious. It was never so much that I struggled. I mean, I found it hard, but I suppose he was in it for the long haul. If he'd bankrupted me, he'd have lost his power. And that was what I realised, over time: it wasn't about the money, or at least, not *just* about the money. It was about the power. He liked that. That sense of power."

"And as Mr Toons became successful, he became a target, too."

"It escalated then. It was just favours from Will at first, but when he started to earn regular money, Jeff was always there. In the background, but a threat that wouldn't go away."

"And when Will threatened to stop paying?"

"He said he'd make sure Will came back into line. He'd make sure Will knew exactly what he was up against."

"Did he assault Terri Murray and then set things up so Will Toons almost got the blame?"

Derek nodded. "He made sure he knew where Will would be. No sense getting him sent to jail, was there? He

238

couldn't keep paying if he was locked up. He knew Will would have an alibi. It was a demonstration;, that was all. Just to keep him in line."

"Terri Murray was fifteen years old." Mac could not keep the anger out of his voice. "You have a daughter. Can you imagine something like that happening to her when she was fifteen?"

Derek glanced up, and Mac could see there was no empathy in the man's eyes, just a look of vague incomprehension. "I always kept my Emily well away from all that," he said. "From Jeff, from dodgy boyfriends, from anything that could hurt her. And it worked, didn't it? She found a good man, got married, had two lovely kids. I kept my daughter safe!"

"And Terri?"

"Not my concern. Not my responsibility. If that sister of hers hadn't let her stay over in Will's house. If she'd not been at that party, if she hadn't been drinking, Jeff wouldn't have been able to get to her, would he?"

"Jeff Mannering would have had to prove his point by raping some other woman, is that what you mean?" Anning demanded.

But Derek made no response. They were losing him, Mac realised, or to be more precise, Derek was losing interest in them. He'd said what he had to say, and he was now withdrawing into himself. His gaze shifted to some point that was not inside this small, cramped interview room, but somewhere far beyond.

"And so you tried to kill Will Toons to stop him confessing. Even though he promised to shoulder the blame," Anning said.

The attention snapped back, just for an instant. Derek said resignedly, "What else could I do? You lot would have got the story out of him sooner or later." He paused and signed heavily. "Then when I heard that he wasn't dead after all, I had to try and finish the job."

And that worked out so well for you.

239

CHAPTER 34

They had tried to talk to him about Fliss Cameron, but after that final burst of interest, Derek had once more retreated into himself and refused even to acknowledge their presence, never mind their questions.

"Someone will have to tell the daughter," Anning said.

"I'll do that," Mac told him. He would take Sergeant Baker, or maybe he would take Yolanda, the idea inspired by seeing her and Andy come through the swing doors.

They were chilled and damp and smelt of smoke from Fliss Cameron's bonfire, but Mac could see that they had recovered something from the woman's house.

"We poked about in the fire, got quite a few pages that hadn't completely burned. Luckily for us, she couldn't finish the job, anyway."

"The neighbours complained about her burning rubbish in her garden," Yolanda said. "Apparently it was well smoky and upsetting the dogs. They threatened they'd call the council and the police and the fire brigade if she didn't pack it in, so eventually she had to stop. There was still a load of stuff in the house. We've got some of it in the car; the rest is on its way."

"Looks like the contents of the box files," Andy said. "Some of the paperwork has Mannering's name on it."

* * *

Later, much later, Mac and Yolanda knocked on the door of Derek's daughter. She knew by then that he'd been arrested, but not the full story. They sat for an hour explaining it all to her and then another hour explaining it again to her husband who had hurried home from work.

As they drove away, Yolanda said, "She still doesn't believe us, does she?"

"No, and I don't suppose she ever will. Not completely, no matter how the evidence mounts up, no matter how other people try to convince her. He's her dad, and as far as his daughter is concerned, that's all that matters. He did a good job for her."

"Pity he got everything else wrong," Yolanda said. "I wonder how Genevieve Atkins's family are taking the news."

"At least they've got some answers," Mac said lamely. He was relieved that the task of informing that other family had been delegated elsewhere.

"Answers," Yolanda said, her tone acid. "Your loved one was killed by a kid too drunk to know where he was and a man old enough to have known better, but who, when he saw what he'd done, made certain she wasn't going to live to tell anyone about it."

"The original post-mortem would have told them most of that," Mac said.

"And now they've got to be told it all over again."

EPILOGUE

Fliss Cameron was picked up a week later when she was recognised by a clerk at a petrol station. Mac walked over to Rina's after work to give her the news.

"Anning's team is doing the interviews," he told her, as they settled in Rina's small front room, her private sanctuary. "Frankly, they're welcome to the job."

"You're sounding very jaundiced," Rina said.

"I suppose I'm feeling it. Will Toons died today. His family took the decision to end his life support. He was injured too badly, and even after the surgery, well, he just lost the battle, I suppose."

"That's sad to hear," Rina said. "One stupid mistake when he was young and the rest of his life ruined. And now ended because of it."

They sat in silence for a short while. Then Rina asked, "What will happen to Derek?"

"His lawyer will probably push the diminished responsibility angle. But he'll still be locked up for a very long time. He's killed three times, no matter how you look at it. I feel sorry for his family, I suppose."

"You suppose?"

"I feel sorry for all the families caught up in this. It all feels messy and somehow unresolved, even now."

"And how are you getting on tracking down the other victims? I assume there were other victims?"

"It looks that way. It's out of my hands. It's going to take a team of forensic accountants to sort that one out, and that's going to take a while. The charity, Caydhill Trust, was definitely a front for Jeff Mannering, but he seems to have had fingers in other pies, too."

He stood up and shrugged into his coat. "It's a calm day; I think I'll walk home around the headland. I need to clear my brain."

Rina nodded. He did indeed look tired and somewhat depressed.

"One interesting thing. Though: it was Fliss that sent the threatening letter to Will Toons. Obviously, she felt she should take over Mannering's business concerns now that he was gone. It seems the pair of them had been an item for years; they'd just been very discreet about it. Fliss Cameron knew exactly what was going on."

Rina stood at her window and watched her friend walking back towards the promenade. The day was grey and cloudy but very still, which probably meant wind and heavy rain later, she thought. Time was, she'd have worried about Mac's black mood, but now she was confident that he'd get over it. After all, he'd found a place to belong, a place where he was needed, and, Rina thought, in the end that was what really mattered.

THE END

THE JOFFE BOOKS STORY

We began in 2014 when Jasper agreed to publish his mum's much-rejected romance novel and it became a bestseller.

Since then we've grown into the largest independent publisher in the UK. We're extremely proud to publish some of the very best writers in the world, including Joy Ellis, Faith Martin, Caro Ramsay, Helen Forrester, Simon Brett and Robert Goddard. Everyone at Joffe Books loves reading and we never forget that it all begins with the magic of an author telling a story.

We are proud to publish talented first-time authors, as well as established writers whose books we love introducing to a new generation of readers.

We won Trade Publisher of the Year at the Independent Publishing Awards in 2023. We have been shortlisted for Independent Publisher of the Year at the British Book Awards for the last four years, and were shortlisted for the Diversity and Inclusivity Award at the 2022 Independent Publishing Awards. In 2023 we were shortlisted for Publisher of the Year at the RNA Industry Awards.

We built this company with your help, and we love to hear from you, so please email us about absolutely anything bookish at feedback@joffebooks.com

If you want to receive free books every Friday and hear about all our new releases, join our mailing list: www.joffebooks.com/contact

And when you tell your friends about us, just remember: it's pronounced Joffe as in coffee or toffee!

ALSO BY JANE ADAMS